ZANE PRESENTS

O9-BTJ-464

ALLISON HOBBS

A NOVEL

MISTY

Dear Reader:

For those of you who are among Allison Hobbs' legions of fans, you are definitely in for another amazing tale spun by the only woman on the planet that I consider to be freakier than me. Allison's ability to draw readers into the characters and storylines of her novels never ceases to amaze me. Yet again, she has stepped up her game with *Misty*.

In the new installment of the lives of Misty and Brick—two of the most memorable characters in the history of books—the drama, confusion, love, and sex are all still running full force. Brick and Misty have a connection that most people would never be able to understand, rather less appreciate. They have been through the fire a few times and have lived to tell the story. Back together again after Brick married Misty's mother and fathered a child with her, things are sure to get heated up this time around. Will they be able to both emerge through the fire one last time?

I guarantee that you will be engaged in this book from page one, and not want to put it down. Hobbs continues to use her imagination for the greater good and she does not disappoint. As always, thanks for the love and support shown to the authors of Strebor Books, as well as myself. We appreciate and love you for hanging in with us for the duration.

Blessings,

Zane

Publisher
Strebor Books
www.simonandschuster.com

ZANE PRESENTS

ALLISON HOBBS

A NOVEL

MISTY

STREBOR BOOKS

NEW YORK LONDON TORONTO SYDNEY

Strebor Books
P.O. Box 6505
Largo, MD 20792
http://www.streborbooks.com

This book is a work of fiction. Names, characters, places and incidents are products of the author's imagination or are used fictitiously. Any resemblance to actual events or locales or persons, living or dead, is entirely coincidental.

ISBN 978-1-59309-469-0
ISBN 978-1-4516-9703-2 (ebook)
LCCN 2014931188

First Strebor Books trade paperback edition July 2014

Cover design: www.mariondesigns.com
Cover photograph: © Keith Saunders Photos

10 9 8 7 6 5 4 3 2 1

Manufactured in the United States of America

For information regarding special discounts for bulk purchases,
please contact Simon & Schuster Special Sales at 1-866-506-1949
or business@simonandschuster.com

The Simon & Schuster Speakers Bureau can bring authors to your live event.
For more information or to book an event, contact the Simon & Schuster Speakers
Bureau at 1-866-248-3049 or visit our website at www.simonspeakers.com.

FOR YVETTE DAVIS
Thank you for a beautiful and true friendship that has lasted decades.

ACKNOWLEDGMENTS

Thank you to all my loyal readers who have let me know in person, via email, and on social media how much you've enjoyed the *Double Dippin'* series as well as my other novels.

A special thanks to these readers and friends who have been super supportive and whom I appreciate so much: Jason Frost, Kat Torres, Johnathan Royal, Chjvon Glass, Vandolin Hilton, Michelle "Chelly" Jones, Myra Payton, Danielle Rameau, Kimberly Haynes, Sharon Simmons, Aaliyah Muhammad, Tara Goodwin-Baruwa, Suretta Johnson, Sue Murray, Danita LaShay Branch, Christina Jones, LaSheera Lee, Crystal Gates, Vanessa Harris, and Stephanie Hunt.

Many thanks to Yona Deshommes, publicist at Simon and Schuster.

I extend my deepest gratitude to my editor and publisher, Charmaine Parker and Zane. Thank you both for your patience and kindness over the years.

Thank you Karen Dempsey Hammond, my sister and friend.

CHAPTER 1

Brick paused in the doorway of Misty's hospital room, frowning in confusion.

Hovering over Misty was a woman dressed in a business suit; she was writing something in a notebook. At the foot of the bed, a man held a camera, snapping pictures of her.

Noticing Brick, Misty impulsively tried to sit up straighter, momentarily forgetting about the paralysis that restricted her movement. Helpless to shift her position, she feebly gestured for Brick to have a seat next to her.

Brick crossed the room. "What's going on, Misty?"

"This is Sharon Trent, a reporter from the *Philadelphia Daily News*. She's writing a story on me." Misty nodded toward the man with the camera. "That's Jack, a photographer for the paper." She smiled at the reporter and the photographer and said, "Sharon and Jack, meet Brick."

"Hello," Sharon greeted, looking Brick over with a curious gleam in her eyes.

Jack grunted a salutation as he continued snapping pictures of Misty.

"Pardon me for being a nosey reporter, but I'm curious about the connection between you and Misty. Are you a relative…a boyfriend? And how do you feel about Misty's new ability?"

Brick ignored the reporter's questions and asked Misty, "What kind of story is she writing?" He glared at the photographer, who had resumed taking pictures of Misty. "Chill, man. Put that camera away for a minute."

Not sure if he should listen to Brick, the photographer looked at the reporter, waiting for her instructions.

Sharon held up a hand. "We probably have enough pictures, Jack. Let's pack it up."

"You want to tell me what's going on, Misty?" Brick pulled up a chair next to Misty's bed.

"Something big. We'll talk after they leave, okay?"

Sharon stuffed her recorder and notepad inside her handbag. "The story should be featured in Friday's edition. I'll be in touch if I need more information."

"Cool. I'm excited about sharing my experiences," Misty said and then turned her attention to Jack. "Are you sure it's a good idea to use my photo in the piece? My face is so damaged; I'm not comfortable being seen like this. Can't you use one of the old pictures I gave you? You know, to let people see how I looked before my face got jacked up?"

"The plan is to put an old photo next to a current one, to garner sympathy, and get some donations pouring in," Sharon said. "The way you've triumphed over tragedy and then survived a coma after trying to end your life is a great, human interest piece. The psychic aspect of the story will fascinate readers."

Brick groaned in frustration. "What psychic aspect? Will somebody tell me what's going on?"

"I'll let Misty fill you in; I have to get back to my desk and start working on the story," Sharon said. With a sense of purpose, she made her way to the door with the photographer lugging his equipment as he trailed behind her.

Alone with Misty, Brick asked, "How'd you turn into a media sensation, overnight?"

"You'll never guess." Misty grinned mischievously.

"I don't feel like playing guessing games. Are you gonna shed some light on the subject? When I left last night, you were feeling sorry for yourself. Now you're grinning like a Cheshire cat. What are you up to?"

"Why do I have to be up to something?"

"Because that's how you do. After all you've been through, please don't tell me you're back to your old tricks."

"Don't be so quick to judge until you hear what happened."

"I'm listening."

"Early this morning, when the nurse woke me up to give me my meds and to take my vital signs, something weird happened."

"Weird, like what?"

"Her palm accidentally brushed against mine, and there was a strange, stinging sensation—popping and crackling—like static when two pieces of fabric connect."

Brick frowned in bewilderment.

"It's hard to explain. It's like, we both felt it, but didn't understand what had happened. The nurse gawked at the blood pressure cuff, as if it had caused the shock. Then she started fiddling with it, and that's when I started seeing this fast-moving video slideshow of her life."

"Where'd you see it—on the wall?"

Misty shook her head. "Images from her life were playing inside my mind. I was able to tell her all sorts of personal information about herself."

"That's crazy."

"It's the truth, and she was in tears by the time I finished reading her."

"Reading her?"

"Yeah, I gave her a psychic reading."

Brick scoffed. "You're not psychic."

"Apparently, I am. The nurse is in her late forties, and I was able to see scenes from her childhood and teen years."

Brick shook his head doubtfully.

"And get this…I even saw her future."

"You shouldn't have messed with that nurse's head like that."

"I'm telling the truth! In my mind, I saw the nurse getting out of a dark SUV and walking toward this cute little house with white siding and blue shutters. There were shrubs and big, yellow sunflowers in front of the house."

"You were imagining things."

"No, I saw that nurse's future. She had on white pants and an orange and white striped top. There were keys dangling in her hand. I knew the house couldn't have been in Philly because I saw a wooden walkway leading to sand and water."

With his eyebrows drawn together tightly, Brick asked, "What else did you see?"

"That's it. But when I told her details about the house, she got excited. She said she'd been looking at property at the shore, and the house I described sounded like a house she fell in love with, but it was out of her price range. She'd tried to get the owners to lower the cost, but she wasn't successful."

"So, what does that prove?"

"It proves that she's going to move into the house of her dreams. She said she doesn't own an outfit like the one I saw in my vision, but that's only a minor glitch in my story."

"I think it proves that you're not actually seeing the future," Brick reasoned.

Misty rolled her eyes. "Why are you being so negative? I know what I saw, Brick; I'm not making this up. Anyway, the nurse said she's read about people coming out of comas with newfound psychic abilities. She was so excited, she called a journalist friend of hers. She asked her to interview me, and as you already know, the reporter I introduced you to is going to write a feature story about me. It's gonna begin with the tragic night that a hater brutally attacked me and left me for dead, and it'll end with me waking up from the coma with the ability to prophesize the future."

Brick shook his head apprehensively. "Are you seriously going to allow people to believe you can predict the future?"

"Yes, because it's true. The reporter said I'll probably start getting a lot of donations when people read about my misfortune. I'm hoping to turn this into something much bigger than mere donations."

"So, the old Misty is back with a brand-new hustle," Brick said sarcastically.

"You're making it sound like I'm going to be scamming people. I came out of that coma with a gift and there's nothing wrong with profiting from it."

"Are you planning to set up shop with a crystal ball and a deck of tarot cards?"

"Think bigger, Brick! First, I need to get my appearance up to par. Get some cosmetic surgery on my face so I can look good—you know, for my clients and also for you."

"I'm not worried about how you look. I told you you're beautiful to me exactly the way you are."

"That's sweet, but I want cosmetic surgery. When I look in the mirror, I want to smile at my reflection, not cringe."

"When you were staying at your mom's house, you told me you didn't care about your appearance anymore. You said you were through with material things and uninterested in earthly pleasures."

"That's because I was planning on killing myself, but if I have to live in this world, then I don't want to look like a monster."

"You don't look like a monster, babe."

"Yes, I do. It's bad enough that I'll never be able to walk again, but having to live with a hideous face is too much for anyone to deal with and not lose their mind."

Brick squeezed her hand reassuringly. "I accept you. Why can't you accept yourself?"

"You didn't turn down cosmetic surgery when my mother offered to get the scar removed from your face, so stop being a hypocrite."

Brick laughed. "Wow, like old times, you're still running off at the mouth. I get that you want to look like your old self, but I'm skeptical about this psychic thing."

"Why do you think I'm lying about being psychic?" Misty asked.

"I'm not saying you're lying, but maybe your mind was playing tricks on you."

"Remember what I told you about being with Shane…around the time I convinced you to help me kill myself?"

A shadow fell across Brick's face. "I don't want to think about that. Those were dark days. At first I thought I had killed you, and after your mom revived you, she wanted me locked up for attempted murder. If you hadn't pulled through, I'd be spending the rest of my life in jail."

"Well, I did pull through, and I'll tell anybody who thinks about accusing you of anything that I took those pills on my own."

"We both know that I helped you try to end your life, Misty," Brick said with a grave expression.

"And no one needs to know. That's between you and me."

"Getting back to this psychic stuff, do you really want the spotlight on you when you should be focused on recovering?"

"I need to focus on something other than lying in bed for the rest of my life."

"You're not going to be confined to bed. I'm going to get you one of those motorized wheelchairs."

"Am I supposed to be happy at the prospect of getting around in a wheelchair? My life is fucked and we both know it; give me some credit for trying to be self-reliant."

"You don't have anything to worry about; I'm gonna take care of you."

"I don't want to have to rely on anyone other than myself. This is a chance for me to lead a productive life and be useful; I don't want to miss the opportunity. So, stop being negative and support me in what I'm trying to do."

"What exactly are you trying to do?"

"With the media coverage, I'll be able to attract clients. Eventually, I'd like to do seminars and group readings. I want to write books…maybe get a TV show. Psychics make a lot of money."

Brick looked at Misty with pity in his eyes. "I don't want you to set yourself up for disappointment. Suppose last night was only a fluke?"

"It wasn't a fluke. Like I was saying, before I came out of the coma, the last thing Shane told me was that I had to come back here so I could touch people's lives."

"Shane is dead; I'm never gonna believe you were actually with him."

"Believe what you want. I know we were together, and I know what he told me."

Brick glanced down at his hand, which was resting gently on hers. "Our hands are touching; do you see my life flashing in your mind?"

"No, but that's probably because I already know everything about you."

CHAPTER 2

"Maybe you should tell that reporter to hold off on the story. Make sure it wasn't a one-time thing before you start broadcasting that you're psychic."

Misty smiled. "I already tested my abilities on another person."

"Who?"

"The housekeeping dude was in here cleaning up, and I asked him if he minded bringing the bouquet of flowers closer to my bed. He brought the vase over to my bed, took a rose out of the bunch, and held it up to my nose, so I could smell it. I tried to hold the flower on my own and my hand brushed against his, and that popping sensation happened again. Then the images started. I saw dude as a little boy, riding a bike. The vision flashed forward and I saw him as a teenager, riding around in a stolen car—"

"How'd you know it was stolen?" Brick interrupted.

Misty shrugged. "I could feel his energy. His friends were excited, but he was scared that they were gonna get caught. Next, I saw him fully grown and traveling on the subway with an attractive woman and a little girl—his family. They seemed very happy."

"Did you see his future?"

Misty sighed. "Yeah, but I didn't tell him that part."

"Why not?"

"Because his future was horrible. He was holding a gun against the temple of a man with dreadlocks."

Brick leaned forward. "What?"

"He seemed desperate, and I don't know if he was robbing the man or what. I didn't know how to deliver that kind of news, so I didn't bring it up."

"Sounds like he got his life together after he became a family man, but I wonder what happened to make him take such a wrong turn."

"He didn't take the wrong turn, *yet*. It's gonna happen in his future; maybe he can change it if I tell him what lies ahead."

"You're not kidding around?"

"No, I really saw it."

"Do you know exactly when he's going to commit this crime?"

She shook her head. "I don't even know if he actually pulled the trigger; I only know what I saw. And the impression I got was that the man with the dreads was messing around with the janitor's wife."

"You should tell him, Misty. Maybe you can prevent him from committing murder."

"So, you believe me?"

"I don't think you'd make up a story for the fun of it, so yeah, I believe you're seeing visions. Whether or not your visions are a glimpse in the future, is a different story." Brick grew quiet briefly. "Do you think you can stop bad things from happening if you give people a heads-up?"

"Maybe."

"You should tell the man what you saw."

"I don't want to tell him that his wife is fooling around. Suppose she hasn't even started cheating yet? I don't want to put ideas in his head. And I don't want to be responsible for him going home and whipping his wife's ass."

"That's exactly why you shouldn't be interfering in people's lives with this supernatural crap."

"I didn't ask for this gift."

"It might be a curse. Do me a favor, and stop touching folks until you figure out if you're really seeing into the future. Wait and see if that nurse moves into the beach house, because the way it stands, you don't know if your visions are accurate or not."

"After the story runs in the paper, people are going to be requesting my services, and I can't afford to turn any money down."

"I have a couple dollars; we're not exactly broke, you know. In fact, I'm gonna look for a place for us when I leave after visiting hours are over. I want you to chill with the readings, Misty. You can't be meddling in people's lives if you're not sure what you're seeing is real. For all you know, this so-called gift of yours might be only temporary. I didn't think you wanted to be in the limelight, and I was hoping this time around, we'd lead a more peaceful life."

"I want a peaceful life, too. But I need to earn money to pay for surgery. It's hard to look in the mirror with a face like mine," Misty said in a somber tone.

"There's got to be another way to pay for surgery. I'll figure something out."

"I got this, Brick. You concentrate on getting us a place, and as soon as I get a consultation with a plastic surgeon and find out the cost, I'll start working on getting the money together."

Brick looked at Misty pityingly.

"Don't feel sorry for me. I love a challenge, and I guarantee you, I'm going to get the money for my surgery."

Brick nodded. "You gotta do whatever makes you happy."

"By the way, what are you going to do about my mother?" Misty stared at Brick intently.

"There's nothing to do. Our marriage is done and over with. She already filed for divorce."

"How long will it take?"

"About ninety days. I'm not contesting anything, and as long as I see my son on a regular basis, I'm good."

Suddenly angry, Misty's eyes narrowed. "My mother's gonna end up old and alone, and that's exactly what she deserves."

"Don't talk bad about your mother."

"It's the truth. She was dead wrong for stealing my man. What kind of mother does that?"

"It's in the past, Misty; let it go."

"I can't."

"We were both wrong. You were wrong for bringing that dude, Dane, to the crib and I was wrong for hooking up with your mom."

"But we have an excuse; we were young and dumb back then. Young people are supposed to make mistakes and learn from them. But my mother was a middle-aged woman, and she not only fucked my man, she stuck the knife in deeper by marrying you and having your baby. That shit was grimy as hell, and I won't ever forgive her. She hurt me to the core." Tears brimmed in Misty's eyes.

Consoling her, Brick kissed her on the right side of her face, the side that hadn't been crushed by the tire iron. "It's you and me, now. We're back—mature enough to deal with everything life throws our way."

Misty sniffled. "It was unbearable living in the same house with you and my mother, and that's part of the reason I wanted to kill myself."

"I didn't know it was hurting you like that; I didn't think you cared about me anymore."

"Brick, I realize I was a selfish person, but I still had feelings. It was a living hell for me to be confined to a bed in the same house where you and my mother were sharing a life together."

"By that point, you'd been with so many different guys—including famous rappers with money—I honestly thought we'd lost our connection."

"Tell me this…"

"What?"

"Did you love my mother?"

Brick didn't respond right away. "I thought I did, but now I realize the only woman I've ever truly loved is you."

CHAPTER 3

Brick arrived at Thomasina's house with a shopping bag filled with toys for his son.

"You should have asked me what he needed before you wasted money on toys," Thomasina said curtly.

"What does he need?"

"He's growing out of everything…his shoes, his clothes."

Brick cut an eye at his son and smiled as Little Baron began playing with the remote control SUV he'd bought him. Returning his attention to Thomasina, he said, "The child support I pay is supposed to cover clothes and his other expenses."

Thomasina threw up her hands in mock surrender. "Forget I mentioned that your son needs clothes and is starting to look like an orphan. I'm sure you'd prefer spending your money on his sister than on him."

"What's that supposed to mean?"

"It means that you and Misty are two of the most selfish people I know. Neither one of you care who you hurt."

"I didn't mean to hurt you, Thomasina, but you had already started the divorce proceedings when you walked in on Misty and me in her hospital room."

"You told me you were over her *before* we got married."

"I honestly thought I was."

"At my age, I should be living for myself and doing whatever I want to do, but now I have to raise your child."

"You don't have to do it alone," Brick assured her.

Thomasina snorted. "Who's gonna help you with him—my invalid daughter?"

Brick flinched. "What's up with you? How can you talk like that about your own flesh and blood?"

"Misty's no daughter of mine. Not anymore. She stabbed me in the back for the last time. And by the way, let her know that her social worker called me about her moving back home and I told her that Misty is no longer welcome here. I suppose she's going to end up in one of those facilities because I know you won't be able to take care of her—not the way I did."

"She's not going into any facility."

Thomasina smirked. "Hmph. Where else is she gonna go? Do you plan on moving her into that hotel with you?"

"I'm not sure about our living arrangements, yet, but we'll figure it out," Brick said.

"Good luck with that. Taking care of a disabled person is a lot of work."

"I'll manage." Brick reached in his pocket and withdrew some cash and handed it to Thomasina. "Buy my little man some new clothes."

As if disappointed that she had nothing else to complain about, Thomasina looked at the money and frowned, and then went into the kitchen.

As Brick played with his son on the floor, he could hear Thomasina opening cabinets, the fridge, and then he heard the rattling sounds of pots and pans. Soon, a delicious aroma began to drift into the living room. Brick felt his stomach rumble; he couldn't remember the last time he'd had a homecooked meal. Forty minutes later, Thomasina returned to the living room and announced it was dinnertime.

"You're welcome to stay and eat with your son if you'd like," she offered.

Thomasina could throw down in the kitchen and Brick was tempted, but his gut instinct told him to decline. Sharing a meal could be mistaken as an attempt to patch up their relationship and he wasn't trying to do that.

"No, I'm good," he told her, though his growling stomach begged to differ.

Disappointment flickered across Thomasina's face, and Brick was confused about her intentions. Was she merely trying to be civil or was she plotting on a way to cause problems between him and Misty?

He picked up Little Baron and kissed him on the cheek. "Daddy has to go, but I'll see you in a couple of days."

"Oh, no you won't," Thomasina interjected in a hostile tone. "You can't drop by whenever it suits you. You have visitation once a week until you get stable housing," she reminded Brick.

Obviously, Thomasina wasn't going to make it easy for Brick and his son to have a healthy relationship. She was lashing out and trying to hurt him the only way she knew how. Realizing it would be a long time before Thomasina got over her bitterness, he decided not to argue with her. He lowered Little Baron to the floor, and said, "I'll see you next week, man. Okay? Are we good?"

"We're good," Little Baron replied.

"High-five!" Brick slapped palms with his son. "Be good, and I'll see you later, man."

"Bye, Daddy."

"Have a good evening, Thomasina," Brick said respectfully, and then sauntered toward the door.

He drove straight to a neighborhood bar on Lancaster Avenue that served food that tasted homemade. He had a newspaper in front of him and was eager to check the classified ads to look for a place for Misty and him. His face was buried in the paper when the waitress came over to take his order. He looked up, noticing that she was a big-boned chick, coffee-colored with sultry, full lips that glistened with cherry red lip gloss. Those lips looked like they could do things that would relieve a lot of stress. She gave him a ready smile that was unmistakably flirtatious.

"What's good?" Brick asked, without looking at the menu.

"I am," the flirty waitress replied with a hand on her hip.

Her body language and the way her lips spread into a sexy smile informed him that she was either a dick tease or she was hot in the ass and looking for a good time. Whatever the case, he hadn't come here to hook up; he'd come to get something to eat.

"In all seriousness, what do you recommend from the menu?" He had too much on his mind; too many pressing obligations to play games with the waitress, who was clearly hitting on him.

Disappointed that her attempt at seduction had failed, her hand fell away from her hip. Mirroring Brick's serious demeanor, the waitress spoke in a more professional tone. "I like the grilled salmon and the crabmeat mashed potatoes. The green beans are good, too," she said without a trace of the smile she'd previously displayed.

"That's what I'll have, then," Brick said.

"What're you drinking?"

"Heineken."

"You look a little down, like maybe you need more than a beer. Will my phone number cheer you up?" she added, making another flagrant attempt to hook up.

Emotionally preparing himself for the hard life with Misty that Thomasina had predicted, he didn't have it in him to start fucking around and getting phone numbers from random chicks. "No, I'm good," Brick responded with an apologetic smile.

The waitress shrugged as if to say, "your loss," and then grabbed the menu and trotted off toward the kitchen.

Left with his thoughts, Brick attempted to make a mental list of Misty's home care needs. She was going to need visiting nurse services, physical therapy, a wheelchair, and a host of adaptive equipment for disabled people. It was a lot to deal with, but he was in for the long haul.

He wondered what the long haul involved. *Not a sex life!* He winced at the idea of giving up sex completely, and wondered if he was capable. It wasn't likely; he was too young to live the rest of his life jacking off to porn for sexual release. Having a side chick seemed like the reasonable alternative, but he'd learned a valuable lesson after being in a relationship with his former lover and partner in crime, Anya. No matter how much a person believed they could be in a sexual relationship with no strings attached, emotions had a way of creeping into the picture.

Truth be told, Anya wasn't the only one who had caught feelings. Brick had strong feelings for her too, but he'd never admitted how much he cared for her. Believing that he was headed for jail, he didn't want to involve Anya in his chaotic life. One of the hardest things he'd ever done was to part ways with her when she pleaded with him to stay.

But everything happens for a reason. Back then, he had no idea that Misty would wake up. Once she came out of the coma, Brick realized his love for her was stronger than ever, despite her physical condition. What he felt for Misty couldn't be described as romantic love; it was love in the purest sense, and it was unconditional. At least that's what he told himself, but he secretly wondered if he was allowing himself to be tied down with Misty out of a sense of obligation. He quickly shook that negative thought from his mind. Misty was the love of his life. Point blank. Period.

He supposed he'd have to get his carnal needs met by prostitutes. Feelings weren't involved when money was exchanged for sex. He knew that from personal experience, when he used to sell sexual favors back in the day.

Putting aside unpleasant thoughts of his past, he scanned the apartment listings of the newspaper that was spread open on the table. Most of the places that caught his eye were surprisingly expensive, and he was grateful that cash wasn't a problem. He had plenty of money in his pocket due to Anya's generosity. Recalling the many ways Anya had held him down, Brick felt a pang of guilt.

He had refused to accept her offer to give him a portion of her inheritance, telling her he'd be all right. Yet, she'd waited until he was distracted and slipped a thick wad of hundred-dollar bills into his travel bag, making sure he was straight until he got back on his feet.

Anya and her sexy-self had been ride or die while she and Brick were together. In another lifetime, their relationship would have worked perfectly. They had so much in common. Both had lost their mothers young, and they were both damaged by their losses, yet they maintained a huge capacity to love. Unfortunately, the timing hadn't been right for Brick and Anya, and he'd been unable to commit to her. He prayed that Anya was healing from all her past hurt and was finally living her life to the fullest in Trinidad. Hopefully, she'd found some clues from her family members that could lead to finding her pops who'd been missing for years. Most of all, Brick wanted Anya to find the true love a fine woman like her deserved.

By the time the waitress brought the food to the table, Brick had circled five apartments that were in his price range and had an extra bedroom for Little Baron when he stayed over. Once Brick was situated, Thomasina would not be calling the shots about how often he could see his son. He realized his relationship with Misty would be confusing for his son, but over time, Little Baron would adjust and learn to accept that his father and his sister were a couple.

When Brick's fork scraped against the ceramic plate, he looked down in surprise. The plate was empty; he'd practically inhaled the food the waitress had set before him. The meal had been so good, he was tempted to order an extra platter to take out and eat later, but decided against it. He wasn't burning calories like he did while working construction, and until he found a new job, he would have to watch what he ate and also start hitting the gym.

Brick chugged down a second beer, and then motioned for the check. The waitress was busy flirting with four male patrons who were sharing a table.

Brick wasn't in a hurry, and so he settled back in his seat and waited. Alone with his thoughts, he recalled Misty's excitement about starting a profession as a psychic. As far as he was concerned, Misty wasn't any more psychic than he was, but she believed that she'd gained the ability to predict the future. Looking on the bright side, it was good for Misty to feel useful, and he didn't think there was any harm in her trying to build up a clientele. People who sought out psychics did it strictly for entertainment, and if they were naïve enough to take a psychic's predictions seriously, then that was on them.

CHAPTER 4

Word had gotten around the hospital that Misty could see the future, and various employees were finding reasons to peek in her room to get a look at her.

When Johanna McBride, the nurse whom Misty had given the reading, came to check on her, Misty complained, "My room has been like Grand Central Station all morning. People are acting like I'm a circus act or something. If one more person pokes their head in that door, I'm going to file a complaint with whoever runs this place."

"You want to complain to the chief of staff?"

"Yeah, him." Misty didn't want to deal with any underlings; she wanted to take her complaint straight to the top.

"That won't be possible; he's an important man."

"And I'm an important woman," Misty countered.

"Of course you are; what I meant was, most of the employees have never even met him. I'm sorry that hospital staff is invading your privacy. I only told one person, but apparently she couldn't keep the information to herself. I tried to be discreet, but I had to get permission from the nursing supervisor before Sharon was allowed to interview you."

Misty sucked her teeth in disgust. "I can't wait to get discharged; I don't like people staring at me like I'm some kind of a freak show."

"The curiosity is going to increase when the story comes out on Friday," Johanna warned.

"I can't deal with all these damn voyeurs who work in this hospital. Can you please put a *Do Not Disturb* sign on my door? I have a right to privacy, you know."

Johanna laughed. "This isn't a hotel, so I can't keep the staff out, but I can make sure that no one comes in here that isn't supposed to."

"Great. Can you take care of that, please?"

"I sure can. By the way, I have some good news," Johanna said, peering over her glasses at Misty.

"Oh, yeah? What's the news?"

Johanna clasped her hands together in delight and broke into a huge smile. "I got approved for the beach home you saw in your vision. I called Sharon, and told her to add that fact to the piece she's writing about you. Even though the story focuses on the horrible assault that paralyzed you and injured your face, I'm sure you're not only going to get inundated with donations for cosmetic surgery, but you'll also get requests from people who want personal readings. Are you prepared for that?"

"As long as they're willing to pay for my services, I'm more than prepared for it."

"Speaking of payment, I have something for you." Johanna opened a drawer of her med cart, and withdrew a sleek iPad. "It's time to connect with the world again, and swiping the screen with a finger is much easier than trying to operate the keyboard on a laptop."

Aw, shit; it's on, bitches, Misty thought to herself. Being paralyzed had robbed her of the will to live, but now she was ready to rebuild her life, piece by piece. She was eager to get the wheels in motion for an exciting new career, and having some use of her right hand, she'd be able to work with the iPad.

"Thanks, Johanna. I'll cherish this," Misty said, her mind racing with ideas. She'd pretended to Brick that she no longer craved the limelight, but that wasn't true. She'd always been an attention whore and being disabled hadn't changed that.

"You can find online support groups to help you learn to live with your disability," Johanna said, offering an encouraging smile.

"Mmm-hmm. Good idea," Misty mumbled distractedly as she tinkered with the iPad and then logged online. She checked out her old website and was relieved that no one had bothered to take it down. She could keep the name: Misty's Place, but she needed to delete the nude photos of the guys who used to work for her and replace them with images of herself—past and present. Like the journalist had said, her facial deformity and paralysis would garner a lot of sympathy. Besides, she wasn't going to be disfigured for long.

Next, she checked her old PayPal account and broke into a smile when she saw the balance left over from her pimping days—a little over three thousand dollars. Not a fortune, but it was something she could put toward her makeover.

Her smile faded when she recalled the small fortune she had hidden inside a safe in her former home. That money could have gone toward her surgery if rapper and entertainment mogul, Smash Hitz, hadn't cleaned her out of all her possessions immediately after the tragedy. He'd wasted no time in getting his people to clear out and reclaim the mini mansion she'd been renting from him. That thief needed to be dealt with, but she decided to leave the past behind her. She was confident that moving on and working as a psychic was going to bring in untold fortune and fame.

Misty glanced up from the screen and asked Johanna, "Is your reporter friend telling readers to send the donations here at the hospital?"

"Yes, this is your home until the social worker finds a facility for you. After you're discharged, the hospital will forward your mail to your new address. "

"Nah, that's not gonna work. First of all, I'm not going to any facility for invalids. My man is gonna find a place for us, but I need to ask you a favor."

"Sure, Misty."

Misty glanced at the hospital-issued phone that sat on a table next to her bed. "Would you call Sharon for me and hold the receiver up to my ear?"

"Not a problem. Why don't you use my cell? I'll put it on speaker." Johanna entered the reporter's number in her phone and said, "Hi, Sharon. I'm in Misty's room and she'd like to speak with you." Johanna set the phone on speaker and placed it on Misty's bed.

Not wasting anytime on pleasantries, Misty got right down to business. "I'm not going to be in the hospital much longer, and so I need you to change the address for the donations. I prefer that donations be sent directly to my PayPal account."

"Oh, I didn't know you had PayPal set up, being that you only recently came out of a coma," Sharon said.

"It's an old account, but it's still active." Misty gave her the email address associated with the account and then said, "One more thing, I need copies of the photos you're using in the article. You can send them to the same email address. Okay?"

"Sure." Sharon sounded a little uncertain. From her tone, she was somewhat taken aback by Misty's aggressive attitude, but Misty was too busy wheeling and dealing to care what the reporter thought of her. She gave a head nod to Johanna, indicating that she was through with the conversation. Johanna picked up the phone and sheepishly told her friend that she'd talk to her later. Then, she stared at Misty.

"What?" Misty asked, playing innocent.

"I didn't realize you were such a go-getter. The way you're handling your situation is commendable; I'm impressed."

"I don't mess around when it comes to making money. And right now, I need a lot of it. How much do think it's gonna cost to get my face fixed?"

"You'd have to talk to a plastic surgeon about facial reconstructive surgery, but I'd estimate it's going to cost somewhere in the neighborhood of twenty or thirty thousand."

"That's not a problem. I'll have that amount in no time," Misty said with assurance.

"I like your confidence, but it might not be a good idea to get your hopes up. Getting that kind of money may take a lot longer than you expect."

"You don't know me very well," Misty commented, the finger of her impaired hand swiping the iPad screen with remarkable dexterity.

"The reading you gave was so fascinating, I'm eager to tell my friends to book a session with you after you're discharged and settled in your new place. Who knows, with the article and word-of-mouth recommendations, you may get more money than you need."

"I'm banking on it. Anyway, thanks again for the iPad, Johanna. Having Internet access was exactly what I needed to start getting my life back on track. I've been down and out for so long, I forgot how much can be accomplished by simply logging online."

Two sharp raps on the door drew Misty's attention away from the iPad. It was about time people started knocking instead of barging in like she was still in a coma with no say-so over the foot traffic that trampled in and out of her room. "Come in," she said with reluctance. She was busy researching plastic surgeons, and didn't feel like being bothered by any of the medical staff. In no hurry to have her blood drawn or to choke down the horse pills the nurses peddled to her several times a day, she kept her head down, avoiding eye contact with the intruder as she viewed the iPad screen.

"How you doing today, Miss Delagardo?" said a familiar male voice.

Misty looked up and smiled in recognition at the cleaning dude, pushing a mop and bucket. "Call me Misty; you don't have to be so formal." Momentarily forgetting how unattractive she was, Misty looked him up and down appraisingly. He appeared to be in his early thirties, but had a shy, boyish quality that was appealing. "What's your name?" she asked softly.

Instead of sounding sexy as she'd intended, her words came out in a horrible lisp, due to the many missing teeth that had been knocked out by the tire iron of her assailant.

"Uh, my name's David," the cleaning guy stammered. From the look he gave her, he was appalled by her flirtatiousness. His look of revulsion was an instant reminder that she was no longer pretty.

Yanked back to the reality of her grotesque appearance, she could have cried. *But I still have Brick, and it's not like I'm hard up for companionship*, she reminded herself. Nevertheless, getting male attention was something she'd always taken for granted. It was her birth right, and she felt entitled to appreciative looks from all members of the opposite sex. *This is fucked up! I don't know how much longer I can handle being ugly. I gotta start stacking money quick, so I can get my looks back.*

"I suppose you've heard what people are saying about me."

"I heard some talk, but I didn't press anyone for details. I do my work and mind my business."

"Good to know. Actually, I'm glad you stopped in; I want to talk to you about something."

He gestured for her to continue, and something in his hand flick was so smooth, confident, and sexy, she was momentarily mesmerized. David had the kind of sex appeal that you didn't see right away; it had a way of sneaking up on you.

Holding onto the handle of the mop, he leaned to the side, waiting for Misty to speak her mind. Her eyes traveled down to his slightly bowed legs, and she was briefly mesmerized. Bowlegged men were known to be well hung; she bet he was a beast in bed. *Oh, God, I want my life back. I can't deal with being a gruesome invalid; I want to be pretty, again!*

"What did you want to talk to me about?" David prompted.

"As you know, I was in a coma…"

He nodded.

"And when I came out, I was blessed with the ability to prophesize."

"I heard a little something about that, but I figured it was only a rumor."

"It's true. Remember when you were standing close to me yesterday, you know, with the rose…"

"Yeah?"

"Did you feel a shock when your hand brushed against mine?"

"I vaguely remember a little spark."

"That's what happens when I get inside your head. Or maybe the connection is much deeper. You know, maybe I'm connecting with your soul."

David laughed uncomfortably. "My soul?"

Misty told him what she saw, describing his childhood bike in detail, even mentioning the black tape that patched a tear in the green seat.

David stared at her in amazement. He glanced around the room nervously when she began to talk about the stolen car he was a passenger in during his teens. "How do you know about that?"

"I see things."

He seemed ready to bolt from her room. "This is creepy."

"I also saw you and your girl waiting for the subway. You were carrying your baby daughter, who was dressed in a pink coat with white butterflies."

"Where are you getting this information? My daughter's five now, but back when she was a baby, we had to get around on public transportation. My wife is going to be shocked when I tell her about this."

"You're married?"

"Yeah, been married for six wonderful years." He smiled with pride. "My beautiful wife is my best friend and my lover."

A streak of irrational jealousy flashed through Misty. She wasn't trying to hear all this best friend and lover bullshit. She was accustomed to receiving compliments from men, not hearing them speak highly of their wives. In the past, she was so admired and idolized by the male species that other bitches didn't exist in a man's mind when he was in Misty's presence. It was insulting for this janitor muthafucka to be singing his wife's praises, as if Misty gave a damn about their relationship.

"What else did you see?" David probed impatiently.

I know this room-cleaning mofo is not trying to rush me. Obviously, he doesn't know that I used to be arm candy for A-list celebrities. I was such a bad bitch, niggas used to rent out their dicks and hustle for me. Furious with David for not seeing past her temporary deformity, she decided to tell him his future in a tactless way.

"You sure you want to hear everything I saw?" she said in a taunting voice.

"Is it bad?" He rubbed his forehead nervously.

"It's not good," she said ominously.

"What's gonna happen?"

"Do you know a light-skinned dude with dreadlocks?"

David shook his head. "No one comes to mind. But, what about him?"

"I saw you holding a gun to his head."

"What! I don't even own a gun," he said in indignation.

"I suppose you'll get access to a gun at some point in the future."

"When is this vision supposed to happen?"

"That I couldn't tell you."

"I don't know anyone who fits that description," he said, shaking his head and frowning.

"Well, maybe your wife does," Misty remarked snidely.

"My wife? How would she know him?"

"I get the impression this dude has something to do with your wife. You need to question her…you know, regarding her fidelity."

David's mouth opened in shock. "Are you saying my wife is fucking around on me with another man?"

"I'm not positive, but that's the impression I got."

"My wife would never—"

"Whatever," Misty said dismissively. "I gave you the info; it's up to you how you use it. Don't be tempted to buy a gun, if you do, you're gonna end up on death row. My duty was to warn you."

"You're fucking with me, right?" His desperate eyes pleaded with Misty to change her prediction.

"Sorry to have to rush you, but I'm extremely busy right now. You can mop in here later today, or better yet, come back tomorrow."

"Are you serious? You can't hit me with this shit and dismiss me."

"Why can't I? I can't help it if your wife has a man on the side."

"My wife wouldn't do anything like that!"

"Believe what you want." Misty glanced back down at the screen. "Do me a favor and close the door on your way out."

David didn't budge from where he was standing. He took deep, angry breaths and glared at Misty, as if she'd put a hex on him. Finally, he pushed the wheeled mop bucket and exited her room.

Pleased with herself, Misty sniggered. *I dare another muthafucka to come up in here, praising another bitch while in my presence.*

CHAPTER 5

Trinidad had been a beautiful paradise. Every morning, Anya woke up to the sounds of birds singing, seemingly, all around her. The different melodies soothed her briefly, but upon fully awakening, she was always struck by an overwhelming sense of loss. The saying that money can't buy happiness was definitely true. Without Brick, she felt incomplete. Her inheritance made life easier, but couldn't un-break her heart.

Her mother's Trinidadian relatives were friendly enough, but thinking that all Americans were rich, they had more interest in getting money from Anya than in actually getting to know her. After only a week in her mother's birthplace, Anya packed up and returned to Indianapolis, Indiana. She needed to regroup and recharge in familiar surroundings before resuming the search for her father in Philadelphia. This time, instead of physically pounding the pavements of Philly, she'd hire a private investigator to do the legwork. It wasn't that she minded putting in the labor, but being back in Philly would be a torturous reminder of Brick and the love she'd lost.

As far as she knew, Brick had turned himself in and was doing time. Then again, he could have patched things up with his wife and resumed life as a married man. In either case, Brick had made it clear that the love she thought they shared was nothing more to him than convenient sex, and he urged her to move on and find true love. As far as Anya was concerned, she'd already found everything she needed in Brick, and she wasn't interested in looking any further. Their lovemaking had been so intense, and her feelings for him were so passionate, the memories of their time together would sustain her.

It wasn't wishful thinking that led Anya to believe Brick had feelings for her that were more powerful than a mere sex connection. When he looked at her for the last time, there was unmistakable love in his eyes. Still, she had to respect his wishes and leave him alone, and for that reason, she didn't allow herself to check the online inmate database to find out if he was locked up. Though she was tempted, she didn't call the hospital to find out if Misty was dead or alive, either. Brick and the people he was attached to were none of Anya's concern.

Hopefully, the money she'd stealthily tucked inside his bag would be put to good use. Good lawyers weren't cheap, and Brick deserved better than a public defender if he had indeed, ended up in jail.

Anya's old neighborhood in Indianapolis seemed more riddled by drugs and crime than when she'd left. Having more than enough money to live in a safe environment, she moved in a furnished, luxury apartment in downtown Indianapolis. At the mall one day, she'd bumped into Natalie, an old acquaintance from high school, and reluctantly agreed to go with Natalie to the hottest new club in the area.

Clubbing was the last thing on Anya's mind, but it was time to get out and try to have some fun. At twenty-one, she was too young to be alone in her apartment night after night. Besides, she had yet to wear any of the pieces in her overflowing wardrobe, and it was time to show off some of her designer clothes.

Driving her new Audi, she honked the horn in front of Natalie's house in the 'hood. Natalie's house was neglected with yellowed window shades. The front of the house looked like a dumping ground. A trash can was toppled over with rubbish and scraps spilling out on the tiny, dirt-patch lawn that was surrounded by a sagging and rusted metal fence. Broken beer bottles and crushed soda cans littered the front of the house, and an evening breeze blew empty cellophane bags around the yard as if they were fallen leaves.

Natalie came out of the rundown house and navigated around the trash and debris as she headed for Anya's car. Having known hard times, Anya gave Natalie a sympathetic smile and said, "Hey, Natalie."

"Is this your car?" Natalie exclaimed, obviously impressed.

Anya nodded and blushed, a sort of apology for doing so much better than Natalie.

Patting the leather upholstery, Natalie said, "You ballin', girl!"

"Not really," Anya muttered as she cruised to their destination. Though her eyes were on the road, she could see from her peripheral vision that Natalie was observing her intensely, starting with her ombre-colored, short, stylish hair, down to her red bottom stilettos.

"Looks like you been making moves," Natalie commented. "Everything about you smells like money. Are you hooked up with a big-time hustler? If so, you need to put me on with his second-in-command."

Anya chuckled softly. "No, I'm not hooked up with anyone. I know how to get bargains when I shop," she said, downplaying her luxe lifestyle.

"You need to take me along on your next shopping trip. I'm

hitting up the club wearing clothes from Wal-Mart while you look like you shopped on Rodeo Drive."

Natalie had an amusing way of expressing herself and Anya laughed again.

"I'm serious. I can't compete with you tonight." Natalie shook her head in defeat.

Anya glanced at Natalie's cheap clothes and bad weave that looked like it had taken only fifteen minutes to put in. Life had not treated Natalie very kindly. "We're about the same size, so the next time we go out, I'll let you borrow something from my closet," Anya offered.

"Cool, I only wish you had told me I could rock something from your wardrobe before you picked me up."

"Next time, I promise," Anya said as she drove around the crowded lot looking for a parking spot.

Natalie perused the parking lot. "Wow, this place is packed for a Thursday. I hope we hook up with some dudes that don't mind spending paper on us."

Anya wasn't interested in a hookup, but she didn't say anything.

"Oh, my God!" Natalie suddenly exclaimed.

"What!" Anya slammed on the brakes thinking she was about to run into something.

"Baller alert!" Natalie shouted excitedly, craning her neck as a Range Rover pulled into the parking area, its gleaming rims spinning. "Sergio and his boys are gonna be up in the club tonight."

"Girl, don't be screaming while I'm driving. I almost ran into one of these parked cars."

"Sorry, girl. I got overly excited because Sergio and his boys are here." Natalie began moving her shoulders to the music that poured from the speakers in Anya's car.

"Who's Sergio?" Anya glanced in the direction of the Range, but the tinted windows prevented her from getting a glimpse of the driver.

"You don't know who Sergio is?" Natalie gawked at Anya. "Girl, you been out of town for way too long. Sergio runs the city, now. He used to be nothing more than a soldier, but he's a boss now that he took over all of Big Marvin's territories. He's a fine-ass Dominican with jet-black, silky hair, smooth dark skin, and hypnotizing dark eyes."

"Never heard of him." She'd never heard of Big Marvin either; she'd never been the type of girl to run after drug dealers.

"Where you been living—under a rock? Everybody knows Sergio." Natalie stared at Anya with widened eyes, gawking at her as if Anya was missing a chip in her brain. Like a lot of naïve young people in the urban community, Natalie viewed drug dealers with the same respect given a politician, a rock star, or a minister.

"Sorry, I don't make it a habit to keep up with the who's who of poison peddlers in our city."

"What do you have against drug dealers? Both my brothers are hustling; they ain't anywhere near Sergio's status, but they making money and taking care of their families."

Anya decided not to judge Natalie. Were it not for the fact that Anya had inherited a large sum of money, she may have been as starstruck as Natalie in the presence of such a powerful man. Her financial security gave her a sense of confidence that she hadn't always possessed.

As she and Natalie walked to the entrance of the club, Natalie was dragging her feet and looking over her shoulder, hoping that Sergio and his friends would catch up.

"Sergio and his whole crew are looking good. We should talk to them before we get inside. Once we're in the club, all the female vultures are gonna be circling around him, making it hard for us to get noticed."

"Stop acting like a groupie," Anya said, nudging Natalie along.

Greeting patrons at the door were a fat bouncer and a much smaller guy who was collecting the admission fee. "Twenty dollars each," he informed.

"Twenty dollars! I thought it was only ten dollars for ladies," Natalie complained to the money collector.

"Ladies Night is on Tuesday," the man replied gruffly.

"It's okay, Natalie; I got the cover charge," Anya offered in a discreet tone.

Anya slipped a hand inside her bag when a silky voice with a Spanish accent said from behind, "Let the ladies in; they're with me."

Anya glanced over her shoulder and took a sharp inhale of breath. The man who had spoken was gorgeous. Distractingly handsome. She immediately snapped her gaze away from him as if looking too long at such an unusually fine specimen might cause her to go blind. Or lose her mind. To get involved with someone with such striking good looks couldn't be good for one's health or sanity.

"Thanks, Sergio," Natalie gushed with a grin that was so wide, all of her molars were displayed.

"It's cool; ma-ma," he replied, and then strode inside with his boys flanking him.

"Welcome, ladies." The bouncer waved an arm, inviting Anya and Natalie inside, free of charge.

"Step it up, Anya. We have to catch up with Sergio and them, so we can drink on his tab tonight," Natalie said urgently.

"I'm not chasing behind that man for free drinks. I can pay for my own."

"Girl, you crazy. You heard him say that we're with him; so, let's join him."

"You can go join him if you want to; I'm good," Anya insisted, noticing that Sergio and his boys had forged ahead into the packed club without bothering to look back at Anya and Natalie. It was obvious to her that if he was interested in their company, he would have waited, but Natalie was too thirsty to recognize that the man had merely extended a courtesy, not an invitation to hang with him all night.

While the crowd parted for Sergio and company, Anya and Natalie had to squeeze and elbow their way through the throng of people to get to the bar to order a drink. Anya had promised herself not to draw attention by flashing money, but with the bartenders obviously too swamped to take her order, and with people bumping into her and stepping on her Louboutins, it was clearly time to put her funds to good use.

"Come on, Natalie, we're going upstairs."

"To the VIP section?"

"Yes. Fuck all this waiting around for a damn drink."

"But I didn't see Sergio and them go upstairs; how are we gonna get a table and bottle service if Sergio ain't pulling out his money?"

"Sergio doesn't run everything."

"But we don't even have a reservation."

"I don't need a reservation." Anya mounted the stairs with her head held high, and Natalie slinked behind, her eyes darting around in paranoia, like she was guilty of stealing something. Natalie hung to the side while Anya furtively made a monetary transaction with a bouncer who was securing the VIP section, keeping common folks from entering the area.

"The air up here is much fresher, don't you think?" Anya said as she and Natalie were being escorted to a table.

Feeling more at ease, Natalie flashed a grin and said, "Smells like morning dew and roses." She comically tilted her chin as she deeply inhaled the air that circulated in the VIP section.

Offered the bottle service menu, Anya selected Patrón Silver.

Happy and impressed, Natalie did a little dance in her seat, and said, "We gon' ball 'til we fall!"

Recalling the luxury experience she and Brick had enjoyed together in the VIP area in a Los Angeles nightclub, Anya dropped her gaze as her eyes clouded with emotion. *Damn, I miss that man.* A sudden feeling of loneliness engulfed her. She longed to feel Brick's arms around her, to hear his voice. But that was a dream. Brick was gone from her life, forever.

The waitress returned and began mixing what she described as "the perfect margarita." One sip and Anya had to agree that the drink tasted like nectar of the gods. The blend of tequila, pureed mangoes, lime, and Cointreau orange liqueur was exquisite. Alcohol coursed through her body, and as if she'd taken a happy pill, Anya's sad expression morphed into a pleasant smile as she observed the elite VIP patrons that mingled nearby.

"This liquor got me feeling good, and I'm ready to get my dance on," Natalie said, getting out of her seat. "Watch my bag," she said, shoving her handbag in Anya's lap and then dancing the entire way down the stairs and onto the huge dance floor below.

Alone at the table, and once again yearning for Brick, Anya took long swallows of the liquor, guzzling it down as if drinking fruit punch.

"Slow down, ma-ma, before you have to get scooped up and carried out of here," cautioned a soft-spoken Latino voice.

Anya looked up and stared into the smoky eyes of Sergio. This time she didn't look away. She took him in fully, and it was a pleasurable experience. His ebony face with striking cheekbones reminded her of photos she'd seen of African royalty. The mass of silky curls that framed his dark-complexioned face gave him the look of someone from India or the northern region of Africa. Dressed in all-white with sparkling gold accessories, Sergio possessed a majestic quality, and despite his occupation that Anya disapproved of, she couldn't deny an appreciation of his uncommon, good looks.

"Drinking alone leads to overindulgence, so if you don't mind, I'd like to join you and keep you safe," Sergio said, confidently pulling out the chair that Natalie had vacated.

"My friend is sitting there."

Sergio looked around. "Your friend must be invisible because I only see you and me."

Anya gave Sergio an amused smile. "She's downstairs, dancing,"

"She can join my friends at my table; I'm sure she won't mind." He pointed across the room where the six handsome men, who had accompanied him inside the club, sat together, laughing and talking. Anya smiled, realizing that Natalie wouldn't protest a bit over spending time with a bunch of good-looking ballers.

Staring at Anya, Sergio reached across the table and rested his palm on top of her hand. "You're heartbroken; I see it in your eyes. Who is the foolish man that left your fragile heart shattered in pieces?"

Sergio was running game, but hearing bullshit spoken in a sexy, Spanish accent was pleasing to the ear, and having nothing better to do, Anya decided to play along with him.

"I'm not pining over any lost love," Anya said sassily. "The sorrow you saw in my eyes was due to regret when I thought the man of my dreams was going to pass by my table without giving me as much as a second look." *Damn, I said that shit like a well-seasoned player.*

Momentarily rendered speechless by the fact that Anya could verbally go toe-to-toe with him, Sergio beckoned the server as he gathered himself. "Bring me the most expensive bottle you've got. I want to celebrate meeting the prettiest lady in the house tonight. And send some bottles to my friends over there." He gestured to his boys.

Anya pointed to the bottle of Patrón Silver and smiled devilishly. "I already bought the best they have to offer."

"My personal stash of liquor is not on the menu."

The server gave Sergio a head nod and quickly disappeared. When she returned she was carrying a silver ice bucket that contained a bottle of Ace of Spades. A few yards away, a different server delivered three bottles of the expensive champagne to Sergio's friends. The sounds of bottles popping echoed throughout the VIP area.

"A toast to the beginning of a beautiful new friendship," Sergio said, and clinked his flute against Anya's. She sipped the liquid and was surprised by the explosion of flavors that slid down her throat with the smooth texture of raw silk.

"I don't usually like champagne, but this is so good," Anya expressed, licking her lips.

"Only the best for you. I'm going to make it my business to heal those scars on your heart."

Anya held out her hands in exasperation. "There's nothing wrong with my heart. Why do you keep insisting that I've been hurt?"

"I know a wounded soul when I see one. I wouldn't be where I am today if I couldn't read people."

"Well, you're wrong about me," she said, and took a gulp of champagne.

"Okay, I'll let it go until you're ready to talk about it. In the meantime, I'd like to ask you something—what's your name, ma-ma?"

"It's Anya."

"Beautiful," he said, reaching for her hand and bringing it up to his mouth. With slightly parted lips, he softly kissed her hand and Anya felt a quickening in the pit of her stomach and a clenching between her legs. *Damn, I miss Brick.* What she was feeling for Sergio was a only a physical reaction. She hadn't had sex in a while and her body was announcing that it was time for her to end the dry spell.

Sergio, with his fine self, obviously had a hard-on for her, so why mince words?

"I'd like to get together with you later on tonight, so my question is…my place or yours?" Anya said with a sexy smile.

More than likely, most chicks went after Sergio because of his money, power, and good looks. But Anya wasn't interested in any of that. All she wanted was some dick for one night only—nothing more. With merely the kiss of her hand, he'd demonstrated that he could make her pussy pucker, and if he could fuck half as good as Brick, then the time spent together would be well worth her time.

"I see that you're the type of lady who speaks her mind; I like that."

Anya leaned back and took another sip of champagne. "And I like the fact that you have very good taste in women as well as champagne."

Sergio laughed at the slick way Anya had given herself a compliment. "Why don't we get out of here?" His dark eyes probed hers.

"I can't. My friend is down there on the dance floor, and I brought her here. It wouldn't be right to ditch her over a strong back and a handsome face." Anya was throwing hint after hint that she wasn't interested in anything more than a good time. A man like Sergio was accustomed to women throwing themselves at him, but he wouldn't have to worry about Anya blowing up his phone or showing up unexpectedly at the places he hung out.

"I'll make sure your friend gets home safe and sound. Excuse me for a minute." Sergio rose to his feet and glided across the room toward his friends.

Moments later, Natalie returned to the table, sweaty and winded. "Girl, you need to get on the dance floor and have some fun." She glimpsed at the bottle of champagne and her eyes widened. "Where'd that come from?"

"Sergio bought it," Anya said with a sly smile.

Natalie immediately scanned the area. Spotting Sergio standing at a table amongst his entourage, she gave Anya a look of delighted surprise. "Sergio bought champagne for us?"

"Actually, he bought it for me and him to share, but you're welcome to have some."

"Hmph. Apparently, all that illegal money he makes ain't so bad after all," Natalie said snidely as she poured champagne.

"Ah, that was a good one; you got me," Anya said with laughter in her voice. Little did Natalie know that Anya's interest in Sergio had nothing to do with his money and status. Sergio seemed like the ideal candidate to put out the fire that raged between Anya's legs whenever she reminisced about making love with Brick.

CHAPTER 6

Sergio returned to Anya's table with a serious-looking dude who had intense, hawk-like eyes that didn't miss anything. He stood with the erect stance of a Marine.

"This is Majid, he's my right-hand man and he'll get your friend home safely," Sergio said. Majid was all business; he nodded curtly, but didn't crack a smile. There was something sinister about him. He had the deadly air of a viper, and Anya glanced at Natalie warily, wondering if she was being left in good hands.

"Natalie, are you okay with this because I won't leave if you're uncomfortable?" Anya said in a hushed tone.

Natalie was looking at Majid with lustful appreciation. "Girl, it's cool; I didn't come out to be grinning in your face all night. I'm like a kid in a candy store being left in the care of all those fine ballers. Don't worry about me, go ahead and do you." She moistened her lips as she surveyed the handsome men who sat at Sergio's table. After catching their eyes, she suddenly bent over, and without warning, she gripped her ankles and started shaking her ass in time to the music, announcing to everyone in the VIP that she was a freak.

Anya looked away in embarrassment. "What's wrong with you, Natalie? Control yourself."

"Girl, I'm having fun. Being in the VIP with a bunch of ballers spending money on me is a fantasy of mine, and I'm gonna make sure this is a night to remember."

"What do you mean?"

Natalie winked. "Know that while you're getting it poppin' with Sergio, I'm gon' be turnt up right here in the club." Natalie cast a glance in the darkened area in the back, insinuating that she planned on dropping her drawers in the public venue. Smiling, she continued to perform her sexy dance. Anya raised a brow, but kept her thoughts to herself. If fucking ballers in the VIP was Natalie's idea of a good time, then so be it.

Majid rejoined Sergio's crew at their table, where the men leaned back in their seats, smiling lustfully as they were entertained by Natalie's twerking and sensual gyrations. Though Majid sat with his boys, observing Natalie's impromptu, dirty dance routine, his expression remained serious and he seemed unfazed.

Soon after, Anya and Sergio left the club, but they didn't leave alone. Noticing that two members of Sergio's entourage walked behind them, Anya glanced nervously at Sergio.

"I don't make any moves without several pairs of eyes on me," he explained.

She nodded in understanding, though she felt somewhat uncomfortable being in the company of a trio of men she didn't know. As she drove to her apartment with Sergio riding shotgun, her eyes kept darting to the rearview mirror, keeping an eye on the Range Rover that tailed them.

"Nothing to be concerned about," Sergio assured her. "My men are discreet; they'll wait for me outside your building."

She let out a sigh of relief. In her mind, she had pictured the two men sitting in her living room, listening to every sound that emerged from her bedroom while she and Sergio got to know each other better.

Sergio's superb bedroom skills had Anya panting, twisting and turning, and yelling profanities. "Fuck me! Take all this wet pussy, it's yours," she declared while caught up in the throes of passion.

"Oh, yeah? This pussy belongs to me?" Sergio said calmly as he slowly and expertly repositioned her body so that her face was down and her ass was up in the air. With Anya in a position of complete surrender, Sergio slow-stroked and spoke to her in Spanish. She didn't know what the hell he was saying but it sounded sexy as shit. With dick deep in her gut, Anya could only moan while she clutched the sheets.

Most men in power positions, preferred to lay back and take, preferring to let the random chicks they picked up, jump through hoops to satisfy them. But Sergio was putting in work. The sweat that trickled down his well-developed body was evidence of that.

With her cheek pressed against the mattress, Anya's eyes landed on Sergio's 9mm that was holstered and placed on her nightstand. The sight of the weapon reminded her of the blood she and Brick had spilled during their rampage of revenge that began in Philly and ended in Los Angeles. Excitement motivated her to buck backward, slamming her ass into Sergio's groin.

"Oh, yeah, throw that pussy at me, ma-ma," Sergio prompted, alternately squeezing her hips and then lightly smacking her ass.

She recalled how she had forced Kaymar Crawford to suck the nozzle of the gun like he was giving head. That memory along with Sergio's dick caressing her inner walls heightened her sexual pleasure. The feeling was so intense, Anya squeezed her eyes shut and gritted her teeth. When she opened them, once again, she was staring at the gun on the nightstand, and the sight of it was a visual aphrodisiac. Her body jerked as an orgasm erupted and tore through her system.

Aroused by the quick, spastic vaginal muscles that continuously gripped his shaft, Sergio quickened the pace of his stroke. His voice rose in volume, as he spoke Spanish even more passionately. His own climax was accompanied by a thunderous roar that completely drowned out Anya's voice as she softly whimpered Brick's name.

As Sergio got dressed, his eyes took in Anya's luxury apartment. "This is a fly little spot you got here," Sergio complimented, looking around Anya's place. "What do you do for a living?"

"Not much."

"So, who's my competition? Who's paying for all this?"

"I pay my own bills."

"I thought you didn't have a job…" Sergio paused as enlightenment brightened his eyes. "Let me guess? You work for a high-class escort service while you're putting yourself through college?"

Anya laughed. "Nah, I'm not into anything like that."

"Then how do you make ends meet?"

Anya's eyes lowered and sorrow softened her voice. "I received an inheritance after my mom passed."

"Sorry for your loss."

"It was a long time ago."

"But the pain is like it happened yesterday," he said knowingly.

"You're right. Anyway, until I figure out what kind of profession I want to get into, I'm simply coasting through life."

"You want to coast with me?" he asked, revealing a look of vulnerability in his dark, mesmerizing eyes.

"What are you asking me?" Naked, Anya lay on her side with an elbow propped up, and her head resting on her palm.

"I'm asking you to spend some time with me. I spend most of

my days and nights out in the streets; it would be a nice change of pace to come home to a shorty that I really cared about."

"But you don't even know me." Anya felt somewhat frantic. She had expected a handsome, major hustler like Sergio to bust a nut and be on his way, but here he was, talking about spending quality time together. The problem was, she wasn't feeling him in the same way.

"What's wrong, don't you believe in destiny? I was standing behind you when you and your friend were about to enter the club. I didn't even have to see your face to know that you were the woman I've been waiting for. I've done my share of dirt, but that doesn't mean that I don't talk with the Man above and ask for forgiveness. I didn't choose this life; it chose me. Generations of my family have been in the game, but we're still human and want that perfect person to love."

Love? What the fuck! "No disrespect, Sergio. We both had a good time, but love is the last thing that I'm looking for. I'm simply trying to enjoy life, and along the way, maybe I'll learn how to smile again."

"I can put that smile back on your face if you give me a chance."

"I don't understand where this is coming from. I assumed you'd smash and keep it moving. I expected you to treat me the way hustlers treat any woman who's willing to give up an easy piece of ass. Love 'em and leave 'em...isn't that part of the game?"

"You're right; but you're different from the others, Anya. I can feel it; I know you're the one."

Anya shook her head. "You don't even know me."

Sergio placed a hand in the center of his chest. "The heart knows what it wants, and my heart is telling me that I should be your man," he responded as he headed for the door.

Sergio exited, leaving Anya in deep contemplation. When she had begun her search for her father, having a man like Sergio, who was worldly wise and who also possessed unlimited resources would have been a godsend. But at this stage of her life, she didn't need a man who couldn't move without henchmen and bodyguards clustered around him. Besides, until she truly got over Brick, there wasn't room in her heart for anyone else.

CHAPTER 7

By the time Johanna McBride found the time to take a break from her nursing duties and bring Misty a copy of the *Philadelphia Daily News*, Misty had already found the article online and had posted it on her website.

Misty glanced up from the screen of the iPad when Johanna proudly set the newspaper in front of her. "I already read the article online," she muttered, ignoring the hard copy.

"Sharon did a great job of portraying what your life has been like since the tragedy," Johanna said, nodding her head briskly as she waited for Misty to agree with her.

"The way she told my story was all right, but apparently it's not compelling enough to tug at the public's heartstrings," Misty commented without looking away from the iPad screen.

"What makes you say that?" Johanna craned her neck toward the screen that Misty was riveted to.

"The contributions have started trickling in, but these cheap Philly bastards don't seem to want to come up off of more than twenty-five dollars a pop. So far, I only have three hundred and seventy-five dollars in donations. At this slow rate, I'll be old and wrinkled before I get enough to pay for my surgery."

"The paper's only been out for a few hours; give it time. You have to be optimistic. Don't forget, before the big donors stepped in, President Obama financed his campaign with small donations," Johanna said, smiling broadly.

Unimpressed, Misty rolled her eyes. "Did you want something else, Johanna?"

Johanna looked momentarily perplexed by Misty's terse attitude. Then her expression brightened. "Oh, there is something I wanted to tell you. Your prediction is so accurate, it's downright uncanny. Do you recall that I told you I didn't have an outfit like the one you said I was wearing in your vision?" The nurse took a deep breath. "You're not going to believe this…" Her eyes widened in excitement. "Drum roll, please…" She imitated beating a drum and Misty could have vomited at the foolish display of joyfulness. It didn't help her disposition that Johanna's protrusive front teeth were hanging over her bottom lip as she beat the invisible drum.

I know I look like a freak, but at least I'm trying to do something about it. This dippy bitch should have invested in some braces a long time ago.

"Would you believe that my sister, who's been packing on the pounds in the last few years, but refused to get rid of her "skinny clothes"—

Misty interrupted with a sigh of exasperation when Johanna made air quotes around skinny clothes. *I wish this nuisance of a woman would get to the point. Ain't nobody ask this ho to come in here and start pantomiming drum rolls and making quotes in the air and shit. If she doesn't hurry up and say what the fuck is on her mind and let me get back to counting my donations, I might have to report her to her supervisor. She thinks she's slick, but I'm not stupid; I know this ho is angling for another free reading, but it's not gonna happen.*

"My sister finally broke down and packed up the wardrobe she can no longer fit," Johanna continued. "Well, you wouldn't believe what I discovered among her discarded clothing…" She paused and folded her arms dramatically and bucked her eyes, as if Misty was hanging on to her every word and waiting in expectation.

At this point in the nurse's long-winded, boring story, had Misty not been paralyzed, she would have leapt out of her bed and commenced to strangling the life out of her.

"Folded up as nice as you please, was a pair of white slacks and the striped orange and white top you said I was wearing when you had the vision."

Misty gave the nurse a blank look while thinking, *Ohmigod; I hate you so much!* "And…," she finally said with impatience evident in her tone.

"And I'm going to be wearing that ensemble tonight when the realtor hands me the keys to my new summer home." Excited, Johanna began clapping merrily and beaming at Misty, expecting her to share her joy.

Misty had had quite enough. She imagined clunking the nurse in the head with the iPad but she didn't want to damage the device that was her only connection to the cheap-ass donors of the Philadelphia area.

"I need my rest, Johanna. Would you please close my door on your way out?"

Wondering what she'd said to upset Misty, Johanna slinked away with her tail between her legs. Misty immediately returned her gaze to the iPad screen and scowled at the latest meager donation that had come in while she'd been distracted by the nurse's stupid story. She'd already told the heifer that she had on white pants and a damn striped top, so why did she feel the need to waste Misty's time telling her something she already knew?

If that bucktooth bitch thought she was going to keep coming in Misty's room, gawking at her and grinning, she was sadly mistaken. She was trying to get way too familiar for Misty's taste. Bitch was starting to act like a stalker, and if she didn't calm herself down and stay in her place as a professional caregiver, Misty would have no choice but to lodge a complaint against her.

The small donations were coming in dribs and drabs and making Misty so disappointed and irritable. She powered off the tablet and closed her eyes, planning to nap for about a half-hour.

"Hey, Sleeping Beauty," Brick said.

Misty's lashes fluttered as she blinked into consciousness. "Hi, Brick," she said, smiling. A glance at the clock indicated she'd been asleep for several hours, much longer than she'd intended.

Brick had a copy of the newspaper tucked under his arm. "I brought you the paper, but I see someone already beat me to it. I read the article and I think the writer did a good job of telling your story and showing how much of a fighter you are. She sort of makes the reader admire you instead of feeling sorry for you. And since I know you don't want to be pitied, I give her props for that."

"Maybe the way she wrote the story is the reason the money is funny," Misty said with her brows wrinkled together. "I only had about four hundred dollars when I drifted to sleep, and to be honest, I expected so much more."

"Don't let that get you down. You're gonna get that surgery if I have to stick up a bank, so stop worrying about it."

Misty laughed.

"I'm dead serious."

"I know you are, but I don't want you to attempt something like that. You're the one person in this world who truly cares about me, Brick, and I wouldn't dream of allowing you to jeopardize your freedom. I'll think of something. You know, me, Brick; I'm always scheming and I'm going to figure out a way to get the money I need. If this article doesn't do the trick, then I'll get in touch with someone from a national newspaper—like the *National Enquirer*—a paper with a much broader audience."

"I have some good news for you."

Misty looked at him curiously.

"We have a place. It's wheelchair accessible, high ceilings, and a nice view."

"I'm not going to need a wheelchair for long," Misty said.

"What are you talking about?"

"While I was asleep, I dreamed I had the ability to heal people. And if I can heal others, I think I should start with myself."

"It was only a dream; I think you're starting to take this supernatural stuff too far. Why don't you focus on getting well enough for the doctor to release you?"

"I really believe I can heal if I tried. My hands are tingling right now, letting me know there's healing power in my hands."

"Are you sure everything's all right in there?" Brick leaned over and gently tapped Misty's forehead.

"How long have you known me?"

"Forever."

"And you've never known me to talk shit I couldn't back up, have you?"

"Making a big deal out of something you dreamed isn't like you. You've changed since you came out of the coma."

"I wouldn't say I've *changed*. I've been enhanced is a more accurate statement," Misty countered.

There was a brief, uncomfortable silence, and then Brick spoke.

"I have to go speak with the director of the Occupational Therapy department."

"Why?"

"I have to set up an appointment for them to make a home visit at our new place."

"I don't understand."

"Before you're released, you're going to have to start having occupational therapy sessions."

"Why do I need occupational therapy? I'm not looking for a job."

"That's not what it means. The therapists can help you with your activities of daily living."

"Such as?"

"I don't know much about it, but from what they told me, you're going to need adaptive equipment to be able to do simple stuff like comb your hair and feed yourself."

Misty grimaced. "Oh, I know what you're talking about. Those crazy-looking, scoop bowls and Sippy cups…spoons with long attachments. Man, I don't want that handicapped-looking stuff in our new crib. No thanks."

"It's for your own good, Misty. I don't want you lying around in bed depressed like you were while you were living at your mom's crib. It's possible for you to lead a near-normal life if you make some effort."

"I intend to lead a perfectly normal life, but I don't want to come home to an apartment that's filled with guardrails and all kinds of special needs equipment. Seeing that stuff will depress the hell out of me."

"But that's what you need to be independent."

"No, I don't," Misty snapped.

"Stop being so stubborn. I have to go talk to those people about the home visit. When I get back, I hope you've had an attitude adjustment. I'm trying to help you, not hurt you."

"I'm sorry, Brick. I didn't mean to raise my voice at you. I get frustrated trying to come to terms with the fact that I'm doomed to be an invalid for the rest of my life."

"But, babe, there's so much technology and modern stuff available, you don't have to think of yourself as being doomed. Look on the bright side…can you do that for me?"

"I'll try."

CHAPTER 8

As soon as Brick exited the room, Misty turned on the iPad to check the status of the donations. To her surprise, she had received a thousand dollars from a single donor and quite a few small donations. But even with the large donation, the sum total was still less than impressive. Bypassing the names of the numerous contributors of small donations, she clicked on the big donor's name: Gavin Stallings. She sent him an email with a thank you note. Almost instantaneously, she received an email from him that listed his phone number and the message: *Call me to discuss your surgical procedure.*

Was Gavin Stallings a plastic surgeon? Misty wondered with delight. Facing reality, she decided he was probably some lonely wacko who wanted to gab on the phone, talking about nothing. She was glad she'd come to her senses before she'd asked a nurse to help her make a call. She'd be furious if she had to listen to Gavin Stallings going on and on about how moved he was by her story. Fuck if she'd be a listening ear to some lonely fool. She had to figure out a way to get other generous people to come out of the woodwork and give money to her cause.

Getting the interest of the *National Enquirer* was her best bet. That paper seemed to love printing stories about medical miracles and posting shocking photos of freaks. She doubly qualified to be featured in the gossip rag, and so she decided it would behoove her to be nice to buck-tooth Johanna. She could get Johanna to contact the paper and tell them about how she had emerged from a coma, inexplicably able to predict the future. Johanna had such an enthusiastic way of expressing herself; she was the perfect person to create a national buzz for Misty.

She'd pretty much kicked Johanna out of her room, but now that she needed her again, she wondered what approach to use to get the nurse to comply with her wishes. *Fuck it, I'll simply apologize and tell her I was in a bad mood. Then I'll make up some shit about her summer home; I'm sure that'll encourage her to help me.*

A soft ping informed Misty that another donation had come in. She struggled to lift her contracted hand and with a partially bent index finger, she tapped the screen and saw that Gavin Stallings had sent another thousand. Maybe she needed to talk to this big spender, after all.

Brick returned to the room with a cheerful expression. "You're a celebrity around here, did you know that?"

Misty sucked her tooth. "These fake-ass hospital employees irk me to my soul."

"What did they do that was so wrong, besides take care of you?"

"They're always skinning and grinning when they come in my room, slyly asking if I would mind giving them a reading."

"You're supposed to be a psychic, aren't you?"

"Yeah, but I'm not reading anyone else without charging them. Plus, I don't want to get too deep into my new profession until I get my face fixed."

"What does getting surgery have to do with helping people with their problems?"

"I don't care about helping anyone with their problems. These people would drain me dry of my powers if I let them. I intend to only read people who can afford my fee, but not until I'm looking presentable. Until then, I have to preserve my abilities."

"You're a trip, Misty, and you're back to being your old self."

"What's that supposed to mean? Are you saying that you fell back in love with the sad, dying Misty, but you don't like the real me very much?"

"I felt sorry for you when you were giving up hope. The feisty Misty is the side of you that I'm most familiar with and I've always loved you, you know that. But I'm not taking any shit off you, either. There has to be mutual respect or there's no point in trying to be in a relationship."

"Don't you think I learned my lesson after you dumped me for my mom?"

"I didn't dump you and you know it. You pushed me away. Now, drop it, Misty."

Misty blew out a sigh. "Brick, I need a cell phone," she said out of the blue. "Oh, I'm sorry; I forgot, you haven't been working for a while and you probably spent your last on the apartment."

"No, I got a couple dollars to tide us over until I get another job."

"How much is a couple dollars?"

"Don't worry about it. I'll get you a phone; that's not a problem. I'll bring it when I visit tomorrow."

"Tomorrow? I was kind of hoping you could get it today."

"I can't, babe. For one thing, I have a job interview in an hour. And after that, I'm going to visit your little brother."

Misty suddenly smiled. "How's Little Baron doing?"

"He's good; getting tall."

"Does he remember me?"

"He hasn't mentioned you, but that's probably because your mom doesn't bring your name up. But his memory will be refreshed when he starts spending time with us at the crib."

"I don't know why my mother is so bitter; she's the one who stole my man—"

"Let's not go there again, Misty. Leave it in the past."

Misty sighed audibly.

"I gotta go." Brick leaned over and kissed Misty on the lips. "See you in the morning."

Misty was curious about the big donor and was ready to talk to him. She pressed the button for the nurse, and less than two minutes later, a young nursing assistant named Paulette entered her room.

"Do you need anything, Misty?" Paulette asked in a cheerful tone.

"It used to take y'all damn near the whole shift to answer when I buzzed you, but now that I'm famous, I see you're Johnny-on-the-spot," Misty said derisively.

"That's not true. We always come as soon as one of us is available."

"Whatever. Do me a favor, Paulette—tell Johanna McBride that I need to speak to her about something. It's urgent, so tell her to hurry up."

"Johanna is on break. Can I do something for you?"

This chick really thinks she's going to get a psychic reading out of me, so I'll have to string her along. "Can I use your cell phone?"

"Sure."

"I need you to call someone for me and put him on speaker."

The nursing assistant retrieved her phone from the pocket of her scrubs. Misty recited the number and after Paulette made the call and set it on speaker, Misty motioned for her to leave. "You can come back and get your phone in about fifteen minutes."

Paulette exited and a male voice said, "Hello."

"Hi, Mr. Stallings; this is Misty Delagardo."

"Ah, Misty! Thanks for getting in touch with me. I read that you're still recovering in the hospital, and I wasn't sure if you'd be able to get back to me."

"Yes, I'm still here, waiting to get the doctor's approval for release. Thank you for the donations; I appreciate your generosity."

"I wanted to do my part to help. Your story touched my heart. And by the way, did they ever catch the monster that did that to you?"

"No," Misty said regretfully. Back when she wanted to die, she wasn't concerned about getting revenge, but she wanted it so badly now, she could taste it.

"I actually cried tears when I saw the beautiful *before* picture that was placed next to the *after* shot. Oh, Misty, my heart bleeds for you, and I'm officially offering to pay for your reconstructive surgery."

"The surgery I need is not as simple as getting a facelift or a nose job. My bones were crushed. My face literally has to be rebuilt and I need extensive dental work. The cost is extremely expensive."

"How much do you consider extremely expensive?"

"For all the work I need, it's going to cost somewhere in the area of two hundred thousand dollars." Misty had done her homework after getting access to the Internet, and the twenty to thirty thousand that Johanna had quoted was far from accurate.

"That's nothing; it's peanuts to a wealthy man like me."

Misty's breath caught in her chest and her heart began to beat rapidly. If this man was on the up and up, then she wanted to get started immediately. But before she got her hopes up, she had to find out a little more about him. "Uh, what do you do for a living, Mr. Stallings?"

"Call me Gavin. In response to your question, I don't do much of anything. I paint a little when the mood hits me, and I travel when I get bored, but I mainly take care of my dogs and wait for Randolph to return."

Who the hell is Randolph? Gavin didn't sound very stable and Misty's heart sank. She hoped he wasn't playing games with her.

"I don't work because I was born into money," Gavin continued. "But believe me, being born with a silver spoon in your mouth is not all it's cracked up to be."

"I bet," she said, still wondering if Gavin could help her.

"I need a reading, Misty. I can't tell you how many so-called psychics I've been to in the hope of locating Randolph. With all the money I've spent, not one psychic has been able to help me. But after reading your story, I have renewed hope."

"Who is Randolph?"

"My life partner. We've been together for years, but he refused to leave his wife until his kids were grown. Finally, his youngest child went to college, and he still didn't have the balls to tell his shrew of a wife about our great love. We had a big fight, and shortly after, my darling Randolph vanished off the face of the earth. I need to know where he is. Can you help me?"

"That's not how my gift works. I see flashes of your life and then I see a scene from your future. I don't know in advance what I'm going to see." She hoped her surgery didn't depend on finding this nutjob's missing lover. Hell, the man probably didn't want to be found.

"I have faith that you're going to be able to tell me where Randolph is. In fact, I have so much faith, I'm going to set up a consultation for you with Dr. Henry Cavanaugh, one of the best plastic surgeons in the area. Leave it up to me, and he'll be there to consult with you in a day or so."

"Really?"

"Yes. I believe in you, Misty. Your story spoke to me, and I'm looking forward to meeting you. You need your rest, so I'm not going to keep you on the phone. Give me a call after your consultation with Dr. Cavanaugh."

"I'll do that," Misty said, wondering if she dared to dream that a new face was in the foreseeable future.

Misty researched Gavin Stallings online and it turned out that he was a descendant and one of the heirs of a great fortune, passed down from his great-great-grandfather, the founder of a well-known American chemical company, established in the early 1800s. Apparently, in an attempt to keep the money within the family, there was rampant incest in the Stallings family, with cousins marrying cousins and even siblings producing offspring.

If Gavin was a kook, he couldn't help it with all that inbreeding in his family. With the kind of money he had, Misty wouldn't dream of holding his craziness against him.

The Stallings family tree was endless, and after reviewing the history of some of the living family members, she learned that numerous members of the prominent family held positions on the company's Board of Trustees. Some played a large part in politics, and most were well-known philanthropists. The only information she found on Gavin was that he was a patron of the arts.

It was good to know that Gavin wasn't a regular rich guy; he had mega wealth! Excitement surged through Misty's body, enlivening her paralyzed lower limbs, making her feel able to walk, skip, dance, and jump with the snap of a finger. With a bleeding heart like Gavin in her pocket, she could be wealthier than she'd ever imagined if she played her cards right.

CHAPTER 9

"Girl, I did all of 'em," Natalie said over the phone in a bragging tone.

"All of what?" Anya glanced at the bedside clock and it was only seven in the morning. "What are you talking about Natalie, and why are up so early?"

"Haven't been to sleep yet. Last night was the bomb. I sucked two of those niggas off in the back of the VIP, and then partied with them later at the Radisson Hotel. I'm still here, chilling in the suite and killing the wet bar."

"You fucked Sergio's boys?"

"Sure did. All of 'em except Majid and the two that left with you and Sergio." She went quiet. "Did you party with them?"

"Of course not. How can you brag about letting those guys run a train on you?"

"They didn't run anything on me that I didn't want to happen."

"Why would you play yourself like that?"

"Girl, you don't know anything about the game."

"School me."

"The way to a man's heart is not his stomach; it's his dick. And Majid told me if I took care of his boys, he'd take care of me."

"That's so twisted. So, let me get this straight: Majid had you fucking and sucking his friends but you didn't do anything with him?"

"Not yet. But I'm gonna get some of that dick eventually. The next time we party, I hope to get with those other two who left with you and Sergio."

"You sound crazy, but you're grown, and hopefully you know what you're doing."

"Oh, I definitely know what I'm doing. Majid gave me five hundred dollars to make his friends happy. How much did Sergio give you?"

"Nothing. It wasn't like that."

"Bye, girl. Sounds like you're the one who got played."

"I value myself too much to ever get played," Anya retorted.

"Yeah, right. Everybody gets played some time or another."

After listening to Natalie's warped way of thinking, Anya felt dirty. Lots of people in Indianapolis had fallen upon hard times, but she doubted if they were whoring themselves out to eke out a living. She needed to rethink her budding friendship with Natalie. A girl who would fuck a man's friends for profit wasn't working with a full deck. And Majid, the man who had paid for the freaky entertainment, had to be a little twisted himself.

After hanging up the phone, Anya tried to go back to sleep, but she could suddenly smell Sergio's cologne clinging to the sheets. It was a pleasant, masculine fragrance, no doubt very expensive. Everything in Sergio's world was expensive, and she supposed that acquiring luxurious possessions was the reason he put his life and freedom at risk. The reason he sold poison to his own people.

So what if he's a drug dealer, I like him, she admitted to herself. Doctors turned more people into addicts than drug dealers did, she rationalized. Still, sensing that an involvement with Sergio would only bring her despair, Anya decided to push him out of her thoughts. She pulled off the layers of bedding and replaced them with a fresh set of sheets and a different comforter. She still wasn't over Brick and having another man's scent in her bed seemed wrong. And even though Brick had encouraged her to move on, it was too soon to get entangled in a relationship.

Taking her mind off Sergio, she decided to focus on the business of finding her father.

Jonathan Whitman, the private investigator from Philadelphia, whom she found online, assured her that he could find her father.

"How can you find someone who has been missing for years?" Anya questioned, speaking to him over the phone. "I looked everywhere and he seems to have vanished from the face of the earth."

"I specialize in finding missing persons."

"Suppose he's dead?"

"Then I'll get that information and let you know." Whitman cleared his throat to fill the silence after his last comment, and then said, "Fax me the info I asked for—a copy of the most recent picture of your father, his approximate height and weight, date of birth, and make a note of any tattoos or scars. You can go to my website and make a down payment of the fee, using a debit or credit card."

After Anya agreed to fax the info and to take care of the down payment, she asked, "How long does it usually take you to find a missing person?"

"At least thirty days. Sometimes sooner; sometimes longer. I'll keep you posted. "

"Okay," Anya agreed. Paying someone that she found online probably wasn't the smartest move, but it was time to resume the search for her father. If Whitman turned out to be bogus, she'd go to Philly personally and find someone who could get the job done.

By early evening, Anya found herself eyeing her phone for a text from Sergio, and she was beyond surprised when the concierge called to let her know she had a guest named Sergio in the lobby.

He was in her building? Suddenly, she was more annoyed than flattered. How dare he pop in on her? She bet he wouldn't be pleased if she showed up at his place without an invitation. "Put him on the phone, please," she said to the concierge.

"Hey, ma-ma. I was in your neighborhood and thought you might want to make a run with me." He sounded completely at ease as if asking her to make a drug run was normal.

He must be out of his damn mind. "No thanks. I'm not interested in your proposition."

"I'm not propositioning you; only asking you to accompany me to one of my favorite places."

"Where?"

"I don't want to ruin the surprise."

"I have to be cautious."

"You win. Look here, an artist I know well and admire is having an exhibit and a party at a gallery not too far from your apartment. I thought you might like to check out his work."

Now, Anya was flattered. A smile crept across her face. "I don't know anything about art, but I'd love to go. What time does it start?"

"It starts at seven, but people trickle into these events through-out the evening."

"What should I wear?" she asked, feeling flustered.

"I'm sure you'll look amazing in anything you select."

"I need at least thirty minutes to get myself together."

"Don't rush, ma-ma. I'll be waiting in the Range outside your building."

She raced to her closet and selected a black cocktail dress. A woman couldn't go wrong in a little black dress. A little makeup, a quick touchup to her hair with the flat iron, and she was good to go.

Holding a beaded clutch, she felt pretty in her black dress and stilettos when she exited the elevator and crossed the lobby. The concierge smiled in appreciation of her classy look, and she smiled back. But her smile vanished when she stepped outside and saw Majid and two other men sitting behind the wheel of a Range Rover that was exactly like Sergio's. She'd forgotten that Sergio required bodyguards to accompany him everywhere.

Like a perfect gentleman, Sergio, looking spiffy in a black suit, got out of his Range and opened the door for her. They made a striking couple, she thought to herself. During the short drive to the art gallery, she found herself constantly looking in the side mirror and watching Majid. He was tailing them for Sergio's protection, but he seemed more like a shark tracking prey.

The party at the gallery was lively and crowded with champagne and finger foods being served to guests on silver trays. The artist was from the Dominican Republic and his work was a vivid reflection of island life. Sergio introduced her to the artist and then the two men chatted briefly in Spanish. Anya drifted away, giving them privacy while she used the time to admire the art that looked vibrant and realistic.

As she stared at a painting of a boy holding up a big fish he'd caught, she felt arms encircle her waist. "See anything you like?" Sergio said softly.

"I like everything. Your artist friend is very talented. I've never bought any original art, but I'm considering getting this piece. It'll look good in my place." She glanced down at the price tag and whistled. "Jesus!" she said in response. "Thirty-five hundred dollars! Wow, that's steep."

"If you like it, it's yours," Sergio said.

"No, I can't let you—"

"Shh." He held a finger to his lips. "Have another glass of champagne while I make the arrangements to have the painting delivered to your apartment."

Sergio strolled away and a server magically appeared with more champagne.

Anya felt so warm and fuzzy inside, she was no longer annoyed by the presence of Majid and the crew. In fact, she nodded her head at Majid, acknowledging him. He stretched his lips into a smile that looked more like a sneer. Anya shuddered.

Sergio returned and draped an arm over her shoulder. "I missed you," he whispered.

She smiled up at him, basking in the warmth of his attentiveness. She was proud to be with such a strikingly handsome man and the way he kept her cuddled close to him, she could tell he felt the same. They admired the paintings together, and Sergio seemed to have a personal experience with every scene depicted in the artwork. He told her interesting stories about Santa Domingo.

"You'll have to go there with me one day; you'll love my island," he told her with a wistful look in his eyes.

"Have you been there lately?" she asked.

"No, I've never gone back since I left. I've been waiting for my princess to be my side when I returned."

Was he inviting her to travel to the Dominican Republic with him? she wondered. Why was such a hot-looking man with loads of money sweating her to such an extreme? She made a mental note to let him know that it wasn't necessary to stroke her ego simply to get her in bed. His sex skills made him more than welcome.

Revealing his bad-boy persona, Sergio swiped a bottle of champagne from a serving tray before they left the gallery. "One for the road," he said with a devilish smile. In his Range, they both sipped from the bottle, laughing as they passed it back and forth. Anya felt naughty and carefree as she drank from the pilfered bottle of champagne.

Back at her apartment, she never got a chance to bring up the subject of him stroking her ego. With him drizzling champagne down the center of her back and letting it trickle down to the crack of her butt cheeks, she forgot all about the conversation she wanted to have with him.

When his tongue stroke followed the liquid trail, she grasped the sheets and bit into her pillow as she surrendered her body to him.

CHAPTER 10

Gavin Stallings' long money and clout had worked miracles. After arranging a speedy consultation with the esteemed Dr. Cavanaugh, he orchestrated a swift date for Misty to undergo surgery. And now, lying on the operating table, Misty was surrounded by Dr. Cavanaugh and his capable team.

"I'm going to make you even more beautiful than you were before," the doctor reassured with a twinkle of confidence in his eyes. That promise had Misty dreamy-eyed and feeling lightheaded before the anesthesiologist had administered the injection.

She woke up to excruciating pain after the ten-hour surgery. It didn't help that each time a nurse checked her pulse and accidentally brushed her palm, Misty would see flashes of light as head-splitting images raced across the screen of her mind. She was too dazed to make sense of the images, but possessed enough awareness to wish she could hit the pause button on her gift of sight. The random images that depicted the lives of people she couldn't even see, due to the mummified bandages wrapped around her face and head, were giving her a migraine.

She released an agonized moan and someone mercifully put her out of her misery with a painkiller injected into her IV.

It was finally time for the big reveal. She'd yet to meet her bene-factor, the mysterious Gavin Stallings, but they spoke on the phone regularly.

Brick was there, holding Misty's hand and maintaining a poker face when the last bandage was stripped away.

"Am I beautiful, Brick?" she asked in a voice strained by anxiety.

"You'll always be beautiful," Brick responded, rubbing her hand.

"There's still a lot of swelling, which is to be expected, but it should go down in another week or so," Dr. Cavanaugh said.

Needing to see for herself, Misty slowly worked her gnarled fingers around the handle of the mirror that was at her side and determinedly brought it up high enough to see her reflection. "Oh, God; I'm still hideous. I look worse than before the surgery," she said, shooting the surgeon an accusatory look.

"I'm an expert in my field and I can assure you that you're going to see evidence of your new, beautiful face very soon," the doctor said.

Misty surveyed her image. "My face is bloated and distorted; I don't look anything like myself," she whined.

"Healing from surgery takes a while, but you must have faith in me and be patient," the doctor said as he began scribbling in Misty's chart. "Trust me, Ms. Delagardo, your beauty will be astonishing," the surgeon said. His voice didn't waver; he didn't blink. He seemed utterly convinced that her face, distorted by lumps, blisters, and bruises would settle into something beautiful.

"If you say so," she said, sulking.

"Oh!" the doctor said, suddenly remembering something. "I have some rather good news for you."

"What's that?" Misty looked at the doctor through eyes with lids so swollen, she could barely make out more than an outline of the man.

"I know you're weary of being in the hospital, and I've spoken with your other doctors and we agree that you're well enough to be discharged, tomorrow."

"Tomorrow! You want me to leave the hospital and go out in public looking like this?" Misty was dumbfounded.

"It'll be all right, babe. It's time to start getting used to doing some things for yourself," Brick added.

"I'm not ready. I can't leave here until I look like myself, again."

The doctor's eyes shifted downward. "Actually," he said, his gaze aimed at the floor, "your coverage won't allow you to continue convalescing here. We can get a social worker to speak to you about long-term care facilities, if you'd like."

"I know you're not trying to put me in one of those places for invalids," Misty said, indignant.

Brick shook his head defensively. "No, that's why I got the apartment for us, so you wouldn't have to go into a facility."

Misty wanted to give Brick an appreciative smile, but was too swollen to manage it. She directed her attention to Dr. Cavanaugh. "What about Gavin Stallings? I thought he was paying for everything."

"He paid for the reconstructive surgery and has promised to pay for extensive dental work once your face has healed," Dr. Cavanaugh replied, writing additional notes in Misty's chart. "Your coverage does include a home health care nurse for a few hours a day," he said with an encouraging smile.

Misty sighed audibly.

"I'd like to see you in my office in two weeks." The doctor left his card on the nightstand, shook Brick's hand, and then squeezed Misty's arm in parting.

"This is some bullshit," she said to Brick after the doctor exited.

"Gavin has enough money to keep me here while I'm healing. Why would he let them kick me out like I'm trash?"

Brick shrugged. "Who knows the ways of eccentric rich folks?" Brick gently placed a hand on Misty's shoulder. "I got you, Misty. You don't have to worry about anything…you hear me?"

She nodded mechanically as her mind raced with terrifying thoughts. Suppose Gavin Stallings was a crazy, vindictive former client whom she'd burned. Misty had been a ruthless pimptress and had hurt a lot of people in her life. Gavin Stallings was a wealthy, gay man and she'd sent most of the boys who hustled for her out on "dates" with men of means. Men who didn't mind paying hefty prices to suck young dick. And some of those men fell in love with her hunky recruits. Oh, God, suppose Gavin was out for revenge and had hired the surgeon to deliberately fuck up her face worse than it already was. The hairs stood up on the back of her neck. Was it possible that Gavin had hired the woman who had tried to kill her and was now intent on making sure she lived a fate worse than death?

She glanced in the mirror again. Ugh! She looked like the fuckin' elephant man. She'd been so stupid to allow a nutty stranger to select a surgeon to give her a new face.

"Brick," Misty said in a whimper.

"Yeah, babe?" He massaged her shoulder. "Stop worrying, you're gonna be all right."

"Remember when you promised to get revenge on the person who hurt me?"

Abruptly halting the shoulder massage, Brick's hand went still. "Yeah, I remember. And you told me to leave it alone; you said you were at peace with everything."

"That's when I was preparing to die, but things have changed, and I need to know who did this to me. I need that bitch and everybody associated with her to be dead." *And that includes Gavin, if he paid for the botched hit.*

"I already took care of that."

"What do you mean?"

"It wasn't a female who hurt you."

"Yes, it was. A tall bitch wearing Louboutins."

"No, it was one of your workers, dressed like a woman," Brick said grimly.

"Which one?" Misty's voice raised several pitches.

"A dude named Horatio."

"Horatio! Are you fuckin' kidding me? Why would Horatio want to kill me?" Then she recalled their trip to Miami and how she had treated him. How she'd gone as far as firing him after he had helped her hook up with mega star, Smash Hitz. *So what? He should have taken it like a man. You win some; you lose some. You don't go around disfiguring and paralyzing people because you got your feelings hurt.*

"He's been dealt with," Brick said, his face tense and with a deadly look in his eyes. "I made sure he suffered. At first that punk was pleading for his life, and then he was wishing he could hurry up and die."

Misty nodded in satisfaction. "What about Smash Hitz? I'm sure he had something to do with it."

"Nah, he didn't. It was a bitch named Juicy who set you up. Her and another woman named Redbone."

"Juicy did this to me! That no good, jealous-ass—"

"She ain't breathing no more. Died of AIDS. And that Redbone chick died a painful death right along with Horatio. Did you really think I'd be able to rest if I didn't track down those muthafuckas?"

"I should have known you would handle it. Who is Redbone, though? Why did she hate me?"

"Her and Juicy were fucking each other. Redbone was part of

the set-up, trying to please Juicy. And that was a big mistake on her part. If the Grim Reaper hadn't gotten to Juicy first, I would have paid her a visit in the hospice place where she was staying and skinned her ass alive before she had the chance to check out peacefully on pain meds."

"I'm relieved that Gavin wasn't involved."

"Why would you even think that?" Brick was baffled.

Misty made a face and shrugged.

"He's not out to get you. Why would he spend all that money for a makeover if he wanted to harm you? That nightmare is over, Misty. It's gonna be smooth sailing from now on."

CHAPTER 11

Late afternoon, Brick had gone to look for work again. There was a tap on Misty's door. The nurse had applied fresh bandages, which sufficiently concealed her dreadful appearance, and Misty called, "Come in," feeling somewhat confident that with her face bandaged, at least she wouldn't scare the bejesus out of whoever was attempting to enter her room.

She was surprised to see David coming through the door with his cleaning cart filled with spray bottles of disinfectant and waste bin liners.

"Come back tomorrow, after I check out," Misty said snippily. She didn't feel like being disturbed while she was watching a rerun of *The Preachers of LA*, a reality show about religious leaders who enjoyed excessive lifestyles that allowed them to live in mansions and own multiple luxury cars. If those pompous jerks could earn that much money from merely yelling Bible verses with passion, then she should be able to live like a queen with her new gift of inner vision.

Hmm. *Inner Vision* had a nice ring to it. Misty's Church of Inner Vision. No, if she put the word "church" in the title of her operation, she'd have to start learning scripture and she didn't have time for that.

The House of Inner Vision. Yeah, that sounded much better. She smiled to herself as she imagined a mega, church-like structure where she'd give readings to desperate people who would pay any price to glimpse their future.

From the corner of her eye, she noticed that David was still lingering in her room. "Are you deaf? I said come back and clean in here tomorrow," she said in an aggravated voice that should have made him scurry away.

But he stood his ground. Grim-faced, his back rigid.

"Let me rephrase my question. Do you have a hearing problem?"

"No, uh, I want to apologize about the way I acted when you told me about my wife and the man with the dreads."

"Apology accepted," Misty said without taking her eyes from the TV screen.

"I was wondering if you could give me another reading."

"Hell, no," she barked. "My services aren't free, and you can't afford another reading. You should have been more appreciative when I was doing giveaways. Like most people, you thought a freebie had no value. Oh, well, it's your loss, not mine."

"Please. I need to know if I pulled the trigger on the dude who's cheating with my wife."

"You don't need me to tell you that. Either you're gonna do it or you're not. Only you know the answer to that."

He began to pace. "I never thought about killing anyone before, but right now, I'm close to getting a gun and killing both of them, and then turning it on myself," David said, looking tortured.

"And then what happens to your little girl?"

David shook his head. "I don't know," he said with a groan.

"It would be real selfish of you to leave your child an orphan simply because your wife cheated. People cheat all the time. It's life; divorce her and get over it."

"But I still love her."

Misty rolled her eyes. "Obviously, she doesn't love you."

"But I do everything to satisfy my wife; I can't believe she's cheating on me with one of her coworkers. I found out they go to lunch together, and sometimes they skip eating, if you know what I mean."

"Look, I don't know what to tell you about your problem. My advice is to figure out a child support and custody arrangement for your daughter's sake, and then move on with your life."

"You're right, I need to move on," David said, staring off into space.

Misty gave him the side eye, thinking to herself, *this muthafucka is crazy!*

Snapping out of whatever zone he was in, he looked at her with a soft smile. "Thanks for listening to me." He took a few steps toward the door and stopped and turned around. "Would it be okay if I left my number with you?"

"For what?"

"In case you see something else in my future," he said, taking a pen from his pocket, prepared to scrawl his number on a piece of paper.

"That's not how this works. I told you what I saw and it's not likely that I'll get a spontaneous read on you with a different outcome."

"Your powers are new, right?"

"Yeah. And…?"

"You never know what might happen. You might see something else."

This janitor with his quiet self has the nerve to be pushy as hell. They say you should look out for the quiet ones. I'm gonna accept his number, so I can get rid of his ass. "Put your number in my phone," Misty said, nodding toward the new iPhone that was on the nightstand. She loved the newest version of the iPhone that Brick had bought her; the very sight of it made her want to shout with joy.

David entered his number in the phone and gave her a head nod before exiting her room.

Suddenly, Misty was relieved that she was leaving the hospital tomorrow. In case David had mentioned her prediction to anyone, she didn't want to be around when the news came out that the soft-spoken janitor had gone haywire and committed a double murder and suicide.

The glimpse into the future that Misty offered folks was definitely not for the weak-minded. Hopefully, her paying clients would be able to handle what she told them and possibly alter any unpleasant future events she foresaw.

The apartment Brick found for them was spacious and sunny and even more important, it was on the first floor, with their front door leading to the outside. There were no worrisome stairs and no vestibule area. The place was more like a townhome than an apartment. Other than mounted TVs in the living room and bedroom, a nondescript chair in the living room, and two stools in the kitchen, there wasn't any other furniture.

"No point in filling the place with a lot of furniture when you're going to need the space to wheel around," Brick explained.

I'm not wheeling around, Misty thought with repugnance. It was unrealistic to think that she wouldn't, but she stubbornly held on to the belief that somehow she was going to walk again.

She sat in her new, shiny-wheeled chair while Brick pushed her from one empty room to the next, pointing to bare walls and reminding her that there were huge portraits of her boxed up in her mother's basement that would look great hanging in their new place.

"Nah, leave those pictures where they are. I want to hire a photographer to take some new shots of the two of us together, after my face heals."

She looked up, checking Brick's reaction to the unselfish way she'd included him in the future photo session, but he didn't seem to notice. Misty intended to have blown-up photos of her and Brick all over the place to taunt her mother when she finally caved (she couldn't stay mad at her firstborn child forever) and came over to visit the reunited couple.

Misty's phone, which was resting on her lap like a beloved pet, began to ring. She glanced down at the display and spotted the 610 area code. "It's Gavin. Put him on speaker for me, please."

Brick reached down and deftly swiped and tapped, and then said, "Hold on for Misty."

"Hi, Gavin," she said.

"Hello, Misty," Gavin replied cheerfully. "How's the new place?"

"It's nice; Brick has good taste."

"I hear you're recovering beautifully."

"That's a lie! My face is as big as a balloon. It's red, black, and blue and has lumps all over it. There's nothing beautiful about me."

"Don't fret," Gavin clucked like a mother hen. "It won't be long before you're restored to your natural state of loveliness."

There was sincerity in his tone, putting Misty's mind at ease. She no longer feared that Gavin and Dr. Cavanaugh had played a cruel trick on her. Suddenly, her heart quickened at the idea that in a few short weeks, she would no longer be hideous. She wasn't aware that she was crying until the salty tears seeped through the gauze bandaging, stinging the puffy, enflamed skin on her face.

"Misty?" Gavin's concerned voice filled the air.

"Gavin, I'm gonna have to call you back," she said, sniffling.

"Oh, gracious, you sound terrible. Are you in pain? Listen, don't try to be brave, my dear. Take the pain meds the doctor prescribed for you, and I'll check on you tomorrow when you're feeling better."

"Okay." She wiped at her nostrils, the only part of her nose that wasn't covered with bandages.

Brick reached down and tapped the screen, ending the call. Baffled, he asked, "What's wrong? You were feeling fine a few minutes ago. Why're you suddenly crying?"

Observing her inquisitively, Brick dabbed delicately at the tears that fell from her eyes.

"I'm crying because I'm happy, Brick. For a moment, I had a bad feeling about the surgery; now I know everything is going to be fine." There was a glimmer of excitement in her teary eyes and the corners of the lips that poked through the bandages, bunched up together in an attempt to smile.

"I never doubted that everything would work out. You being psychic and all, shouldn't you have already known that?"

"Not really. I can't foresee my own future; I can only predict snatches of events in other people's lives, but *you* already know that."

"I'm only messing with you." He brushed the top of her hand that was contracted so badly it seemed to be balled into a fist.

Misty regarded her deformed hands. "My hands are going to have to be broken and operated on if I expect to be able to fully use them again. But a different kind of surgeon will have to work on my hands."

"All in good time, Misty. Don't start worrying about that."

"I'm not worrying. Dr. Cavanaugh said I should wait at least six months before I get that work done."

"Good advice. So, what do you want to do? Wanna watch TV? Want me to make you something to eat before I go out?" It wasn't unusual for Brick to take care of Misty. One way or another, he'd always taken care of her.

"I can eat when the nurse gets here. Where're you going?"

"Second interview at the site where the new prison is being built."

"What new prison?"

"I keep forgetting you've been out of it for so long, you don't know about the different things going on in the area. You know they shut down twenty-three schools in Philadelphia; they cut out sports and art programs and laid off four thousand teachers, yet the state is spending millions to build a new prison in Collegeville. Folks are pissed, saying that since they're depriving kids of a proper education, they won't have any choice but to end up incarcerated in the new prison. It's in Montgomery County—only a thirty-minute drive from here. It pays thirty an hour. Not bad, right?"

"That's good, but don't get too comfortable working there."

"Why not? Do you see me hitting the lottery in the future?" Brick joked.

"I need you to work with me once I get my business up and running. I'll pay you a whole lot more than thirty an hour."

"Is that right?" Brick said, smiling as he indulged Misty's fantasy.

"You think I'm playing, but you'll soon see how serious I am."

Still smiling, Brick strolled toward the door. "Call me if you need anything."

CHAPTER 12

Brick wasn't hired for the construction job in Montgomery County, but he did get a job at a site in Old City, Philadelphia. Eager to start earning a living, he left the apartment at practically dawn. Audrey, the home care nurse, arrived at seven and was scheduled to care for Misty for four hours. She dressed and groomed Misty, prepared breakfast for her, and dispensed her meds. Then she transferred her to her wheelchair, planning to park her in front of the TV for the remaining hours of her shift.

Audrey never commented when the tiny prickles occurred whenever her flesh connected with Misty's. Apparently, she hadn't read the article about Misty and maybe she hadn't noticed. Whatever the case, Misty was glad the nurse didn't pester her with a request for a reading. She'd seen Audrey's boring life review, but oddly, hadn't seen the woman's future. It didn't matter, Audrey's future was no doubt as boring as she was.

Audrey was in her mid-thirties, but had an old lady way about her. She wore big, goofy, thick-lensed glasses. Her complexion was dreadful with acne scars on her cheeks and a fresh cluster of adult acne on her forehead and chin. Her crinkly-textured hair was pulled tightly into a plain, low bun. Her clothing was dreary and shapeless and she wore black, orthopedic-looking nurse's shoes. Audrey was the epitome of old-fashioned, and with those thick glasses, she reminded Misty of an ugly schoolteacher she'd once had named Ms. Peabody. Laughing to herself, Misty began calling Audrey "Ms. Peabody" in her mind.

Misty fiddled with her iPad while Audrey knitted something uninteresting and chuckled through a rerun of *Two and a Half Men.* The doorbell chimed, startling both of them.

Audrey eyed the door suspiciously. "Are you expecting company?"

"Looking like this?" Misty pointed to her bandaged face and scowled beneath the gauze.

The doorbell sounded over and over, as if someone was persistently jabbing the button.

"Someone sure is impatient," Audrey remarked. "It's probably one of those cable companies trying to get you to switch." She grudgingly hefted herself out of the chair and moved swiftly toward the door, intent on getting rid of the annoying salesperson.

"Hello. I'm here to see Ms. Delagardo," said the familiar soft-spoken voice that Misty had only heard over the phone. Gavin had taken it upon himself to come to her apartment, unannounced and uninvited. His money allowed him to take liberties, she supposed.

"And who should I say is here to see her?" the nurse inquired.

"Tell Ms. Delagardo that her secret admirer is here," Gavin said in a joking tone, apparently unwilling to divulge his identity.

"He's a friend of mine; let him in," Misty said in a voice as loud as she could manage with bandages nearly covering her mouth.

Gavin glided toward her with the entitled air of those who've inherited wealth, and Misty was instantly struck by his golden handsomeness. Well over six feet tall, his frosted blond hair hung past his chin and was coifed in a style that looked carefully tousled. His pale gold slacks matched the highlights in his hair and his china blue silk shirt, which complemented his eyes, billowed behind him, giving him the appearance of a nobleman from a previous century—a count, a duke, or perhaps a marquis.

Misty glanced at the gold watch on his wrist and imagined it must have cost as much as a luxury car. He reeked of money and unlike some rich folks who downplayed their wealth, slopping around in faded jeans and T-shirts, Gavin had a great sense of style and was very well put together in rich fabrics and expensive, sparkling jewelry.

"Well, well. Aren't you a striking figure," Misty quipped. "You look so aristocratic, I feel like I should be addressing you as Sir Gavin."

Pleased by the compliment, Gavin pursed his lips, suppressing a proud smile.

"Have a seat." Misty pointed to the lone chair that had been occupied by the nurse.

"Would you two like some coffee or tea?" Audrey asked, needing to occupy herself now that the unexpected visitor had made himself comfortable in the only chair in the living room.

"Nothing for me, but I'd like to speak to Ms. Delagardo in private, if you don't mind," Gavin said, his sultry mouth turned down apologetically.

"Oh, all right; I'll watch TV in the bedroom," Audrey said and gathered the big canvas bag that contained her yarn and needles.

In an authoritative tone, Gavin said to Audrey, "Why don't you take a thirty-minute break? Go outside and get some fresh air," he suggested.

"Sure, if that's okay with you, Misty?"

"I don't mind. Why don't you make it a forty-five-minute break? Gavin and I have a lot to talk about," Misty replied.

Gavin's blue eyes swept around the apartment, making sure Audrey had vacated the premises before he spoke. "I hate to barge in on you like this…especially while you're convalescing," he began, "but I'm dying to get a reading. I had a dream last night that Randolph and I were back together and I'm so excited, I had to see you and hear every detail about the wonderful future my beloved and I are going to share." He eagerly scooted to the edge of his seat, intertwining his long, elegant fingers.

Misty wasn't in the mood to do a reading. The flashes of light that accompanied the images had become blindingly painful since the surgery. But she couldn't refuse the man who had financed her new face, and so she lifted her good arm as high as she could, and said, "Give me your hand."

Gavin gently grasped Misty's crippled hand and uttered a soft gasp when he felt the sting. Misty closed her eyes and winced as the flashing lights preceded the slide show of Gavin's life.

She saw Gavin as a baby wearing a Philadelphia Flyers shirt and knit cap. He was crying as if offended by the hockey attire. Time progressed and he looked to be around seven or eight, and there he was, wearing a football uniform, out on the field, holding a football, limply. Misty got the impression he would have been more comfortable holding a Barbie doll. During his college years, Gavin looked much more comfortable in his skin. He was a dashing young man, the center of attention in his small circle of eccentric friends, artsy types. And later, she observed him fall in love for the first time with a Frenchman while vacationing in Paris.

Misty closed her eyes tightly as she viewed Gavin's future. There were two people struggling in the shadows, Gavin and someone else. Gavin hit the floor. "Christ," she muttered upon realizing that yet another violent future was unfolding before her all-seeing eyes. She was grateful for the bandages that hid the grimace on her face as she watched a silver candelabra being wielded like a weapon. The candelabra was covered in blood and blond hairs. Was it Gavin's hair? Misty wondered. Was someone going to bash in Gavin's skull? Oh, for fuck's sake, how was she supposed to tell him this bullshit?

Misty opened her eyes, inhaling in gasps and exhaling frantically, as if she'd emerged from battle. The readings exhausted her, but viewing bloody, murderous visions made her pulse race and it was beginning to take a toll on her emotional well-being.

Gavin sat grim-faced on the edge of the chair, as if he knew his future was fraught with horror. "Misty, you seem petrified. Something rattled you terribly. What was it; did you see something ominous? Please tell me what you saw," he urged her anxiously.

"I...uh, I saw you as a baby dressed in a hockey uniform. And when you were older, maybe eight or nine, I saw you playing football without much enthusiasm."

"Ugh. I've always hated seeing baby pictures of me dressed in sportswear, and it breaks my heart that my parents forced me to play Little League football when they were clearly aware that I loathed all games that required strength and physical prowess. I tried; I really did," he whined pitifully, "but my coach hated me and kept me on the bench. And being on the bench was where I belonged; it was my preference. But my dad wanted his boy to play. He threatened the coach and the entire county with a lawsuit if I wasn't allowed to play."

Gavin swallowed hard and closed his eyes in agony as he recalled the brief period when he attempted to play football. "I was such a disaster on the field; I had no idea of what I was expected to do with that damn football. And running in those heavy cleats..." His words trailed off briefly as he shook his head at the painful memory. "Running in those things was a nightmare. To this day, my gut clenches and my hands shake if I see anything associated with that sport."

Misty gave her best impression of nodding in understanding when she actually didn't give a damn about Gavin's poor-little-rich-boy childhood. "But you became comfortable with yourself in college," she said encouragingly. "You found friends with similar interests who accepted you as a gay man."

"That's so true. You're amazing. How do you see these things? Do you read minds?"

Misty chuckled. "No, I get visuals and feel your sensations during the time period I'm viewing. It's kind of hard to explain."

"Your process is interesting," Gavin said, crossing his legs. "So tell me, what else did you see?"

Unable to give a full smile due to the bandages, Misty lifted one side of her mouth and tried to inject warmth into her eyes. "I saw you fall in love for the first time in Paris. The language barrier between you two was not an obstacle. You communicated with your eyes, gestures, and the fiery passion you shared in your hotel room."

Gavin placed a hand upon his heart and dramatically said, "Philippe, oh Philippe. *Mon amour, mon amour.* How I loved that man. You are spot on, Misty. Philippe couldn't speak a word of English and my French was terrible, but that didn't stop our great love affair."

"Yes, I sensed that you two were deeply in love."

"Yes, we were deliriously happy," Gavin said with emotion, his eyes closed as if enraptured.

"Well, what happened; why did the romance end?" Misty asked, deliberately avoiding any discussion regarding Gavin's disastrous future.

"Our story is as tragic as Romeo and Juliet." His eyes became watery as he reminisced about his first love. "It was time for me to leave Paris and return to school, where I was studying international finance. What a bore," Gavin said disdainfully. "But it was absolutely impossible for me to leave my beloved behind, and so I decided to drop out for a semester, telling my parents that I needed more time in Paris to study art, which was my true passion.

"They indulged me for one semester only, and then insisted I return to the States, threatening to cut off my allowance if I didn't. I couldn't survive without my parents' money, and so I had to tell my dear, sweet and beautiful Philippe goodbye. It was heartbreaking and I despised my insufferable parents for forcing me to abandon my true love. It was as if they'd ripped out a piece of my heart."

"But you survived and found true love once again, right?"

"Oh, yes. Many times but nothing could compare with the love I shared with that dear, sweet boy."

"Not even Randolph?"

Gavin's face hardened. "What Randolph and I had was different. He's much older than me, and to be honest, he pretty much stole my youth. I wasted ten good years of my life with that man, and for him to abandon me the way he did is unconscionable."

"I'm confused; I thought you wanted to find him because you love him."

"I do love him, but I'm furious with him at the same time. I need an explanation from him." Gavin dabbed at his eyes, which had filled with tears, again. "What did you see in my future? Do Randolph and I have a happy ending?"

"I'm not sure who the groom was, but I saw you getting married. The wedding was fabulous—really over the top; a platinum wedding and no expense was spared," Misty lied, telling Gavin something she hoped would delight him.

"Oh, my God, I'm getting married? Who is the lucky groom?"

"No idea."

Gavin let out a happy laugh. "Can you tell me when is the wedding supposed to take place?"

"Sorry, I didn't get a sense of the date."

"Do you at least know the season?"

"Um, it appeared to be an autumn wedding."

Gavin's mouth turned down. "I don't like autumn colors. I'm more into pastels; I'm a spring-and-summer-type guy."

Misty shrugged, indifferently.

Gavin stuck out his hand. "Read me again. I need more details about my wedding."

This bitch must be crazy; I'm not trying to see him meet a bloody, bludgeoning death, again. "I can't. I'm tired; I really need to rest."

"Please."

"No!" Misty said sharply. "I have no strength left, and I'm in pain. It's time for my medication." She allowed her shoulders to slump, emphasizing her exhaustion.

"Tomorrow, then?"

"That's too soon. I actually shouldn't be doing any readings while I'm recuperating. The flashes of light are painful. You're going to have to wait until I've healed."

"How long did Dr. Cavanaugh say it's going to take?" Gavin asked, quietly seething. Apparently he was accustomed to getting what he wanted.

"Two to three weeks. Maybe a month."

Gavin shook his head mournfully. "I don't know how I'm going to be able to wait that long."

"The healing process might speed up if I had more nursing care," Misty said slyly. "My coverage only pays for four hours daily." Misty had no idea when Gavin was going to meet his gruesome and untimely demise, but it behooved her to work quickly and get as much of his money as she could, as soon as possible.

"I can cover the cost of nursing care around the clock, if that will hasten the healing process."

"I don't need care around the clock, but I do need someone who can do other functions as well as nursing. You know, like cooking for me and my man, running errands, and doing some house-keeping duties."

"That's not a problem. I'll call an agency and get you a nurse slash maid as soon as possible."

"Great, but I want to keep Audrey from seven to eleven. The other person can start her shift when Audrey's ends and work from eleven to seven."

"Fine. Would you like to interview the applicants?"

"Yes, Audrey and I will interview them together. Audrey can ask them all the nursing questions and find out if they're up to par."

"Good idea."

"Another thing."

"Certainly."

"I need some furniture in this place. My boyfriend didn't get any because he thinks I need the space to wheel around in here. He expects me to learn how to operate a motorized wheelchair."

"Sounds like a good idea."

"I don't have any intention of sitting in this wheelchair for the rest of my life."

Gavin's eyebrows drew together in puzzlement.

"I'm going to walk again," Misty affirmed.

"Wasn't your spine damaged beyond repair? There's no surgery for your type of injuries, is there?"

"Not that I know of. But I saw my future in a dream, and I was walking." She nodded her head adamantly. "I was walking in heels."

CHAPTER 13

Putting in a hard day's work was invigorating and made Brick feel like a man, but he was hungry as a bear, and could go for a hearty meal. Not much of a cook, there wasn't any point in going home and trying to put together an edible dinner. Preparing food for Misty was easy since she wasn't able to chew anything of substance; her diet consisted of nutritional drinks, soup, oatmeal, scrambled eggs, and other soft foods. He thought about stopping at a deli and getting a hoagie or a cheesesteak with an order of large fries, but that kind of take-out food seemed more suitable for lunch. He sure missed Thomasina's good food, and he also missed going home to his son after a hard day's work, but he'd destroyed his stable home life when he tried to grant Misty's wishes and give her a dignified death. It took breaking up with his wife to make him realize that his feelings for her had diminished.

Funny how things worked out. Never in a million years would he have imagined him and Misty cohabitating together again. When she first came out of the coma, it seemed as if she'd been enlightened. She seemed warmer, her heart filled with love. But ever since she got that iPad, she had gone back to her old, devious ways. She wasn't happy unless she was swindling someone out of their money. She was running a big con on that rich dude, and Brick wasn't about that life anymore. He knew in his heart, he couldn't be a part of Misty's shady dealings. He wouldn't tell her right away; he'd wait until she felt more confident about her appearance. Once she had her looks back, she probably wouldn't even care that Brick wanted to end their relationship.

There, he'd admitted it to himself. He didn't want to be with Misty, anymore. He'd changed, but she hadn't. He was satisfied with working hard and leading an ordinary life, but she still wanted the moon, the stars, and the sun. She wanted attention and to shine so badly, she was willing to pretend to be psychic as a way to get her hands on other people's money.

He wouldn't leave her helpless; he'd find her an assisted living facility. There had to be agencies that could help find her suitable housing. He'd heard of wheelchair communities throughout the city that catered to young people. Misty wouldn't like it, but over time, she'd adjust. She had no choice. Once he got her situated in a safe environment, he was out! He didn't need the big, expensive apartment they were living in; he'd be perfectly comfortable in a smaller place.

Brick entered the apartment carrying an extra-large pizza with the works for himself and a large order of cheese fries for Misty, something she'd always enjoyed since childhood. He figured cheese fries were the kind of finger food that she could grasp and feed herself and were also soft enough for her to chew.

To his surprise, the living room was fully furnished. Brick put the pizza and fries down on the kitchen counter and then poked his head in the bedroom. Misty was sitting up in bed, hunched over the iPad as usual.

"Where'd the furniture come from?"

"Gavin paid for it and had it delivered."

"I could have bought furniture, but I thought you needed room to wheel around."

"I don't want to wheel around."

"Okay, there's no point in arguing about it. I picked up one of your favorite snacks," he said, making his voice sound more cheerful than he felt.

"What?" she asked without looking up.

"Cheese fries."

"Oh, I'm not hungry. The nurse whipped up a banana and strawberry smoothie and I'm still full from that." Misty pointed to a milky concoction inside a tumbler with an adaptive handle that allowed her to pick it up, and the long, bent straw inserted in the no-spill lid, also assisted in her self-feeding.

Noticing she'd only drunk half of the smoothie, he said, "The nurse left at eleven and it's five-thirty; aren't you hungry?"

"Nope, too excited to be hungry."

Brick looked at her thoughtfully. "Excited about what?" Misty's mind was always busy, and she stayed plotting and scheming. He braced himself for what she would pull out of her bag of tricks.

"Gavin surprised me with a visit today."

"That was nice of him."

"Not really; he wanted a reading."

"And…"

"I gave him what he wanted."

"That man spent a fortune getting you the surgery that you desperately wanted, he sent furniture over, and you repay him by playing head games with him?"

"You don't get it, do you?"

"Yeah, I get it. You still only care about you, and I was gullible enough to believe that your brush with death had made you a better person, but you'll never change, Misty."

"Why don't you believe me? Do you really think I'm crazy enough to keep a lie like this going?"

"How long have I known you?"

"Since forever."

"That's right. And there's never been anything psychic about you. I went along with that crazy story about the janitor because I thought you were hallucinating. But I can't pretend to believe in this crap any longer."

"I don't need your pity, Brick. Sorry you refuse to believe me, but that's your problem. I didn't ask for this gift of sight, but I have it and I'd be crazy not to milk it for all it's worth."

"I hope this shit doesn't backfire on your ass. That rich dude may seem nice, but I bet he'll show you a totally different side if he finds out you're running a game on him. Rich folks like to sue and they have access to high-powered attorneys—the kind that throw around expressions like fraud and embezzlement—"

"Embezzlement? You sound stupid. How am I going to embezzle anybody? I don't have access to that man's money."

"All right, well 'embezzlement' wasn't the right word, so let me put it in terms that make more sense. Handicapped or not, that dude and his team of lawyers will put your ass underneath the jail if he finds out you've been taking him for a ride."

"I'm trying to be optimistic about my life. Trying to move forward without feeling sorry for myself, and here you are, talking all this doom and gloom bullshit. Tell me, Brick, what do you prefer that I do—lie in this bed and watch TV all day or make myself useful?"

"I want the best for you, Misty, and you know it. The other day when you told me you could pay me much more than I earn on my job, well, the conversation brought back some unpleasant memories for me. If you think I'd ever allow you to pimp me in any way, you're a lot crazier than you're acting."

"Ain't nobody trying to pimp you, Brick," Misty said with disgust. "Damn, I was young and wild back then. Give me some credit for maturing and changing my ways."

Brick gawked at her. "You were pimping a whole stable of dudes right before you got hurt."

"But after that tragedy, I saw the error of my ways. I would never use people like that again. From now on, I'm going to earn a living with my God-given talent."

With a smirk on his face, Brick reached out and touched Misty's hand. "Make me a believer. Give me a reading."

"I'm coming up blank. I can't get a reading on you."

"I didn't think so," he said smugly, and walked out of the bedroom.

Sitting in the chair in the living room and using an empty box for a table, he watched *The First 48* as he wolfed down pizza along with Misty's cheese fries. With a slice from the second box in hand, Brick was suddenly snoring.

Brick dreamed of being in Trinidad. Anya was dancing in the moonlight; swinging her hips to the rhythm of an island song. Brick had no idea that Anya could dance like that. People were clapping, men were leering at her. Watching her move so seductively made Brick's dick hard, and when she silently led him away from the crowd, taking him to a private area of the beach, Brick eagerly dropped his pants and lay on top of her glistening body that was sprawled out on the sand. Grunting, he made love to her, whispering her name over and over again. "I'm glad we're back together, Anya."

"Shh! Don't talk! Fuck me!" she demanded.

Giving her what she wanted, Brick drove himself more deeply inside her.

Jolting awake, Brick cussed when he realized he'd had a wet dream and his inner left thigh was sticky with ejaculation.

CHAPTER 14

Sergio was a breast man; there was no doubt about that. The way he cupped Anya's tits, almost worshipfully, was a turn-on. With his lips tugging on her nipples while his tongue swirled around the knotted flesh, hot moisture instantly accumulated between her legs. Something needed to be inserted inside her pussy, to take the edge off. Her hand drifted downward, her middle finger poised to penetrate.

Sergio's strong hand grasped hers. "Leave that pussy alone."

"But…" Anya squirmed with desire.

"I'm gonna take care of it in a minute. Be patient, ma-ma."

Abiding by his wishes and surrendering to his skillful tongue, she looped her arms around his neck, her fingers combing through his silky hair. His lips returned to her breasts, and he nibbled and sucked until Anya was beseeching him to fill her with dick.

After an eternity of pitiful begging, Anya's pleas turned into moans of gratitude when Sergio inched downward, positioning himself inside the space between her thighs. She was more than ready to get fucked, but would accept the rhythmic in and out strokes of a thick finger while a skillful, wet tongue twirled around her swelling clit.

But Sergio had other ideas. Using only the tip of his tongue, he licked at her sensitive bud, teasing her into slow madness. Making growling sounds, she arched her back, lifted her butt off the bed, trying to make her pussy flush with his face, urging him to tongue her deeply. But Sergio continued the slow lick that had her thrashing, cursing, and pleading for mercy.

"It's too soon, baby. You gotta keep making that honey for me," he whispered in a soft Latino accent.

The honey he was referring to was pouring out of her pussy, and as far as she was concerned, there was more than enough to satisfy him. Anya had come to learn that Sergio loved sucking the sweetness out of her pussy, and he did it in a manner that was noisy, like he was slurping oysters. The way he ate pussy was super sexy, had her ass on fire and ready to turn him over, get on top, and ride him like a stallion.

"That's enough, Sergio," Anya whined, unable to endure any more of the sexual torture he was putting her through.

"Not yet," he insisted, swiping a finger between the crevice of her pussy lips, checking the amount of moisture. "It's nice and juicy in there, baby. Open your legs wide for me," he instructed.

Unsure if she could handle a dizzying and drawn-out, pussy-eating performance, Anya did the opposite of Sergio's request, and pressed her thighs together tightly.

"Come on, ma-ma," he coaxed. "Let me taste that honey."

Slowly, hesitantly, she widened the space between her thighs. She bit down on her bottom lip and squeezed her eyes shut, praying she didn't pass out from sheer pleasure. Sergio was a master at cunnilingus, but surprisingly he'd never allowed her to suck his dick.

The first time she made the attempt, he scolded her. "No, I don't want you to do that. It's nasty. There're plenty of dirty bitches out there who give blow jobs and whatnot. But you're my woman, and I kiss you...I need the lips that I kiss to be pure."

Anya didn't understand Sergio's aversion to fellatio; she figured it must have been a Dominican thing, and she didn't probe him for an explanation.

Right now, she was fighting to stay conscious while he sucked and tongued her nearly to death. Finally, his appetite was satisfied and he grabbed her hand and aimed it toward his dick. Obligingly, she wrapped her palm around his hot flesh.

"You feel how hard you got me, ma-ma?"

"Yes, and I want you so bad," she whimpered.

"How bad do you want this dick?"

"More than I want money. More than food. More than…" She paused as she tried to come up with more examples, but her mind went blank. It didn't matter because Sergio wasn't listening anymore. He was breathing hard and guiding his dick toward her heated center. Once he pushed inside her, and she wrapped her legs around his waist, they both began groaning, speaking irrationally, and yelling nonsensically.

And when it was over, Anya rested her head on Sergio's chest, he wrapped both arms around her and cooed to her in soft-spoken Spanish.

In the morning when Anya opened her eyes, Sergio was leaning over her with his lips brushing her cheek. "Go back to sleep; I'll call you later."

"Okay," Anya murmured.

"Tomorrow night, I'm gonna take you somewhere fantastic. Okay, baby?"

She smiled and nodded, and watched as he sauntered out of the bedroom.

It was evident that Sergio genuinely cared for Anya. Each time they got together, he splurged on her, taking her to the finest restaurants and always surprising her with gifts. She asked him not to, but he ignored her wishes, showering her with lavish presents: expensive Dominican art, a rose gold bangle, embellished with brilliant diamonds, an ostrich Prada bag, exquisite Clive Christian perfume, and an Hermès vintage silk scarf. Whenever they were together, he treated her as if she were as delicate as fine china, opening doors for her, holding her hand as he helped her out of his enormous SUV. He was completely attentive to her, checking in daily and asking if she needed anything.

Most women would give anything to have a fine man like Sergio catering to their every whim, but Anya was terribly uncomfortable with the way he doted on her. She felt guilty because all she really wanted from him was sex. He was good in bed and she was using his body as a way to forget her troubles.

The investigator had yet to find her dad, which was deeply troubling, and not knowing whether Brick was incarcerated or not, weighed heavily on her heart. One night when the uncertainty became unbearable, she went online and did a search on the Pennsylvania Inmate Locator site. She was relieved when Brick's name didn't come up.

Where is he—back with his wife? Anya asked herself for the hundredth time. Thankfully, she could always rely on Sergio to ease her pain when her yearning desire for Brick caused her eyes to fill with tears.

It was surprising that a hustler and a known womanizer like Sergio had so much free time to spend with her. He was never too busy to wine and dine her, making Anya keenly aware that his feelings exceeded a mere sexual attraction. She wished she felt the same, but she didn't. She liked Sergio a lot; their sexual chemistry was amazing, but she was still in love with Brick.

Maybe in time, she'd be able to give a little more of herself to

Sergio, since it was obvious that he wasn't going anywhere, any-time soon.

And neither was Natalie.

Anya had politely tried to ease out of her friendship with Natalie, ignoring her calls most of the time and when she did pick up the phone, she'd quickly tell Natalie she was busy and couldn't talk. But Natalie wouldn't take a hint and was relentless, leaving long-winded messages in which she bragged about her continued sexual adventures with Majid and several other men employed by Sergio. The sex acts Natalie described were disturbing, and Anya wondered if Natalie possessed all her mental faculties.

Feeling sorry for her friend and planning to offer her some advice about her wanton conduct, Anya agreed to meet Natalie for drinks during happy hour at a club called Skippy's in downtown India-napolis. According to Natalie, the venue was trendy and offered free appetizers and specialty martinis that only cost three dollars, which Natalie considered a big plus.

CHAPTER 15

At the club, Anya located Natalie at the buffet table, loading up a plate with hot wings and meatballs. She noticed immediately that Natalie still had a shabby look about her and her weave was as tacky as ever.

"Hey, girl," Natalie greeted. "Get yourself a plate 'cause the food disappears quick."

"I'm good." Anya had heard stories about the germs that accumulated in food served buffet style. She followed behind Natalie until her friend's plate was piled so high, Anya looked around in embarrassment.

Natalie pointed to an empty table with an empty martini glass. "I saved that table for us. This place is going to be packed in a few minutes."

They meandered over to the table and a waitress stopped by and took their drink orders.

"I'll have two more chocolate martinis. What do you want, Anya?"

"Um…chocolate martini sounds good. I'll have the same, but only one."

"Girl, you need to drink up. The drinks are cheap tonight; they usually cost ten dollars apiece. Besides, I'm paying the tab, so you don't have to act like a miser."

"Whoa. Check you out, big spender," Anya teased. "Seriously, though, I only want one martini. I have to drive."

Natalie shook her head as if Anya were a fool. The waitress trotted off and Natalie leaned in. She spoke in a low, conspiratorial tone. "I'm getting money, girl. I'm working for Majid."

"Selling drugs?" Anya asked with a shocked expression on her face.

"No. He put me on the payroll to take care of him and his friends."

"I already know that. You've left a lot of very descriptive messages, but I thought you were having fun being freaky. I didn't know Majid was pimping you out."

"He's not pimping me out," Natalie replied, offended. "We're in a relationship that's both business and pleasure."

"So, you're Majid's girl, now?"

"Majid sees a lot of different women, but no one is wifey. That could be my spot if I let him groom me the way he wants to."

"Groom you? What are you talking about?"

"He wants his main chick to be open-minded, sexually, and he's trying to help me get over my hang-ups."

"I didn't think you had any sexual hang-ups."

"I have a few that I need to work on."

"Like what?"

"I'm not going to get into all that. That's between me and my man. Like I said, Majid is teaching me quite a few things and he's also making sure that my money is right." Natalie smiled brightly. "I feel like I've finally found the man of my dreams."

Majid seemed more like a nightmare, but Anya didn't say anything. Not yet. She decided to wait until she had a little bit of liquor in her before she got the heart to tell Natalie it sounded like Majid was only using her.

"I think I proved myself last night," Natalie said. She had such a ridiculous smile on her face, Anya wanted to smack her.

"How'd you prove yourself?" Anya braced herself to hear about more of Natalie's deviant behavior.

Natalie took a deep breath and grinned, as if she was about to reveal a wonderful love story. "Last night, I let Majid's friends fuck me with beer bottles. Those niggas couldn't believe how deep my pussy is."

Appalled, Anya gasped and recoiled. Anya attempted to speak, but could only cover her mouth in horror. Natalie was a hot, ratchet mess. The girl had no self-esteem whatsoever and was quite possibly, a lunatic. Finally finding her voice, Anya said sternly, "What you're doing is dangerous, Natalie. And it's unsanitary. Why would you allow those men to degrade you like that? There's no amount of money worth your dignity. Something is seriously wrong with you, girl; you need to talk to a professional."

Natalie sucked in her breath indignantly. She became so infuriated, her nostrils flared. "I hate when bitches judge me. People been judging me all my life and I'm sick of it. I invited you here to have a good time, not to listen to you criticize me. Who do you think you are, talking to me like you think you're my mother?"

"I'm not trying to act like your mother; I'm only saying—"

"You don't have any right to judge me!" Natalie snapped, pointing a finger at Anya as she made her point.

"Damn. Simmer down, sis, and get your fucking finger out of my face."

Natalie lowered her finger.

"Look, girl, it's your life, and if you like it, I love it," Anya said, making a final decision to cut Natalie loose. Before the evening ended, she was going to be straight up, and tell her that she didn't want to associate with a deranged person. Until Natalie got some help, she needed to lose Anya's number. But Anya needed her liquid courage to express her sentiments. She scanned the room, looking for the waitress. Driving or not, she desperately needed another drink.

Eager to smooth the slight friction between her and Anya, Natalie said in a gentler tone, "So, anyway, girl, I'm glad you came out to have drinks with me. It's nice to have a best friend who can listen without passing judgment."

I'm not your best friend, you psycho! "What, uh, happened to the girls you used to hang with from the neighborhood?"

"I don't mess with none of these bitches in Indianapolis; somebody's always starting rumors about me, so I keep to myself."

Anya could understand why people gossiped about Natalie; the girl's behavior was crude and scandalous. She craved attention, any kind of attention, which led Anya to surmise that something traumatic had happened during Natalie's childhood. Having lost her mother at a young age, Anya could relate to dealing with a tragic childhood. If she knew more about Natalie's family life, maybe she could understand what made her tick.

The waitress arrived and set their drinks on the table. Natalie proudly extracted a five and a ten from her wallet and told the waitress to keep the change.

"Thanks for the drink, Natalie," Anya said.

"You're welcome. There's plenty more where that came from. Girl, I'm ballin'," Natalie bragged, her lips twisted arrogantly, her neck and shoulders moving in time to the music that the DJ played. Then, her expression and her tone of voice suddenly softened. "I'm glad you came home, Anya. I hope we can start being more like sisters than friends."

Natalie was acting really thirsty, and the way she was trying to latch on and get close to Anya was pitiful. Anya could be cold-blooded when she needed to. Hell, she could kill if she had a reason to, yet she felt a tug of sympathy on her heartstrings. Natalie was practically begging for her friendship, and Anya didn't have the heart to turn her back on such a misguided, poor girl.

After another round of drinks were served (the last one, Anya promised herself), Natalie once again began talking about her relationship with Majid. "I'm getting long paper working Majid's private parties."

"Where are the parties held?" Anya asked and took a sip of her martini. It was obvious Natalie wanted to talk about her perverted lifestyle, and Anya needed liquor to be able to tolerate listening to the disgusting details.

"Different places. Usually all men, but sometimes other women are there."

"Do the other women get paid to entertain the men like you do?"

"No, they're only there to have fun."

"What kind of fun do they have?"

"They like watching the different things I do with the men. Sometimes Majid gets me to serve one of the bitches at the party."

A perplexed look appeared on Anya's face. "Serve? How?"

"Eating pussy," Natalie said in a matter-of-fact tone. "I'm not crazy about going down on girls, but it makes Majid happy and gets his dick hard, so I do it for him."

Anya's mouth fell open. "You eat pussy in front of everybody at those after-hour parties?" she asked, appalled.

Natalie nodded. "It's all good; I get big tips for that."

"Ohmigod, Natalie," Anya mumbled, shocked and repulsed by Natalie's startling admission. It was a shame the way Majid was taking advantage of Natalie. She thought about complaining to Sergio, and then changed her mind, deciding to mind her own business. Natalie was a grown-ass woman, making grown-ass decisions.

"Don't tell me you never been with a girl before?" Natalie searched Anya's face closely, as if daring her to lie.

"Absolutely not and I don't intend to."

"Chile, that's how you keep a man. I bet Sergio would love to see you involved in some girl-on-girl action."

"Does Sergio attend those parties?" Anya asked in a shaky voice.

"He hasn't attended any so far, but I wouldn't put it past him to show up at some point."

"Why do you think that?"

"I'm saying, if his boys are into all that freaky stuff, he must be too. You know what they say…birds of a feather," Natalie said tauntingly as she licked the end of her straw.

CHAPTER 16

"As you can see, the crib could use a feminine touch," Sergio said as he took Anya on a tour of his palatial home that was decidedly masculine with a color scheme of brown, gray, and deep maroon. Ethnic pottery and wood carvings of animals were set upon tabletops and shelves. A pair of tribal drums was used as end tables, and a shimmering silver chest with dangling locks and a rich, leather trim made an impressive coffee table. The walls were adorned with interesting pieces of Caribbean art, and Anya was able to discern the pieces that were painted by Sergio's Dominican friend. Everywhere Anya looked, there was something unique to admire.

Sergio was probably accustomed to women losing their minds when they saw the luxurious way he lived, and if she were a materialistic person, Anya would jump at the bait and start plotting on a way to move in with him.

"Hmm," Anya murmured with a faint smile, but declined to comment. The champagne she'd been served not only tasted delicious, it put her in a fantastic mood. She couldn't remember the last time she'd felt so happy and giggly.

"Maybe one day you'll be the lady of the house and add your special touch." Sergio eyed Anya with a glimmer of mischief in his eyes. He was dangling a carrot and waiting for her to jump at the opportunity.

"So far, every room I've seen is decorated with style and elegance—your home isn't lacking anything."

"It's a big house, ma-ma. Some of the rooms are empty."

"I'm sure your interior decorator has great ideas for the empty rooms," Anya said, refusing to even entertain the outrageous notion of moving in. It was much too soon to even consider the idea.

When they approached the kitchen, there was the distinct sound of chopping, and mouthwatering aromas drifted in the air. She and Sergio didn't enter; they stood in the doorway of the cathedral-ceiling kitchen with white marble counters and white cabinetry, observing the chef and his two assistants preparing what smelled like a scrumptious meal.

"Appetizers will be served in exactly fifteen minutes, Mr. Travares," the chef commented respectfully as he chopped vegetables at an amazing speed.

"That'll work," Sergio replied and guided Anya away from the kitchen.

"Whatever they're cooking smells divine. You went all out for me, and I'm really flattered."

"Only the best for you," Sergio said, as he led her down a hallway. Soft music piped through the speakers, adding to the ambience of the romantic evening he had planned.

He stopped outside a room with pure white carpeting and described it as his chill spot. The room was decorated in soft hues of gray and blue and there were large, plump pillows on the floor.

"This is where I relax when the weight of the world comes down on me. Whenever I have big problems that require tough solutions, I come in here and meditate on the situation." The sadness in his tone didn't escape Anya. She supposed there was a lot of pressure being a drug kingpin.

"While I'm in here trying to get answers to business problems, I should also try to find the answers to what's going on between you and me."

"What do you mean?" She dropped her eyes uncomfortably.

Sergio lifted her chin with a finger, forcing her to meet his gaze. "I don't know what else I can do to convince you that I want you by my side."

When he removed his finger, she swallowed more champagne.

"No comment?" Sergio prodded, gazing at her with a serious expression.

The air was suddenly tense. Anya cleared her throat and said, "Well…it's a little soon to even consider shacking, don't you think?" She laughed in an attempt to lighten the mood.

"But is that something you would consider?" His brows furrowed questioningly.

"I like you a lot, Sergio, you know that. But I don't understand why you're trying to speed things up. I thought players enjoyed their freedom." Nervously, she chuckled again.

"I'm a reformed player."

"Since when?"

"Since the night I met you."

Anya had no reply. Blushing, she glanced away.

"You're real cute when you blush, you know that? Eventually I'm gonna break through that tough exterior and find a way to your heart. That's a promise." Bristling with confidence, he winked at her, and then placed an arm around her waist and escorted her through double doors that led outside to the pool area.

"It's beautiful back here." Anya's gaze went from the lush greenery to the Olympic-size pool and the Jacuzzi next to it. Sergio was doing a thorough job of showing her how long his money was, and though she was impressed by his lifestyle, she wasn't a gold digger. She'd never gone after any man for personal gain.

They sat on chairs near the pool and quietly enjoyed the view. "I like what I see; you're a beautiful young lady," Sergio said, breaking the silence.

"Thank you." She smiled in appreciation as she observed his smooth, ebony skin, which contrasted nicely with his white shirt and light gray suit. The gold and diamond-encrusted chain around his neck added pizzazz to his look. It was nice to be alone with him without Majid or his other bodyguards lurking in the shadows or sitting outside in cars, the way they did whenever Sergio visited her at her place. When she'd asked Sergio about his security team, he'd said that where he rested his head was his refuge and the only place where he didn't feel the need to be guarded.

Facing Anya, Sergio moistened his luscious lips and said, "I'm trying to take us to the next level. Why're you fighting me, ma-ma? Is that other man still on your mind?"

"I'm not going to lie to you, Sergio. I do still have feelings for someone else, but he'll never be in my life again."

"So, all you need is time to purge yourself of those old feelings?"

Anya nodded and sighed. "But, it's not only that."

"What else is on your mind?" Sergio furrowed his brow thoughtfully.

"You lead a dangerous lifestyle, Sergio. And I'd be foolish to get too deeply involved with someone like you. You could never really settle down while you're handling business in the streets. Why can't we simply enjoy each other's company and leave it at that? I mean, why is it so important for you to put labels on us?"

"I'm twenty-nine years old and I've been on these streets for seventeen years."

"Really?"

"I started hustling when I moved here from the Dominican Republic when I was only twelve years old. I'm going to be thirty on my birthday next month, but I've seen so much and dealt with so much bullshit in my young life, it feels like I'm about to turn forty. The way I'm living is every young hustler's dream. To actually achieve that dream is practically unheard of. Most hustlers either get killed or wind up behind bars while trying to make that climb from small-time soldier to being at the top of the food chain. I've been lucky, blessed, some would say. But this blessing is often like a curse. Besides a few close associates, a man in my position can't trust anyone."

"It's lonely on the top; is that what you're saying?"

"Exactly."

"But you can have any woman you want? Why me? I look good… I know that," Anya said, laughing a little. "But I'm not above average."

"What mirror have you been looking in? You're above average to me."

Anya ducked her head down as a quick smile appeared on her lips. "I would expect a man like you to want arm candy, and that's not me."

"Arm candy is disposable. But a beautiful woman of substance is rare. I sense you have principles and values that are important to you, but I also get the feeling that you have a warrior's heart." He looked at Anya closely. "I'm rarely wrong about people. I need a woman like you by my side, especially now that I plan to go legit."

"You're thinking about getting out of the game?"

"I'm easing my way out. I'm co-owner of the club where we met—a silent partner. And I'm venturing into several other endeavors. If my plan works out, my money should be washed clean in less than a year."

The information Sergio imparted put a different spin on things.

She touched his hand. "I like the direction you're moving toward, but I'm not ready to commit to a serious relationship. It's too soon."

Sergio held up his hands in surrender. "Okay, I can't force you. All I can do is keep trying until you tell me to stop."

"I want things to progress naturally. If we're meant to be, nothing in the world is going to stop us, and if we're not, nothing is going to keep us together." Her thoughts turned to Brick, and how badly she'd wanted him, but destiny had other plans for them.

One of the chef's assistants came out and announced that dinner was ready. Sergio and Anya followed him into the house and to the dining room, and to Anya's surprise, two violinists were standing near the table. With a nod from Sergio, they began playing their instruments.

Anya smiled delightedly. "This is really sweet of you, Sergio. Makes me feel so special."

"You're very special to me," he said, pulling out Anya's chair.

CHAPTER 17

Dr. Cavanaugh maintained a serious expression after removing the bandages from Misty's face.

"Well?" she said impatiently.

With his head cocked, he scrutinized her face through discerning, squinted eyes. "You are a stunning beauty. I've exceeded my expectations. Have a look." He placed a large hand mirror in front of Misty.

The face reflected in the mirror was flawless. Jarringly beautiful. "Is that really me?" Enchanted by what she saw, she spoke in an awestruck voice that was barely above a whisper.

"It's the new and improved you," Dr. Cavanaugh responded.

"I can't thank you enough, doctor," Misty said as her eyes watered. "You and your future wife, Erin, are going to have two handsome sons," she blurted, giving the surgeon an unsolicited reading. She'd seen his future numerous times when he touched her, and now felt the desire to share what she'd viewed with him. Although he'd been paid handsomely, she was so grateful to have her beauty restored that she wanted to give him something from the heart. Smiling, she looked at Dr. Cavanaugh, waiting for his reaction.

"I don't know anyone named Erin." He shook his head, turned his nose up a little, somewhat annoyed by the prediction.

"You'll meet her soon. Your oldest boy is going to devote his life to helping others, and your youngest is going to be a surgeon, like you."

"I've heard rumors about your abilities, but I'm a man of science, and I don't believe in predestination or anything that can't be explained."

"Neither did I before I was given the gift. Anyway, you'll become a believer when Erin accepts your ring and agrees to marry you."

"I'll keep an eye out for this woman named Erin," he replied with a good-natured laugh. Misty laughed, too, presenting a mouthful of chipped and broken teeth. Dr. Cavanaugh's forehead wrinkled in concern. "Your transformation won't be complete until we've done something about your smile. I can recommend a top-notch oral surgeon if you'd like."

"Absolutely. I value your opinion, doc."

"Dr. Nathanial Arden uses cutting-edge dental techniques that will give you a dazzling smile in no time at all."

Under anesthesia, Misty found herself back in the blissful, pictur-esque, alternate reality she'd explored with Shane. And once again, worldly desires seemed childish and insignificant. In this reality, she had a clearer understanding of the real meaning of love, and she didn't want to leave.

"You have to go back," Shane told her.

"I don't want to go back. I get greedy and materialistic when I'm back in physical form. The things that matter to me are so superficial. All I think about is beauty, money, and power."

"You're definitely not grasping the lessons you were supposed to learn when you were sent back. You see things clearly when you're on this realm, but when you're back in physical form, you fall right back into old patterns of behavior. You have to change the way you perceive life.

"*You're so smart, Shane. So wise and kind. You were completely different when you weren't in spiritual form.*"

"*I didn't know any better when I was in my physical body, but you know better. We had numerous discussions the last time you were here with me. If you recall, you agreed to rise above material yearnings, to embody the spirit of love. You were given a second chance, Misty, and with that opportunity came the ability to heal.*"

"*I've been giving a few readings, but I have to do that sparingly because people will drain me dry if I let them.*"

"*Why aren't you healing people? All you think about is yourself and your own well-being. You never give for the sake of love.*"

"*I do my part. I try to heal by telling people what I see. It's not my fault if bad news surfaces while I'm doing a reading.*"

"*I'm not talking about your gift of prophesy; I'm talking about your ability to physically heal the human body.*"

"*I don't have that ability. I can see past and future life events, but I can't heal anyone. If I could, don't you think I would have spared myself from suffering through two separate surgeries?*"

"*You were so busy focusing on superficial wants and desires, you failed to realize that your hands possess the power to heal.*"

"*My hands are deformed, Shane. I can't even open them fully. I'm going to have to go through another painful surgery to get them to function normally. Life is so much easier here; why can't I stay with you?*"

"*You're not ready and it's not your time.*"

"*No offense, but I don't understand how a messed-up person like you is existing on a higher realm. There wasn't anything spiritual and selfless about you when you were in human form. You were a womanizing ho, and you committed the vilest sin when you betrayed your twin brother and got with his wife. So, how come you get to stay here? What did you ever do in your life that was beneficial to others?*"

"*You're right; I wasn't a good person, and so I agreed to help you—to be your mentor and guide. From the soul's perspective, I could see that your narcissistic tendencies would land you at death's door. When you were feeling sorry for yourself and contemplating suicide, I visited with you in dreams, trying to show you the beautiful life that awaited you after you finished your journey on earth. You misunderstood and thought I wanted you to join me here much sooner than you were supposed to. And that's why I was here waiting for you, gently coaxing you to go back."*

"And you succeeded. I went back, but I swear I don't want to go back again. Being here is so peaceful."

"Life is not about having a smooth journey where everything goes your way. It's about meeting challenges and overcoming obstacles. You got a second chance to do better, so get over yourself, Misty. The world doesn't revolve around you. Help people—not for monetary gain, but for the pure joy of sharing the love that shines within."

"I can do that here," Misty said. "I can help another misguided soul the way you've helped me. I can't be an invalid again, Shane. Even though I got my looks back, it's horrible not being able to walk or even move my legs."

"You can't stay here; you have to finish your soul's journey in the physical realm. And always remember that you have the ability to heal and ease the pain of others."

"Agh!" Misty emitted painful, strangled sounds. Her gums, jaws, her entire mouth hurt unbearably.

"I know you're in pain, and I'm going to write a prescription for something that will make you feel better," the oral surgeon said.

Whimpering, Misty nodded. In addition to the pain, she felt lightheaded and disoriented as though she had one foot in two different worlds. There was a deep sense of loss as she glimpsed a fading, indistinguishable shadow from the corner of her eye. She had the vague memory of a dream she'd had about Shane, but couldn't recall what she'd actually dreamt.

During the limo ride home that was the courtesy of Gavin Stallings, Misty's nurse asked the driver to stop at a pharmacy so she could get Misty's prescription filled. While Audrey was inside the pharmacy, Misty felt an annoying, tingling sensation rippling through her hands. It was similar to the sensation that people refer to as a hand or a foot falling asleep, but more severe, like a thousand pins pricking her palms and the top of her hands.

She rubbed her left hand with her right and watched in astonishment as the contracted hand straightened out. With widened eyes, she examined the fingers of her left hand, balled and unballed the fist that she'd previously been unable to move.

It was a miracle! Her left hand was cured.

By the time Audrey returned to the limo, Misty's right hand and both arms were fully functional. Bewildered but also curious to see what other body part she could heal, Misty ran a palm along her jawline, instantly eliminating the pain in her gums. Next, she placed her hands beneath her denim skirt and gently stroked the flesh of each damaged thigh. She gasped as she felt her lower limbs becoming revitalized. Checking to see if she'd been able to repair her legs, Misty stretched them out and then bent them at the knee.

I'll be damned; it feels like I could walk if I tried.

The driver opened the door for Audrey when she returned. She slid into the backseat, holding up a bottle of water. "I bought this in case you need to take a pain pill right away," Audrey said with compassion in her eyes.

"Thanks, but I can wait," Misty answered.

"Are you sure?"

"I'm positive."

Audrey watched Misty curiously throughout the ride to Misty's apartment. When the limo glided into the parking lot, Misty sat in the back, in a state of awe as the driver and her nurse fiddled around in the back of the limo, retrieving her wheelchair. The driver swiftly lifted Misty and lowered her into the chair and Audrey fussed with Misty's clothing, making sure that her skirt and top were perfectly adjusted.

"Do you want to take your pill and lie down?" Audrey asked once they were inside the apartment.

Unwilling to endure the process of being transported from the chair to her bed, Misty shook her head. "No, I'm going to sit in the living room and watch TV. You can have the rest of the day off."

"But…"

"Turn the TV on and then you can leave. I'll be fine until the second shift nurse arrives."

Audrey retrieved the remote that was stuck between cushions on the new couch and clicked on the TV. "What do you want to see, *Maury? Wendy Williams?* A movie?"

"It doesn't matter."

Audrey surfed through channels, finally settling on *Judge Judy*. Misty watched the TV screen, pretending to be engrossed.

"Is there anything else I can do for you? I don't feel comfortable leaving you all alone."

"I'll be fine." *Get out, Ms. Peabody; I need time alone!*

Audrey slung the strap of her large tote bag over her shoulder. "Okay, I'll see you tomorrow." Shifting from foot to foot, she gave Misty a questioning look.

"Bye, Audrey," Misty said dismissively, keeping her eyes glued to the screen. She released a sigh when Audrey finally opened the front door. The moment the nurse left, Misty grasped her phone. With a straight and steady finger, she pressed a button, calling the home health care agency and then cancelled her afternoon nurse.

Then she gripped the handles of the chair and slowly lifted herself up. Standing on shaky legs, arms flailing, she attempted to balance herself, like a toddler struggling to take its first steps. She took three wobbly steps and then drifted backward and collapsed into the wheelchair, panting and gasping. Learning to walk again was exhausting work.

Determined, Misty gauged the distance from the wheelchair to the kitchen. She blew out a sigh, and then took staggering steps toward the kitchen. When she reached it, her shoulders sagged in disappointment. Fatigued, she needed to sit down and rest for a moment, but there were no chairs, only stools and she'd be damned if she was going to try climbing up a tall stool. Chest heaving up and down in exhaustion, she leaned against the fridge until she caught her breath. Minutes later, she made the trek from the kitchen to the bathroom, where she regarded her image in the mirror and smiled.

She had no idea how she was managing to walk again, and could only conclude that it was another ability that had something to do with coming out of a coma. She'd completely forgotten the visitation she'd had with Shane while under anesthesia. Had no recollection that she'd promised to use her abilities for the good of others without expecting compensation.

Finally, she toddled to the bedroom, where she flopped down on the bed and took a well-deserved nap.

CHAPTER 18

After work on pay day, Brick and the fellas congregated at their preferred spot to eat and then hopped in their cars and headed over to their favorite strip club. They were all grimy with layers of dust and specks of concrete clinging to their work coveralls, but it didn't matter, not with their pockets filled with crisp one dollar bills provided by the bank when they'd cashed their pay checks.

Going to the strip club was a way for Brick to unwind as he threw back beers while enjoying the delectable sights. A couple of his buddies, however, had it bad. A dude named Lance would lap dance away every cent of his pay, and his work buddy, Doug was dangerously in love with one of the dancers, a big-busted girl with hypnotic eyes and succulent lips. Her name was Mo-Monée, and that name alone should have warned Doug to steer clear of her, but he always sat in his car after the club closed, waiting to drive Mo-Monée home. By Monday, both Doug and Lance had to borrow money to buy their lunch and pay for petroleum to get around in their gas-guzzling, big cars with V8 engines.

Ordinarily, Brick would have been rushing home to make sure Misty was straight, especially a day like today when she'd gone through the ordeal of oral surgery, but he knew she'd be okay. Misty had that rich guy, Gavin, wrapped around her finger, and he was not only paying for expensive medical procedures, he was providing Misty with nurses who didn't mind pitching in and doing a little cooking and cleaning. Brick wasn't sure if they were paid extra or if Misty was manipulating them the same way she manipulated everyone else.

Although Misty was back to looking like her old self—even better—Brick wasn't feeling her at all. All she talked about was building an empire and putting together some type of nonreligious mega church. The shit she talked gave him a headache. He'd been listening to Misty's schemes since they were in third grade, and frankly, he was sick of it. He didn't share her desires for money and power.

On some real shit, it was only a matter of time before he rolled out, but he needed to be sure that she was being cared for adequately. Needed to know he wouldn't have to worry about her after he left.

He bought the first round of beers for him and his boys and sat back in his seat, ready to enjoy the tits and ass show. The MC announced a dancer who went by the name, Island Girl. She pranced onto the stage while Caribbean music blasted from the speakers. Accompanying her set was a backdrop of sand, seashells, and tropical foliage beneath clear blue skies, and when she started swaying her hips, Brick had an instant feeling of déjà vu.

Island Girl didn't have a long weave like the other dancers; she wore her hair in a short and sassy style. The way she moved her hips in time with the music was a sensual sight, giving the impression that she was actually fucking. Something about her reminded him of Anya, and he suddenly remembered the dream of Anya dancing in the moonlight. He recalled the way he'd cum all over himself and felt a bout of shame, but one glance at Island Girl and his mind filled with lust while his dick grew unbearably hard.

Brick was usually a mere observer, but Island Girl turned him on, prompting him to get out of his seat and walk up to the stage, where he made it rain with fifty one-dollar bills.

His buddies, unaccustomed to Brick spending money on anything but beer, clapped his back and cheered him on when he returned to his seat. When Island Girl's set was over, Brick wasn't the least bit surprised when she strutted in his direction.

He welcomed her onto his lap, enjoying the feel of her soft body, the scent of her perfume. He stuck a five in her bosom and took the liberty of squeezing her titties and stroking her nipples. Island Girl let out a soft moan, and moved one of his hands down to her crotch. Feeling her clit pressing against the soft fabric between her legs, Brick stroked the nub with the pad of his finger, while his lips found their way to her neck. But in his mind, it wasn't Island Girl who was rubbing her butt against his crotch. All he could think about was Anya and her sweet deliciousness.

He drove home slow as a snail, careful not to swerve or show any signs of being intoxicated. He hoped that when he got home, Misty would be sound asleep and not waiting up to show off her new dental work. Now that her physical appearance was up to her standards, she was going to start her new clairvoyant practice, and the dude, Gavin, was going to loan her the money to get started, and Brick wasn't opposed to the idea. As soon as Misty was financially stable, Brick would have a clear conscience about telling her goodbye.

The lights in the apartment were dim when Brick arrived home. He could hear the sound of water running in the bathroom. Had the health care worker left water running in the bathtub when she left earlier in the evening? He rushed down the hall, expecting to see water flooding out the bathroom. But he encountered a sight far more bizarre, a sight that staggered him.

Misty was in the bathtub, covered from the neck down in soapy bubbles. Her hair was piled on top of her head, with tendrils cascading to her shoulders and sticking to her soapy skin. She sent a glorious smile his way. Her smile revealed teeth that were even and pearly white. She looked more radiant and beautiful than ever before. And what was even more amazing was the fact that she was moving her arms with ease as she bathed herself. With a look of triumph in her eyes, she leisurely stretched out an arm and soaped it up with a bath sponge. And while Brick gawked at her, she sensually propped up a leg on the ledge of the tub.

He blinked a few times before managing to speak. "Misty," he said in a choked voice that was filled with awe. What the fuck was going on? He realized he was slightly drunk and everything, but how the hell did a holographic version of Misty get in the tub? Eyes bulging and his heart pounding, Brick's head swiveled in the direction of the bedroom, irrationally expecting to see the real Misty, unmoving, lying in bed. When he saw that their bed was empty, his head jerked toward the tub. Mouth gaping, he made sounds but was unable to form an articulate sentence.

He cleared his throat and finally said, "What the fuck is going on? How are you moving your arms and legs and shit?"

"I'm healed, Brick. I'm not paralyzed anymore." She slid her leg back into the bath water and then drew her knees up to her chest.

"I don't understand."

"I healed myself, Brick. No doctor operated on my spine. No one in the medical profession could help me; you know that. I told you something wonderful happened to me while I was in a coma. I told you I had gained psychic abilities, but you refused to believe. Are you a believer, now?"

Brick nodded mechanically, while his mind raced with questions.

"Would you hand me a towel, Brick? I'm ready to get out."

Misty rose out of the water and stood. Brick turned his head away, giving her privacy.

"Don't be afraid to look at me, Brick. I'm back, baby. This is the real me. I'm not crippled or sickly anymore. And I want to make love to you. I want to show you how I feel."

With his eyes aimed toward the floor, Brick gave Misty a towel. "I don't know about all that, Misty. It's too soon. You need to talk to your doctor; find out if it's all right."

"Fuck my doctor! He didn't do shit for me, so why do I need his permission?"

Brick rubbed his forehead in frustration.

"Help me out of the tub, baby. I'm still a little unsteady on my feet."

He reached out a hand. "This is crazy; feels like I'm in the twilight zone."

"I don't understand it any more than you do, and I'm not trying to figure it out. My hands started tingling in a weird way and I touched my left hand and it straightened out."

"But that's some sci-fi shit; it doesn't happen in real life."

"I'm living proof that it does." She stopped drying her shoulders, and handed Brick the towel. "Help me dry off, and then let's get in the bed."

Ever since she'd gotten hurt, whenever Brick attended to Misty's care needs, it was in a clinical way, and never, ever did he perceive her in a sexual way. "I can't do that, Misty."

"Why not?"

"I gotta take a shower, to get this dirt off of me."

"Fuck that. Do you think I care about a little bit of dirt after being dead below my waist for so long? All that time you were with my mom, I dreamed about this day. I want to feel you inside me. I really need you right now."

Brick shook his head. "Something's not right about this, and I can tell you in advance, my dick is not gonna get hard."

Misty's mouth fell open. "What are you saying?" She made a scoffing sound. "I'm all fixed up, better than before, so don't tell me you're repulsed by me."

"No, it's not that."

"Then, what is it?"

"When I left for work this morning, you were paralyzed. Now you're standing up and moving around, and I can't wrap my head around any of this."

Misty snatched the towel from Brick's hands, and wrapped it around her body, cinching it above her breasts. "Can you carry me to the bedroom? I'm starting to feel a little weak."

Brick swooped her up into his arms and as he took strides down the hallway, Misty began kissing and licking his neck. "Can you imagine how tight my coochie probably is?" she whispered in his ear, trying to arouse him.

He placed her on the bed gently, eyes averted, unwilling to take a good look at her. "Do you want me to get a nightgown or something for you to put on?" he asked, his eyes darting in the direction of the bureau drawer that contained her nightwear and her panties and bras.

"I like sleeping nude. How could you forget that?"

Brick sighed and sat on the edge of the bed, holding his head, in despair.

"Why don't you want me, Brick?" she asked, rubbing his back and caressing his shoulders.

"It's too soon," he mumbled, studying his dusty boots.

"But I need you, Brick; it's been so long."

He sighed again, realizing that Misty wasn't going to let up until she got what she wanted. To be able to please her, he started thinking about the stripper, Island Girl, and then he thought about the dream he'd had about Anya. When his dick jerked to life, he stood up and began slowly peeling off his work clothes and underwear.

CHAPTER 19

S oon after Brick left for work, Audrey arrived, using her key. With her knitting bag in hand, she was looking forward to a routine day of getting Misty groomed and fed and then watching hours of TV, along with intermittent naps throughout her work day.

But Misty had other plans for the nurse. "I'm in the kitchen, Audrey," Misty called out cheerfully.

"What are you doing in the kitchen?" Audrey asked as she closed the front door, rushing toward the sound of Misty's voice. Even though Misty didn't sound like she was in distress, the sight of her empty wheelchair in the living room filled Audrey with dread, and she imagined her patient sprawled out on the kitchen floor, badly injured.

Finding Misty sitting on a high stool, leisurely drinking tea, Audrey dropped her knitting bag, the metal needles spilling out and clattering onto the floor. "How in the world—"

"Don't freak out, Ms. Peabody," Misty said sternly, accidentally using the offensive nickname she'd given Audrey. "I've already had to deal with Brick's shock, and I need you to get a grip and listen to me carefully."

Audrey frowned in bewilderment as she nodded her head. "Are you okay? You called me Ms. Peabody...do you know who I am?" Audrey asked with a worry line etched in her forehead.

"Of course I know who you are. Ms. Peabody is my pet name for you. Anyway, what you're witnessing is a miracle. I have healing power in my hands. I don't know how or why this happened to me but I know there's a reason. I'm thinking about starting a business venture, but I'm going to need my benefactor, Gavin Stallings, to help me with it."

"What kind of business venture?"

"I don't want to talk about it; don't want to jinx my project. Anyway, I need to look my best when I approach Gavin for a loan. He's very much into art and beauty, you know, and I think he'll be more inclined to help me if I looked more polished and up-to-date. This junk my mom picked out for me while I was paralyzed needs to be dumped in the trash." Misty looked down at her no-brand jeans and scowled. "You and I are going to get in your car and drive straight to the mall, and I'm going to finally put some of my donation money to good use."

"The mall isn't open yet," Audrey replied in an awestruck voice, gazing at Misty with adoration as if she were a heavenly creature.

"We're not going to a nearby mall. We're going to King of Prussia, and having to deal with rush-hour traffic on Seventy-Six West, it might take about an hour and a half to get there."

"Right," Audrey murmured, still staring at Misty. "Your mouth, uh, your teeth—the dentist did a wonderful job."

"Yeah, he did and he was paid a small fortune for his expertise. I want to keep you on as a helper because I get tired easily, but I called the agency and fired that girl that comes after your shift ends. Now that I can chew food, I need someone who can do more than light cleaning and grinding up fruit and vegetables in a blender."

"If you're hungry, I can make you some breakfast before we leave," Audrey offered.

"Nah, I'm good. I want to eat at the food court in the mall; it's been a long time since I've done that."

Misty slid off the stool with ease and grace. She walked across the floor effortlessly and put the mug in the sink. Audrey peered at her in fascination.

"Now that I'm back on my feet, this place is gonna get a lot messier," Misty said. "But I'm going to be far too busy to deal with housework," she added.

"I'll clean up for you." Eager to please, Audrey hustled over to the sink, picked up the mug, rinsed and dried it, and then placed it inside the cabinet. For good measure, she wiped the countertop and inside the sink.

Misty dazzled her with a charming smile.

As the two women passed through the living room, Audrey paused at Misty's wheelchair. "Do you think we should take it with us; you know, in case you want to get off your feet?"

"Hell, no! I want that thing in the trash along with every boring piece of clothing in my closet."

"Instead of throwing everything away, why don't I box it up and take it to Goodwill?"

"I don't care where you take it, as long as it's out of my line of vision."

"Pardon me for staring, but I can't help it; you're as beautiful as an angel." She shook her head in bafflement; her lips twitching into a crooked smile. "I'm in shock; I don't know what to make of all this."

"Me either, but I'm not going to keep questioning it. I'm not looking a gift horse in the mouth. You dig?"

Audrey nodded, lingering near the wheelchair as if unwilling to leave it behind.

Misty glanced at the wheelchair and sneered. "I'm not a cripple anymore, and I don't need this despicable chair. The only thing I need right now is some retail therapy."

With each purchase, Misty handed Audrey the bag, and the nurse didn't seem to have a problem lugging Misty's purchases. She actually seemed honored. When eleven o'clock approached, Audrey called the medical clinic, where she worked full-time, and pretending to be sick, she told someone on the other end of the phone that she needed the day off.

"It's so exciting being with you, I don't want to go to my dull job at the clinic."

Misty nodded in understanding as she observed her reflection in a full-length mirror inside Neiman Marcus. Had she not been in such a rush to shop, she could have stared at her image for an extended period of time.

They walked a few paces and another mirror beckoned Misty. Unable to resist, she stood in front of it, running her fingers through her hair and admiring the new plumpness of her lips. The subtle slant to her eyes. There was even a slight change to the shape of her face; her bone structure was absolute perfection.

She couldn't help checking on her appearance each time they approached a mirror. It was if she had to be absolutely certain that the former, grotesque mask she'd been forced to wear, had not reappeared.

"Are you tired, Misty?" Audrey inquired.

"A little."

"Do you want to go to the food court, relax and get something to eat?"

"Not yet. I'll rest while I try on shoes," Misty answered and sauntered toward the shoe department.

Audrey's tendency to dote on her was the precise reason Misty had kept her employed. Now that she had her looks back, she expected everyone she came into contact with to bow down and treat her like royalty. Once again, all men would adore her and females would either envy her or develop a girl-crush. She suspected that Audrey was smitten, and who could blame her?

Misty sat in a comfortable chair while Audrey sprang into action, rushing back and forth, bringing her various shoes from the display table, and returning shoes that didn't meet Misty's approval. Serving as Misty's mouthpiece, Audrey also spoke with the shoe clerk, providing him with Misty's size and inquiring about shoe colors.

Audrey had always been kind and attentive when she considered Misty a helpless patient, but something in Audrey had changed, and Misty sensed the nurse had begun to admire her, and it wouldn't be a stretch to say she believed Audrey now idolized and revered her.

"My feet are starting to cramp a little," Misty complained, testing Audrey's devotion.

"I'm so stupid; I shouldn't have let you do so much walking," Audrey responded, berating herself for her lapse in judgment. She set a few of Misty's bags on the carpeted floor and she placed several bags in the seat of empty chairs. Then, she sat next to Misty. She placed Misty's right leg upon her lap, removed her shoe and began administering to her foot with a gentle massage. This drew the attention of other shoppers, but Audrey seemed oblivious to the curious glances.

When the sales clerk returned with boxes of shoes, Audrey was working on Misty's left foot, and seemed reluctant to stop.

"You can finish when we get back to my place, okay, Ms. Peabody," Misty said with laughter. Audrey laughed along with her.

The dutiful nurse ushered Misty inside her apartment and made sure she was comfortably seated on the sofa with a cup of herb tea before she began lugging in Misty's purchases. After several trips from the car, she noticed Misty wincing.

"I think you overdid it today. Too much walking for someone who hasn't been on her feet in such a long time."

"You may be right." Misty flinched and grimaced.

"What's hurting—your feet?"

"Everything hurts. My hips, my legs, my back—everything."

"Do you want to take a pain pill and lie down?"

"No. I'm afraid of getting addicted to those things." Misty sighed. She covered her face briefly and then looked up at Audrey with tears in her eyes.

"What's wrong?"

"It's sort of embarrassing to talk about."

Audrey scampered over to the sofa and sat next to Misty. "You can confide in me, Misty. Please talk to me. I'm here for you."

"I thought Brick would be thrilled about the miracle that has happened to me. We haven't been physical in such a long time, and so when he came home last night, and after he got over the shock of me being healed and all, I asked him to make love to me." Misty sniffled and shook her head. "He didn't want to, and I practically had to beg him. It was so humiliating, Audrey." Misty covered her face again and made crying sounds, though she couldn't quite manage more than a few tears.

Audrey rubbed her back and murmured that Brick probably didn't want to hurt her and she was sure everything would be all right in time.

Misty shook her head. She dropped her hands from her face and wiped nonexistent tears from the corners of her eyes. "He's not attracted to me anymore. We had sex, but his heart wasn't in it. He got his, but he didn't even care that I wasn't satisfied."

"That's terrible. I don't know where he thinks he's going to find another woman as beautiful as you?"

"I know, right? Apparently, my looks don't matter to him. I knew it was too soon to be on my feet for so long, but I thought a new wardrobe would make me more appealing to him."

"You can't jeopardize your health for that man. You have to take care of yourself, and I'm going to help you. Your transformation is a gift from above. You're obviously one of the chosen, and Brick should be honored to have a woman like you."

"He used to worship me." Misty shook her head regretfully.

"As he should have," Audrey said in a hostile tone.

Misty sighed and stood up. "I'm really tired. I should go lie down for a little while. Would you mind helping me get out of my things? I'm too weak to do anything for myself right now."

"You don't have to do anything for yourself when I'm around. I'm serious, Misty. I'll do whatever you need me to do." Audrey put a supportive arm around Misty as she guided her down the short hall.

In the bedroom, Audrey helped Misty remove her top, jeans, and her shoes.

Misty turned around, signaling Audrey to unclasp her bra. She rolled down her panties and stepped out of them.

"Do you want to put on a nightie or something?"

"No, I want you to look at my body and be honest with me," Misty said as she lay on her back.

"Be honest about what?"

"Does my body look all right?"

"It's more than okay; it's perfect," Audrey said, dropping her eyes self-consciously.

"Do you think I'm sexy?"

Audrey looked embarrassed. "Everything about you is sexy, Misty," she admitted with a bit of embarrassment.

Misty drew her legs up and spread her thighs. "Does my coochie look all right?"

Standing over Misty, Audrey bent at the waist and observed closely. "Uh-huh, it looks very nice," she said with a mixture of shyness and excitement glimmering in her eyes.

"Well, what are you waiting for, Ms. Peabody? Kiss it, so I can start feeling better about myself."

Fully dressed, Audrey climbed awkwardly on the bed and eased into the space between Misty's thighs. As Audrey administered to Misty's needs, Misty grabbed two handfuls of the nurse's hair, yanking her head right and then left, making sure her lips touched exactly the right places, and controlling the nurse's movements as if she were operating the steering wheel of a car.

CHAPTER 20

"U ncle Fabian and my Uncle Diaz took care of me when I arrived here in the States. They taught me everything about the game," Sergio said as he cruised along the highway. The sun had not come up yet, and Anya and Sergio were only twenty-five minutes into a three-hour drive to the upstate prison where Sergio's Uncle Fabian was serving a life sentence for murder and drug trafficking.

Prior to asking her to accompany him upstate, Sergio had never spoken about his family, other than mentioning that generations of his relatives had been involved in the drug game.

"Did your parents send you to live in America because they thought your uncles could provide a better life for you than they could?" Anya asked, perplexed as to why parents would send a young boy to live with two criminal uncles.

"My parents were both killed in a drug war back home. A car bomb," Sergio said softly, and Anya could hear the grief in his voice. "I saw it happen. My parents and I were going to visit my grandmother at the hospital. I didn't want to go; I wanted to stay behind and play soccer with my friends. My father insisted, saying my grandmother was very ill and that it might be my last time seeing her. I didn't think my grandmother was sick enough to die, and I figured he was exaggerating, and so I dragged my feet, sulking as I walked toward the car. My mother motioned for me to hurry up and then my father turned on the engine. Boom! The car exploded and went up in flames right before my eyes."

Anya touched Sergio's arm. "That's horrible; I'm so sorry to hear that."

"Going through something like that at twelve years old was rough. My grandmother died shortly after my parents and that's why I was sent to live with my uncles." Sergio stared ahead with a grim expression. "My heart was cold for a long time. I believed I had nothing to live for, and so I took risks that a young kid wouldn't normally take. My lack of fear is how I was able to move up the ranks so swiftly, advancing higher in position than either of my uncles ever made it in the game."

"What happened to your other uncle? Is he in prison also?"

"No. Uncle Diaz was serving a ten-year sentence when he got knifed by inmates from a rival crime family." Sergio held up a hand as if to say, *that's how it goes.* "Uncle Fabian is my only living relative, and I want him to meet the woman who has put a smile back on my face."

With Sergio being so candid with her and sharing his painful past, Anya felt comfortable enough to talk about the tragic loss of her mother and the pain of not seeing her father in years. "I was very young when I lost my mother, and I was led to believe that she was shot to death in the midst of a robbery. But I discovered the truth only a few years ago. I learned while reading court transcripts online that my mother was kidnapped from the underground parking lot of her job. She was brutally raped, beaten, and then stoned to death by two psychopathic teenagers."

Anya's eyes welled with tears and Sergio reached for her hand, caressing it tenderly.

She refrained from telling him that ten years after the crime, she'd been able to exact revenge on one of the killers—that she'd tortured the man and left him bound and bleeding to attract rats that would surely eat him alive. Nor did she mention that she'd participated in a double homicide when her ex-lover, Brick, retaliated on the people responsible for disfiguring and paralyzing his childhood girlfriend. Not wanting Sergio to know about the vengeful side of her nature, she kept that information to herself.

"I sensed when I met you, that the two of us shared a painful past. The loss of parents is something a child never recovers from."

Anya nodded solemnly. "You're right. I've always felt completely alone in the world with no blood relations who cared about my well-being."

"You're not alone anymore," he said softly.

She squeezed his hand.

Uncle Fabian was an older version of Sergio. They shared the same dark skin, the same bone structure, and the same ink-colored, silky hair. The uncle, who looked about ten years older than Sergio, had a thicker Spanish accent.

"Good to see you; how are you, nephew?" his uncle greeted. "This must be Anya," he said, his dark eyes quickly looking her over.

"Yes, I'm Anya. It's very nice to meet you." She gave him a hug.

"When I talk to my nephew on the phone, his speaking voice sounds like he's singing, and I asked him to introduce me to the lady who put music back in his heart. And here you are," he said, beaming at Anya.

Uncle Fabian was a charmer, and Anya couldn't hold back a broad smile.

Throughout the hour-long visit, Sergio and his uncle reminisced about the Dominican Republic, and his uncle encouraged him to revisit the island to preserve some ties with his birth place.

"I plan to," Sergio said, glancing at Anya.

"It's a nice place to take a honeymoon, one day. Your new bride could learn the culture and learn firsthand how to cook the meals you used to crave when you first arrived in the States," Uncle Fabian said, winking at Anya.

"Uh, we're not married," Anya informed.

"Not yet. Would you allow me to speak the truth?" Uncle Fabian asked.

"Go ahead," she said.

"You favor my beautiful sister—Sergio's mother. I'm not surprised my nephew fell so hard for you. You seem like exactly the kind of woman he needs. Feminine, loyal, and ride or die. I could live out my prison sentence with peace of mind if I knew he was with someone who had his back."

Anya squirmed visibly, wondering why Sergio's uncle was pushing so hard for her and Sergio to marry. She was relieved when Sergio cut in, "Hey, stop pressuring my girl. You're starting to embarrass me, Uncle Fabian."

His uncle backed off, and the conversation took another direction. As she listened to the two men laughing and joking, it occurred to her that the uncle saw the venomous side of her nature that Sergio didn't know about. Somehow he knew that beneath her pretty face and sweet façade, she was a killer, as was Uncle Fabian and most likely, Sergio, too. Though Sergio hadn't openly admitted it, he had certainly alluded to being involved in serious crimes. Common sense told her he couldn't be in the position he was in without getting his hands dirty. Eventually, she would have to tell him about her past. He deserved to know the ugly truth about her, and if the truth didn't scare him away, if it actually appealed to him, perhaps there was a future for them.

The hour zoomed by and while they were saying their good-byes, Uncle Fabian said to Anya, "Take care of my boy, and I look forward to seeing you the next time my nephew comes to visit."

During the drive back home, Sergio seemed pensive. "Are you okay, Sergio?" Anya inquired.

"Yeah, I'm all right. Visiting my uncle always leaves me depressed. He and I both try to stay in good spirits during my visits, but it's really hard for me to see him caged up like that."

"I know, but on the bright side, you still have him. You can talk to him regularly and see him whenever you have time to make the long trip. I have distant relatives in Trinidad, but we hardly know each other. I also have a play aunt in Indiana. She raised me, but she's not blood, you know. She has her own kids to worry about, and after I turned eighteen, I was pretty much on my own."

"You're not on your own anymore. I'm going to look out for you, Anya. Make sure you're always all right. As far as money goes—"

"I'm okay financially," she interrupted. "I told you I received a large inheritance when I turned twenty-one."

"That money will disappear over time if you don't have other finances coming in. I want to take care of you and share my wealth with you," he said sincerely.

"That's not necessary, Sergio."

"I want to." He lit a thin cigar and blew out a stream of smoke. "Make a list of your monthly bills and I'll handle them from now on."

"But—"

"No buts. Look in the glove box," he instructed her.

She opened it and saw an envelope. "Open it," Sergio said.

She didn't know what to expect, and was completely surprised to find the exclusive, American Express Black Card with her name engraved on the front.

"There's no limit on that card; that's for your shopping sprees. I'll cover the bill."

"I can't let you do that."

He held up a hand, silencing her. "I plan to do a lot more for you in the future."

"Why?"

He shrugged. "I love you," he said, matter-of-fact. "It's a man's job to take care of the woman he loves."

For the duration of the trip back home, Sergio was cheerful, opening up about his future dreams as well as sharing personal secrets. He told her where his money was hidden and even divulged the location and combination to his safe. Anya felt both privileged and a little nervous about being privy to such personal information.

"There's a special room in my house you haven't seen. I'll show you when we get home."

"Okay." Though his house wasn't exactly home to her yet; she had been spending a lot of time there, staying over at least three or four times a week. It was clearly only a matter of time before Anya took the plunge and moved in. She was tempted to tell him everything about herself, right there on the spot, but decided the time wasn't quite right for her shocking confession. Only a few moments ago, he'd told her that he loved her, and she wanted to bask a little longer in the glow of his adoration. She wasn't ready to risk seeing a dark cloud come over his face when he discovered that the girl of his dreams was capable of killing without so much as blinking an eye.

CHAPTER 21

Misty summoned Gavin, pretending she was eager to show off her beautiful face and equally excited to give him a second reading when she actually wanted to discuss the business venture she wanted him to invest in. He had no idea of her miraculous healing, no clue that she was now able to walk.

Pledged to secrecy, Audrey opened the door for Gavin and led him to the living room where Misty sat in her wheelchair. For shock value, Misty planned to suddenly stand up and strut across the room; she couldn't wait to see the look of astonishment on Gavin's face.

Looking magnificent in blue, python print lounge pants and matching camisole, Misty greeted her benefactor with a dazzling smile.

"Look at you! You have the face of a classic beauty…someone like Grace Kelly or Greta Garbo."

"I think she looks like Halle Berry," Audrey chimed in, smoothing down an errant strand of Misty's hair. Seeming unsure of what to do with herself if she wasn't doting on Misty, Audrey began fussing with the straps of Misty's camisole, adjusting them obsessively.

Feigning modesty, Misty lowered her eyes and murmured, "Thank you both for the compliments." She turned appreciative eyes on

Gavin. "And thanks to your generosity, Gavin, I have a new life. I can actually start earning income now that I'm presentable enough to be seen in public." She looked him in the eye. "I want you to know that I intend to pay back every dollar you've spent on me."

"That's kind of you, but I doubt you'll ever earn enough to repay the exorbitant amount I spent to make you beautiful again," Gavin said with friendly laughter followed by a dismissive wave of his hand, informing Misty that he was unwilling to discuss any kind of compensation.

He leaned forward, fingers interlaced. "Let's pick up where we left off; I've been anxiously anticipating my second reading." He cut a suspicious eye at Audrey, who hovered near Misty. "If you don't mind, I'd like some privacy during my reading."

"That's not a problem," Misty said. "Would you excuse yourself, Audrey? You've done more than enough for me today. Go home; I'll see you in the morning."

A look of surprise came over Audrey's face. "All right." Reluctantly, she gathered her bag of yarn and needles. She fluttered her fingers in a sad, parting wave before exiting the living room.

After Audrey left, Gavin looked at Misty and frowned. "I didn't think you'd dismiss her for the rest of the day; I only wanted privacy for thirty minutes or so. A walk around the block or a quick errand would have sufficed. Who's going to help you out until Brick gets home?" Gavin seemed horrified by the possibility that he might have to assist Misty in any capacity.

"Don't worry; I'll be fine," Misty said with a smile of amusement sparkling in her eyes. She held out her hand, her arm fully extended. In his excitement at getting another reading, Gavin failed to notice the full range of motion in Misty's arm.

Their hands made contact and an electrical charge rippled through their hands. A kaleidoscope of color burst behind Misty's eyes moments before the slide show of Gavin's life began.

With her eyes closed, she began to describe what she was seeing. "The décor of your childhood bedroom is a sports theme. There's a large, green area rug that's a replica of a football field. Team banners adorn your walls. One wall has a life-size mural of basketball players in motion, running down the court. A ball being passed from one player to another is hovering, mid-air. Your pillowcases and bedspread continue the theme, decorated with images of various jersey numbers and team logos. Football helmets, signed baseballs, basketballs, and footballs are displayed on shelving throughout the room."

This is more of the same boring bullshit. I'm sick of seeing scenes from his past. Gavin feels persecuted because his dad expected him to enjoy being a boy. What an ungrateful, spoiled brat!

"I hated my room," Gavin said bitterly. "Being in my room was like being imprisoned inside a sports stadium. To this day, I get physically nauseous merely hearing the cheer of a crowd during any kind of sporting event."

Misty held up a finger, silencing Gavin. "Now I see a woman entering your room. She has curly dark hair and she's carrying a plastic storage container—a big one. She places it on the floor and bends over to unfasten it." Misty leans forward, as if getting a closer look. "Oh, I see what's in there. The container is filled with Barbie dolls and the dolls have an extensive wardrobe," she said with an amused smile.

Gavin's involuntary intake of breath informed Misty that he was experiencing a fond recollection of what she described. "You're talking about Elsa, my nanny. She was the only person who understood me. She was such a sweet soul," he said softly. "But my dad fired her; he kicked her out of the house when he discovered her allowing me to play dress-up. I had on a yellow princess costume with a gorgeous tiara and sparkly heels."

Gavin pressed a monogrammed handkerchief to his tear-filled eyes. "Elsa was sent packing and I was banished to football camp for an entire summer in the hopes that the coach and counselors would change my mindset and rough me up enough to get the girlishness out of my system."

"We're moving forward now."

"Yes, let's fast forward. I hate reliving my painful childhood." Gavin sniffled and wiped his nose with the hanky.

Yeah, well, it's painful for me to listen to this silver-spoon dickhead talking like he had it so hard.

Misty continued the reading, informing Gavin of her observations. The bedroom of his first apartment was a stark contrast to the theme of his childhood room. The space was painted a soft peach color, frilly curtains hung at the windows, and fluffy pastel pillows decorated the bed. His personal art, splashes of vibrant color that seemed to have been splattered on canvases without rhyme or reason, adorned the walls.

"You were happy in your first apartment," Misty said.

"I was deliriously happy. My father had disowned me by then; he wanted to cut me off financially. Luckily, the family fortune is from my mother's side of the family, and whether my dad liked it or not, it was stipulated in the will of my deceased great-grandfather, that all his direct descendants be provided for." Gavin pursed his lips in satisfaction, and then began to pout. "I want to know about Randolph. What do you see in our future together?"

Misty groaned involuntarily and scowled in revulsion as she once again witnessed Gavin's future. Nothing had changed. Gavin was going to piss someone off and end up with his head bashed in.

"What are you seeing? What's wrong?" he asked in a shaky whisper.

"I'm a little jealous of the great love you and Randolph share," Misty improvised.

"Are you saying that we'll be reunited soon?"

"Yes. I see you two together on the beach in Saint-Tropez. You're both tanned and smiling with umbrella drinks in your hands."

"Really? Randolph hates the sun, and he's so envious of my love affair with Philippe, I'm surprised he agreed to vacation in France."

"From what I can see, he becomes more self-assured and trusting in the future."

"Oh! That's wonderful news, but I need to know exactly when he's coming back to me," Gavin said anxiously.

Misty's eyes snapped open, indicating the reading was over. "Time is tricky, you know. I don't see dates or anything like that. You have to have faith that the future events I see are your destiny."

"I have faith, but I've been waiting for months for Randolph's return, and I'm growing impatient," Gavin whined. "Look at you, your face is perfection. I made that possible with the expectation that you would lead me to Randolph."

"Reconciliation with your beloved is inevitable, but you need to take your mind off him and focus on something else for a while. The more you worry, the farther away you're pushing your reunion."

"I don't understand."

"The energy around you is fearful and negative. You'll draw him to you sooner if you relax a little and allow yourself to be happy. I know what I'm talking about, but you have to have faith in my visions." *Wow, I sound really convincing; like I've been dabbling in mysticism for years.*

"You're right," Gavin conceded. "I've been obsessing over Randolph and that isn't healthy."

"It's not healthy at all," Misty agreed.

The look on Gavin's face was unmistakably sad. "I miss him so much," he said, covering his face with his hands as he broke down and sobbed.

CHAPTER 22

"Girl, these are the best hand-me-downs I've ever had," Natalie said, patting the two shopping bags of designer wear that Anya had generously passed on to her. "But what about some shoes? We wear the same size and I know you have plenty pairs of hot-looking shoes," Natalie said, with a look of greed glinting in her eyes.

"I'm a shoe freak. I can't give up any of my precious shoes."

"I only want one pair," Natalie whined, trying to persuade Anya by putting on a sad face.

"Nope. I'm serious. I can't part with my shoes."

Anya had no idea what Natalie was doing with the big bucks she claimed to be making from Majid's after-hour parties, but being that she always looked a hot mess, it was apparent that buying clothes, shoes, and getting her hair done at a salon weren't top priorities.

As obnoxious as Natalie could be, Anya had a soft spot in her heart for her and hoped that she could help elevate her friend's self-worth by giving her a more fashionable wardrobe. Hopefully, having more confidence would open her eyes and allow her to see that Majid was not looking out for her best interests at all. He was using and abusing her, treating her like scum, yet Natalie's loftiest goal was to be his number one chick. It was becoming unbearable to even listen to Natalie talk about the sex parties and the sordid activities Majid had her involved in.

The sex games Natalie described were becoming increasingly dangerous, and in Anya's opinion, it was only a matter of time before Natalie got injured or even killed.

The two women sat in Anya's living room, drinking mimosas, when Anya said, "I want your opinion on something. Be right back." She set her drink down and trotted to her bedroom, returning with a very expensive-looking, oblong box.

"Check it out; this is the birthday present I bought for Sergio."

Natalie opened the box and scowled with confusion. She lifted the elegant Mont Blanc pen from its packaging and inspected the geometric pattern of the sleek pen. "It looks expensive. How much does something like this cost?"

"It wasn't cheap, I can tell you that," Anya replied vaguely.

"Is it real gold?"

"Yep. Fourteen carat with a platinum-plated cap."

"That's nice," Natalie said unenthusiastically.

"I know Sergio's taste and he's gonna love it," Anya said defensively. Finding a suitable birthday present for the man who has everything had been challenging.

Rotating the pen between her thumb and index finger, Natalie continued to examine it. "It's pretty and everything, but you should have bought him a big glitzy chain or a ring with diamonds and other jewels. It's not like you can't afford it."

"Sergio already has a lot of jewelry. Besides, he wouldn't want me spending a large portion of my inheritance on something he already has in abundance."

"I don't get it. What is he gonna do with a pen? That man is busy moving bricks; I know he's not sitting around writing love letters."

Anya laughed. "Look, this is not any ordinary pen. The salesperson wouldn't even call it a pen; she referred to it as a writing instrument."

"Umph," Natalie grunted, unimpressed.

"This pen is gonna come in handy when Sergio starts writing lots of checks—when he goes legit."

Natalie stared at Anya inquiringly, and Anya immediately regretted having repeated what Sergio had told her in confidence. Sergio's secret wouldn't have slipped out if Natalie hadn't had her on the defensive about the gift she'd bought him.

"Is Sergio planning on getting out of the game?" Natalie asked with a raised brow.

"Well, um...," she stammered. "They all have to get out of the game, at some point, right? Everyone knows that the end result is either death or jail."

"That's a negative way of looking at your man's livelihood. What's up, you trying to jinx him or something?" Natalie shook her head disapprovingly.

"Of course not, but I have been hinting for him to get a real job. I'd be much more comfortable if he was in a less dangerous profession," Anya said, making it sound like it was her idea for Sergio to get out of the game.

Natalie burst out laughing. "Keep dreaming, girl. That man's gonna ball 'til he falls. Do you really think he would give up his power to go work in the corporate world? Or would you prefer for him to flip burgers for a living? It seems like you're wishing the worst for him," Natalie accused with her face twisted in a scowl.

"That's not true, but why don't we change the subject? I'm not comfortable talking about Sergio's personal business."

"I feel you on that. Majid would have a fit if he thought I was putting his business out there." Natalie glanced at the pen once more and then set it on the coffee table.

Anya was surprised to hear Natalie speaking as if she and Majid were in a serious relationship. First of all, Natalie was not Majid's main girl; she was one of many side pieces and was nothing more than a sex toy to him. Secondly, Natalie *had* put his business out there when she disclosed that he hosted after-hour freak parties. But Anya didn't say anything. She reached over and returned the pen to the luxurious, cushioned box.

"So, how are you gonna celebrate your man's birthday? You should rent out the entire VIP area at the club and have a private party for him," Natalie suggested.

"I have other plans. Something quiet and romantic."

"Like what?"

"I was thinking about baking him a cake from scratch and—"

"Ohmigod, that's so boring. What's wrong with you, girl? You're smashing the biggest hustler in the area, and the only thing you can come up with for his birthday is a damn cake? That's corny."

"That's not the only thing I'm planning to do. I'm trying to learn how to cook Dominican food, and I'm gonna surprise him with one of his favorite dishes—Pollo Guisado. That's chicken stew with a lot of flavor. It's served with rice and beans."

"Girl, if you don't stop being cheap and take your man out for a juicy steak and lobster instead of that crap you're talking about. You gon' fuck around and lose Sergio to a bitch who knows how to treat a man."

"I know how to treat a man. Trust," Anya said with certainty. "It's not always about how much something costs, Natalie. It's about the effort involved in showing how much you care. I know Sergio, and he wouldn't want me to spend a fortune on an elaborate birthday gift. We're going to spend a quiet evening at home on his birthday and the fact that I'm taking the initiative to learn how to cook the food he loves will mean a lot to him."

"Oh, so you're gonna be cooking at his crib?"

Anya nodded. "You should see his house; it's stunning and huge with a pool and an outdoor Jacuzzi. And the kitchen looks like something out of a magazine. It's completely white with top-of-the-line appliances. I'm gonna love moving around and rattling pots and pans in his big, beautiful kitchen."

"I thought material things didn't mean anything to you and Sergio," Natalie said snidely.

"Obviously, we both like nice things, but I decided to cook for him. Something from the heart would mean more to him than something store-bought. After all, what can I buy Sergio that he can't buy himself?"

"Something better than a pen. If I had your money, I'd buy him a pure gold, Dookie chain to match the one he wears. That would look hot."

"No, I'm sticking to my gut and keeping it simple." Changing the subject, Anya said, "You know what he told me the other day? He said before he met me, he hardly ever stayed at home; he was always out in the streets. He said the place was so big, he felt lonely in there all alone. But now that we're seeing each other exclusively, he enjoys spending time at home." Anya went quiet briefly and then smiled. "Lately, I've been at his place a lot. He asked me to move in with him."

"Are you?"

Anya shrugged. "I don't know. We're getting really close, and I have to admit, I've been giving it a lot of thought. But I don't want to ruin what we have by moving too fast. You know what I mean?"

"I have no idea what you mean. Shit, Majid wouldn't have to ask me twice. I'd be up in that bitch so fast…sitting in a plush chair with my feet up before he could blink his eyes." Natalie demonstrated by comically propping her feet up on Anya's coffee table.

Anya burst into laughter, and in the midst of it, she glimpsed the soles of Natalie's shoes and noticed they were painted a glossy red, mimicking Christian Louboutins. Sadly, the chipped and cracking paint was a dead giveaway that the shoes weren't authentic.

Anya had several pairs of Louboutins and wondered if Natalie was trying to compete with her. Embarrassed for her friend, Anya glanced away from the cheap, hand-painted soles.

"So, how are things with you and Majid?" Anya asked, pretending that she considered their warped sexual union as a genuine relationship.

"We're doing good; except for the fact that he got this bitch named Heidi who thinks she's running shit when Majid isn't around."

"What do you mean?"

"When he's taking care of business with Sergio, he can't personally attend the parties. So, the chick, Heidi, tries to get shit popping by telling Majid's other bitches what to do." Looking disgruntled, Natalie twisted her lips. "It's one thing for Majid to tell me whose dick to suck and whose pussy to eat, but I don't appreciate that bitch, Heidi, giving me orders."

"Are you really okay with the lifestyle you're leading?" Anya asked, choosing her words carefully. "I don't think it's emotionally or physically healthy for you to be tricking for Majid."

"I'm not tricking," Natalie protested.

"What do you call it?"

"Having fun, working parties."

"But you're not having fun."

"It's a lot of fun when I make my baby happy. But when Majid's not there, I don't like that bitch ordering me around."

Natalie's warped way of thinking was outrageous, but despite her flaws, Anya had grown to like her. She also felt sorry for her, and had come to the conclusion that Natalie was mentally slow. She hoped her friendship and guidance would steer her in the right direction.

"There's no reason for you to allow this Heidi chick to degrade you."

"There's nothing I can do about it."

"Yes, there is." With patient weariness, Anya touched Natalie's hand. "You have to stop selling yourself to entertain people who don't care about you. You have to start loving yourself."

"I have to keep Majid happy."

"No, you don't. You have to keep yourself happy."

"Who are you supposed to be, my therapist or somebody? Look, I have a plan and one day I'm gonna be in Heidi's position. I'm gonna be the one calling the shots. But right now I have to stay humble and play my part."

"I'm scared something bad is gonna happen to you, Natalie."

Natalie dismissed that idea with a hand wave. "Ain't nothing gonna happen to me. Now that I'm getting money, I don't have to make my rounds to different churches on Sunday."

Anya stared at Natalie blankly. "What are you talking about?"

"Me and my brother used to go from church to church sitting through boring sermons, waiting for the collection plate to come around."

Anya gasped. "Don't tell me…"

"Uh-huh. That used to be my hustle," Natalie said proudly. "Money snatched from the collection plate would pay for our weed for a whole week."

Natalie's confession was so unexpected, Anya was startled into laughter. "You stole from the church to buy weed?"

"Sure did. Don't judge! The preacher's doing the same thing, but he's taking a lot more than weed money," Natalie rationalized.

CHAPTER 23

Misty waited patiently for Gavin's tears to subside, watching as he dabbed his eyes and returned the handkerchief to his pocket. Deciding that he'd sufficiently pulled himself together, she addressed him.

"I've made a recent discovery," she said, gazing into Gavin's red-rimmed eyes. "It's a huge money-making venture."

"I already have money; I'm not interested in any venture, especially if it involves you giving public readings like a gypsy at a carnival," Gavin said with a look of repugnance.

Misty chose not to take offense to the verbal jab, at least not at the moment. She'd pay him back for insulting her when he least expected it. At present, she needed him to be on her side.

"Your income, though immense, is doled out to you on a semi-annual basis. Wouldn't it be awesome to earn billions of your own?"

"Billions?" he asked with a smirk. "I doubt if there are any clairvoyant billionaires."

"I'll be the first," Misty said confidently. "I've made a recent discovery that will rock the world, but I don't want to go public, and that's where you come in. Through your family's connections, you have access to some of the wealthiest people in the world. I plan to do business with only the affluent; I want a select and very elite clientele."

"You can't be serious. You expect me to contact business tycoons from the *Forbes* Billionaire List and tell them about your marvelous ability to see into the future? A nebulous future without any sense of a time frame, I might add," he said sarcastically. Frowning in disapproval, Gavin made a scoffing sound.

"I have more than the ability to foretell the future. I have exactly what the filthy rich are not able to buy," Misty said knowingly.

"And what might that be?" Gavin gave a weary sigh. "Love? That's such a cliché. Believe me, money can buy you a wonderful illusion of love, and with that in mind, I've decided to self-medicate my love sickness by taking a solo trip to Brazil. I'm sure I'll meet a buff young, hottie on the beach—someone who'll take my mind off Randolph for a while. That's the kind of instant gratification that money can buy."

"I can offer something much more lasting." Misty gripped the arms of the wheelchair and slowly, dramatically pushed herself up until she was standing upright.

"You…you're standing. How is that possible?" Gavin stammered, his face suddenly deathly pale. Stunned to the point of shaking, his trembling fingers began to fidget with his collar, and then the buttons of his crisp, light-blue shirt. "I don't understand how you're managing to stand."

Showing off, Misty took graceful steps and even twirled around.

"I knew you had some movement in your arms, but I thought you were completely paralyzed from the waist down." Gavin's vocal tone changed from shocked to indignant, as if Misty had been faking her inability to walk.

"The medical profession couldn't do anything for me. Doctors said I was doomed to sit in this disgusting chair for the rest of my life…" She paused and angrily gave the chair a hard shove, knocking it on its side. "But I cured myself." She stretched out her arms. "With these hands, I'm able to heal. People spend fortunes going to fake-ass healers. I've done my research and I know what I'm talking about. Sites of so-called healing water springs and wells are scattered all over the world, and hordes of desperate people travel far and wide to get the magical water to rid themselves of AIDS, cancer, blindness, all types of maladies. I read online that up to ten thousand people a day visit this place in Mexico. They stand in long lines for hours to get a bottle of the *supposedly* miracle water. They're fools, but that's on them. Initially, I wanted a mega church that would attract thousands for readings. But after acquiring this new ability, I decided to cut to the chase. Instead of exhausting myself with all the work involved in building a following, and getting a lot of small sums of money from the working stiffs, I'm going to offer my services only to the super-rich and get paid a big chunk of their ever-accumulating wealth."

Misty sat on the couch. Wearing a smirk, she faced Gavin, leaned back and crossed her legs. Watching him closely, she noticed a spark of interest in his eyes.

"This may be a great idea," he said, stroking his chin thoughtfully.

"It's an amazing idea. Go on and admit it," she said with teasing laughter. "Even the richest of the rich get sick. And they want a quick cure for what ails them and their loved ones. The starting price of my cure will be one million and upward, depending on the severity of the illness."

"Okay, I'm interested. But I need to know that you can really heal before I put the word out. Also, you and I have to legalize our partnership."

"You better pump your brakes, Gavin. I didn't say anything about a partnership."

"You couldn't possibly think I'm going to hand over an elite clientele out of the kindness of my heart. I've already paid to restore your beauty, and I didn't ask for anything in return except to learn the whereabouts of Randolph, and you've failed to hold up your end of the bargain."

"You didn't do anything out of the kindness of your heart. You want me to be your personal fortune teller, but you had ulterior motives, also."

"I did not!"

"Yes, you did. You're so fastidious and squeamish, you wouldn't have been able to look at me without having to fight the urge to vomit, so don't pretend that you're all merciful and full of grace, because you're not."

Gavin lowered his eyes guiltily. "Okay, I admit that when I saw the picture on your website with your face caved in on one side, you were an eyesore, Misty. It would have been extremely difficult to look at you without gagging. But despite my motive, I helped you. You can't deny that."

"You're absolutely right, and that's why I'm going to pay you ten percent of my earnings."

Gavin opened his mouth to protest, but Misty shut him up before he could speak. "Hey, ten percent of a billion dollars is a lot of paper, so don't turn your nose up."

He leaned forward in his seat. "Do you honestly expect to make a billion dollars?"

"Several billion," Misty said smugly. "I'd be one of the new billion-aires featured on next year's *Forbes* list if I was willing to go public, but I'm not trying to put myself out there like that. I'm not trying to give Uncle Sam a cut of my hard-earned money."

Gavin nodded while deep in thought. "I have an aunt who's suffering from Alzheimer's. She doesn't recognize her own children, and it breaks their hearts. Do you think you could reverse the effects of that disease, and you know, give her back her mental faculties?"

"I'm positive. But I'm not giving away any family freebies. Your aunt has to come out of her pocket, like everyone else."

"But she's not capable of handling financial affairs."

"Get the money from her kids."

"That's not possible. Her children—my cousins—have their own inheritance and their mother's money is being handled by the executors of the Stallings estate. I couldn't possibly convince them to write a large check—"

"I don't accept checks. I need my money in cash," Misty said with an excessive frown.

"Cash? You're being completely unreasonable. This business venture doesn't have to be handled like an illegal drug operation, you know. There are ways to get around the IRS. We can set ourselves up as a religious organization or a nonprofit group."

"There you go with that 'we' shit. Ain't no *we!* You work for me, Gavin, and I call all the shots. That nonprofit mess you're talking will involve attorneys and a whole bunch of other people wanting a piece of my pie. That is not gonna happen. If those rich muthafuckas want what I can offer, then they better make a huge withdrawal out of their Swiss bank accounts."

Gavin sighed heavily. "You're impossible, Misty. You seemed so sweet when I first met you, but now your true colors are showing. You're greedy, mean, and narcissistic." He shook his head. "I'm not surprised that someone tried to take your life."

"Since you want to be mean and insulting, I'll take back my generous offer. I don't need you to generate business. I figured I would expedite matters by having a member of the prestigious

Stallings family as my mouthpiece, but you know what? Fuck you, Gavin! The billionaire list is public information, and I'm perfectly capable of seeking out every person on that list on my own."

Gavin resorted to tears again. "I want to be a part of this. I spoke out of anger and I apologize," he whined, pulling his mono-grammed hanky from his pocket, again. "I'm tired of living on a stipend from my family. It's demoralizing. I tried to make it as an artist, but I failed. I know I could succeed as a..." Gavin went silent. "What is my job title, exactly?"

"If I decide to hire you, you'll be my assistant."

"Assistant? That sounds so lowly. I need a much more prestigious title."

"How about director of life enrichment?"

Gavin smiled. "Hmm. I like that."

"Good, glad you like it. Okay, so, you're hired, but only on a trial basis. Use your resources to get me wealthy clients, and please use discretion. Clients don't need to know my full government name; they can simply refer to me as Misty."

CHAPTER 24

I n less than a week, Gavin called Misty with a lead. "There's this software guy named Jeffrey Backus; he has a thing about aging—"

"I never said I had access to the fountain of youth; I said I could cure diseases and shit," Misty hissed.

"His disease is age-related. He has rheumatoid arthritis. His hands are horribly misshapen to the point where he can't play golf anymore. He's had surgery on one of his hands, but it's still infirm and causes him a great deal of pain. Not to mention embarrassment. He wears gloves to hide the deformity."

"A pair of fucked-up hands should be a piece of cake to heal, but don't tell him I said that. I'm gonna need a million upfront to lay hands on dude."

"I don't know if I'm comfortable asking him for money before he's been, uh, treated."

"Trust me, if he wants to play golf bad enough, he'll come up off that cash. Two million is like two hundred to a billionaire. Call me back when you've made the arrangements. Tell him he can come to a hotel here in Philly or he can fly me and my people to his location. It's his choice."

"Your *people?*"

"Yes, I get fatigued if I'm on my feet too long, and I need my nurse with me. I also need you to handle the money transaction, and I need a bodyguard to look out for me. I'll never travel without one ever again. If I'd had a bodyguard with me the night I was assaulted, the punk who tried to kill me wouldn't have been able to get to me. But you know what they say: live and learn."

"It's politically incorrect to use the word *punk*," Gavin said dryly.

"I don't care about being politically incorrect. By the way, when you talk to the software guy, make it clear that I don't want a commercial flight; tell him I require a private jet."

"I'm feeling more like an assistant than a director of life enrichment," Gavin complained.

"Whatever. Handle the details and call me back."

Misty hung up, feeling satisfied and superior. She was making it abundantly clear to Gavin that she didn't feel indebted to him in the least. He could stop thinking of her as his charity case now that he was working for her. Hopefully, he wouldn't meet his brutal demise before she earned her first billion.

Brick was avoiding Misty again. On his side of the bed, he had his back to her and was sleeping so close to the edge, it was a wonder he didn't fall on the floor. Misty was horny as hell. It seemed like her coochie was vibrating, sending off waves of need in Brick's direction, but he was stubbornly ignoring the signals.

Ever since she'd become unparalyzed, her sex drive was amped up, as if trying to make up for all the time she'd gone without sex.

"Brick," she murmured, tapping him on the shoulder.

"What?" he said grumpily.

"I need you."

"Nah, I'm not feeling you like that."

"This isn't working," she said with a sigh.

He sat up, his back propped against the leather headboard. "I know the way I'm acting isn't fair to you, but I can't fake feelings, Misty. Something is off between us. It's not your fault. It's on me. When you came out of the coma, I was so relieved that you made it. I mistook that feeling for love. To be honest, I love you in the purest sense—like family, but not as my woman. That kind of love died a long time ago."

"Well, thanks for finally letting me know," Misty said, throwing the covers off of her. "I'm leaving; going to get a hotel room until I can find my own place."

"You don't have to leave, Misty. I'll go."

Misty laughed and the sound held a bitter ring. "Please. You're living from paycheck to paycheck; you can't afford to go anywhere. Keep this dump. I'm moving on to bigger and better things." She clicked the bedside lamp on, got out of bed, and went to the closet to pick out something to wear.

"It's after midnight, Misty. Why don't you wait until morning?"

"Don't try to act like you care."

"I don't want anything to happen to you. Look, I'm sorry it turned out like this, but don't run out of here in the middle of the night because you're mad. It shouldn't be like that between us." Brick got up and grasped Misty's wrist. "I don't blame you for wanting to leave, but let's discuss it, first. I need to know where you're going, so I can be sure you're all right."

Misty yanked her hand away from Brick. "You don't get to know my whereabouts, Brick; it doesn't work like that. You may not want me, but I guarantee you, a hundred other muthafuckas will be lining up to get some of this."

"I know, Misty. Like I said, it's not you, it's me."

"Don't use that tired-ass line on me; it's insulting and degrading!" Indignant, Misty placed a hand on her hip. She angrily walked to the closet and slipped into a pair of jeans that still had the tag dangling on the side. The top she selected also bore a sales tag. In fact, everything in the closet was brand-new. "I don't have any luggage, so I'll be back tomorrow to pack up my shit. You can keep the furniture. Consider it a goodbye present."

"No, that's your furniture that your friend bought for you. I'll keep it here until you get a place of your own. I'll do whatever I can to make sure you're straight."

Misty smirked. "I don't need your help. You don't get it, do you? I don't need this bullshit furniture and I don't need your little bit of money. I'm about to become a billionaire, baby. You have no idea of the kinds of moves I'm making."

Brick shrugged. "All I can say is, I wish you well, Misty. That's from the heart."

"Yeah, whatever. All I can say is go to hell," Misty said spitefully as she picked up her phone to call a cab.

With a few of her clothes and personal items stuffed in a large LV bag, Misty sat on the couch in the darkness, waiting for the cab to arrive. Bitter tears rolled down her cheeks. Brick had no idea how badly he'd hurt her, and no idea that there were severe consequences for breaking her heart.

The cab dropped her off at the hotel and after Misty went to her suite, she munched on a banana from the complimentary fruit basket. When it occurred to her that she needed sexual relief, and not something to eat, she furiously hurled the banana against a wall. She had a big, comfortable bed in her room and no one to help steam up the sheets. She could call Audrey and ask her to come over and give her some head, but getting a tongue-job would not satisfy her cravings tonight.

She needed some dick. Hard-hitting, deep-penetrating dick with sustained strokes and staying power. Damn, she wished she knew how to get in touch with Troy. That ashy muthafucka with his elongated dick always gave her a thorough workout in bed. Unfortunately, she had no way to contact him.

Suddenly, her thoughts shifted to David, the janitor from the hospital. He didn't have a lot of personality and seemed a little timid, but she would bet money that he was a beast in bed. David had made it clear he wasn't feeling her when she was a patient, but she had no doubt he'd fall hard for her now that her image had been greatly improved.

Recalling that he'd put his number in her phone, Misty pulled up her contact list and tapped on his name. He answered sleepily on the fourth ring.

"Hi, David. This is Misty. Remember me? I was the patient who gave you a reading."

"Misty? Oh, yeah. What's going on?" he asked groggily.

"I need to see you about something I saw."

"You saw something about me?" he whispered in the phone.

"Yes, I did, but I can't talk about it over the phone. I'm at the Omni Hotel on Chestnut Street."

"Downtown?"

"Yeah, Fourth and Chestnut. I'm in room twelve-zero-seven. Have the front desk call me when you get here."

David didn't say anything for a few moments, and Misty heard a woman, most likely his cheating wife, speaking in an annoyed voice in the background.

"I'm not going to be able to make it. It's pretty late, and—"

"You need to hear what I have to tell you about your future," Misty said, cutting him off. She wasn't about to allow his bitch of a wife to stand in the way of her getting some dick. "It's urgent, David. I'll be waiting."

CHAPTER 25

"I thought you'd be in a wheelchair," David said, peering at Misty.

"Surprise," Misty said with a smirk.

"I'm confused; I thought you were paralyzed."

"That was a temporary condition. I'm good, now."

David observed her closely. "Your face…" His words trailed off. "You look like a totally different person. And you're so pretty."

"I had a little nip and tuck here and there to get my looks back. Glad you approve," she said nonchalantly. Misty's eyes roamed from his close-cropped haircut down to his white Nikes. "You look a lot different, too," she acknowledged.

"Yeah, I'm out of my work uniform," he said, gesturing toward his clothes with his eyes lowered bashfully.

Sitting on the bed, Misty smiled invitingly. David's shyness was attractive, and his sex appeal was much more apparent with him dressed in jeans and a close-fitting shirt that accentuated his slim but athletic build.

Instead of sitting in the chair opposite Misty, David stood by the window in her room, slouched against the heating and cooling unit, and twisting his wedding ring around his finger in anxious circles. "What did you want to discuss?"

Misty began to recite the story she'd prepared in advance. "I had another vision, but this time it lasted longer. I want to make sure that my vision is correct."

"You want to read me again?"

"Yes," she said, rising from the bed and approaching him with her arm extended. She touched his hand and saw a different set of clips of his life. The life-movie paused at key moments, like when he moved from his mother's house and went to live with his dad and stepmother. Misty sensed that David dreaded having to live with his father, but his mother thought he needed a male influence.

The scene that revealed his future remained the same, with David holding a gun against his wife's lover's head.

Unwilling to spoil their evening together with bad news, Misty made up a future that deviated from what she had originally told him. "So, uh, I saw an extended version of your future, and this time I heard the dude with the dreads pleading for his life. You had a change of heart and took your finger off the trigger and lowered the gun. You were angry, cursing, and threatened him, but you didn't harm him. I called you tonight because I thought it was important for you to have that information. You know, so you could stop worrying about being a murderer."

"And what about my marriage. Does it end?"

"I got the feeling you forgave your wife and that the two of you will be able to work things out," she said, telling him more of what he wanted to hear.

David dropped his head in relief. "I hope so," he whispered. "Knowing what she's been up to, but keeping it to myself is killing me."

"You haven't said a word to her about her affair?" Misty asked, incredulous.

He shook his head. "I've been acting like everything is all right, hoping if I don't say anything, my wife will come to her senses and keep our family together by ending things with dude." David dropped his head and squeezed his eyes shut tightly, as if disgusted by his weakness.

Seizing the moment, Misty consoled him by caressing his forearm and murmuring, "It'll be all right." She moved closer. "You need a hug," she whispered, wrapping her arms around his lean and muscular back. She slipped her hands beneath his shirt, her palms traveling up his smooth, bare flesh. He flinched and gave a deep intake of breath when she scratched his skin lightly, teasingly.

His mouth glided down the side of her neck. "I want you, but I shouldn't. It's not right," he whispered and then pressed his lips against hers. His tongue probed and then slid along hers.

Misty could feel his erection straining against his fly as it sought release. Taking the initiative, she unzipped his jeans and slipped her hand inside. David made feeble protests, but Misty ignored him, capturing his dick, taking it out of his pants, and then openly admiring it. It sort of reminded her of her ex-lover, Troy's long dick, only thicker and without the layer of ash.

She caressed it and felt a shiver of excitement running up her spine. "I bet you know how to use this thing, don't you, baby?" Misty looked up at David and smiled. "It looks tasty, but I'm not gonna suck it."

"Why not?" he asked in a quavering voice.

"It's been a long time since I sucked a dick and I don't trust myself. I might fuck around and try to eat the whole thing," she said with laughter.

"Suck it, please," he begged.

"Nah. My pussy is spazzin' out; you gotta take care of it. Can you do that for me?"

"Yeah, I can take care of that pussy for you," he mumbled in a low, husky voice as he moved Misty toward the bed. He pulled his jeans and briefs down and allowed them to pool around his ankles, and then sat on the edge of the bed. Misty kicked off her jeans and climbed on his lap, gripping his length and guiding it to the opening of her pussy. Squatting down, she took him in fully. She took him in so deeply, she could have sworn she saw stars. Her muscles tightened around him and he began to lift off the bed with each harsh thrust.

He was fucking with wild abandon, giving her such forceful thrusts, she was bouncing up and down so vigorously, she had to wrap her arms tightly around his neck to keep from being thrown off his lap.

"This is what I'm talking about," she murmured with her face buried in the space between his neck and collarbone. Brick had given her an uninspired and lackluster sexual performance, but David wasn't holding back, he was giving her exactly what she needed. When he hit a particularly sensitive area, she sank her teeth into his shoulder to keep from crying out and calling for Jesus.

He must have enjoyed having his neck bitten because he went berserk, breathing heavily, bucking and fucking like an animal out of the wild. Since he seemed to like it, Misty decided to put her expensive dental work to good use, biting him over and over on his neck, his shoulder, and his back. The harder she bit, the harder and faster he fucked.

Finally, Misty felt a wonderfully familiar pressure in her loins and realized it wouldn't be long before she climaxed. Wanting to thoroughly enjoy the moment, she whispered for David to slow down, which he did. Getting stroked at a leisurely pace, she wrapped her legs around his back and with her coochie stretched wide, she instantly exploded in ecstasy and David shot a load two seconds later. She tumbled off him, and collapsed on her side. Gazing up at him, she noticed that one side of David's upper body was covered with bite marks.

She stifled a giggle, wondering how he'd explain the teeth indentations to his wife.

They fucked in various positions and all over the hotel room until the sun came up, and Misty still hadn't had enough. Apparently, David hadn't either; he required only minimal coercion to call in sick at his job. With the entire day to themselves, Misty and David ordered room service, took naps, and fucked some more. At six in the evening, with her sex craving finally satisfied, she encouraged David to go home to his wife.

"Can I see you again?" he asked, running his fingers through her hair and kissing her cheek and earlobe.

It was apparent that David couldn't get enough of her, which was exactly how Misty wanted him to be, but she'd had enough of him for one day. "I don't want to interfere with your marriage, so go on home and patch things up with wifey. She's probably furious that you stayed out all night," she said, making up an excuse to get rid of him.

"With all the dirt my wife's been doing, I don't care how she feels. I can do whatever I want."

"But for the sake of your child, you should try to make it work," Misty said, sounding compassionate, even though she didn't give a damn about his marriage or his kid.

"There's such a strong connection between us; I don't want to leave. I didn't expect to fall for you the way I have, but now that it's happened, I don't feel I should have to apologize. Not after the way my wife has been doing me."

"You and your wife should talk about the situation."

"She can have him. I don't care anymore, now that I've got you." He stared at Misty dreamily. "Look at you. You're so sexy and beautiful. Is this real or should I pinch myself?"

This is the same muthafucka who looked at me all crazy when I had a messed up mug and tried to flirt with him at the hospital. I'm gonna have to pay him back for hurting my feelings. I'm gonna turn his ass all the way out. He's gonna jump when I say jump, and he's gonna be crawling on all fours before I'm through with him. This dude is gonna be trained exactly like Brick used to be before my stupid mother interfered and undid all my good work, turning a good man bad. I hope David doesn't get locked up for putting a bullet through the dreadlock man's head before I have my fun with him.

"Give me another kiss before you leave," Misty said with her lips puckered. David embraced her and covered her mouth with his, putting his heart and soul into his kiss.

After Misty pulled away, he asked, "Is it all right if I call you later on tonight? You know, to touch base and say goodnight?"

"Not tonight. Make peace with wifey. When you make love to her, I want you to pretend that you're making love to me."

David frowned. "I don't want to have sex with her. My eyes are open now, and I'm sick to my stomach over the way I allowed her to play me. I don't care about her and dude. They can have each other because I want you."

Damn, my coochie must be the bomb. This muthafucka is tryna leave his family so he can lay up in bed with me.

"If you really care about me, you won't get me mixed up in your marital problems. Now, please go home and be nice to your wife so she won't go through your phone and find my number. The last thing I need is for a jealous female to be calling and harassing me."

"I won't let that happen," he promised.

"Good," Misty said, cracking open the door. "We'll get together later this week, okay?"

"When?" he asked eagerly.

"I'm not sure. But we'll get together before the week is out."

David exited her room quite reluctantly and only after Misty promised to call him first thing in the morning.

CHAPTER 26

Paloma, Sergio's housekeeper, who had recently arrived from Santo Domingo, had provided Anya with the recipe for pollo guisado. Paloma was a kind woman in her early forties, though she appeared much older. Probably from a lifetime of domestic labor that began in her childhood.

Like Sergio, Paloma was dark-complexioned with a helmet of soft, curly black hair. Her Spanish accent was melodic and soothing, and Anya enjoyed listening to her speak.

Taking her friend Natalie's criticism to heart, Anya decided that a one-course meal wasn't grand enough for a milestone birthday, and so she hired Paloma to stay overtime and cook a feast of Dominican food for the private festivity.

The two women worked together in the kitchen with Paloma multitasking as she prepared numerous Dominican dishes. Anya was impressed with how organized and efficient the housekeeper was in the kitchen. Meats that were marinating in special sauces were refrigerated, beans that had soaked overnight were poured into a pot and placed on the stove, and baked bread was taken out of the oven. Meanwhile, Paloma chopped garlic and numerous vegetables—many of which Anya could not identify—with the speed of a seasoned chef.

Simply watching Paloma in action made Anya's head spin, and

so she concentrated on mixing the cake batter and getting it in the oven. Once that was done, Anya went through the steps of preparing the chicken stew. While tending to the feast, Paloma managed to keep an eye on Anya, offering helpful advice, such as: "a little more salt; don't forget the bouillon cube; don't dice the onions, cut them in rings."

Finally, with the chicken browned and all the other ingredients mixed in, Anya turned the burner on low.

"Can you taste this and tell me what you think?" Anya asked, inviting Paloma to sample the contents of her simmering pot.

Paloma dipped a wooden spoon in the mixture and tasted. "Very good. Are you sure you're not from the Dominican Republic?" Paloma teased.

"No, but my mother was from the Caribbean. She was born in Trinidad."

"Well, that explains it. You have Caribbean cooking in your blood," Paloma said with a warm smile.

Anya beamed with pride as she frosted the cake she'd taken from the oven. This was going to be a birthday Sergio would never forget. His attentiveness and patience had won her heart. Though she'd never forget Brick, she was finally ready to move on. Tonight, she would tell Sergio she was ready to take the plunge and move in with him. But first she would entertain and entice him with a sexy little birthday strip-tease she'd learned from a burlesque-dance DVD.

"Would you keep an eye on my stew while I take a shower and get dressed?" Anya asked. "Sergio will be home soon and I want to look nice."

"Not a problem. Go make yourself beautiful for Mr. Sergio; I'll make sure your dish doesn't burn."

Anya showered and changed into a black patent leather, body-hugging strapless dress with a long, side zipper that she planned to unzip slowly during her striptease. Beneath the dress, she had on a frilly push-up bra and a thong with a removable rose petal in front. Sergio was going to love the second phase of his birthday celebration.

Paloma brought out the pollo guisado. "This was prepared by the hands of your fine lady," she told Sergio.

"With Paloma's help," Anya added. She wanted to devour all the food that had been prepared, but feared if she ate another bite, her tummy would protrude unattractively during the burlesque routine she planned to entice Sergio with after the meal. She declined the chicken stew and asked Paloma to hold off on the rest of the food. "Bring out the cake next; I want Sergio to have a slice before he gets too stuffed from all this food."

Sergio tasted the chicken and nodded his head in approval. "This tastes like my mother's cooking," he commented.

Flattered, Anya smiled, though she knew he was only teasing. "Stop messing with me, Sergio. Seriously, does it taste okay?"

He took another mouthful and he closed his eyes blissfully. "It's delicious."

Anya watched with delight as Sergio devoured the food she'd cooked. Paloma cleared away the dishes and brought out the coconut and chocolate birthday cake, which Sergio raved over.

"How much longer is it going to take for you to make up your mind about settling down, ma-ma? After tasting your cooking, I'm interested in more than shacking up; I'm ready to make it official and tie the knot."

These words were spoken half-jokingly, and Sergio and Anya laughed together. Despite the laughter, she saw earnestness in Sergio's eyes and wondered if he really was thinking about marriage. She hoped not because she wasn't ready. At least not yet. What she was ready to do was to take the birthday celebration to the next level.

"Your presents are in your bedroom. Are you ready to join me upstairs?" she asked, forming her glistening lips in a sensual pout.

Eager to oblige, Sergio wiped his mouth with the napkin and stood. Joining hands, they exited the dining room. "You look so good in that dress, baby. I can't wait to peel it off of you," Sergio murmured as they climbed the curved staircase.

In Sergio's room, a bottle of his favorite champagne was sitting on ice and two gold-rimmed flutes bearing Sergio's monogram set next to the gold ice bucket.

In the center of the bed, a gift that was wrapped handsomely in navy paper and tied with a small gold ribbon was placed in the center of his bed.

"What do we have here?"

"Open it and see."

Anya watched with eagerness as Sergio unwrapped the present. He took the pen out of the cushioned box and appeared to be impressed with the luxury writing instrument. "This is classy," he said, inspecting the pen. "It's perfect for the new life I'm building. It would have never occurred to me to invest in something like this, and you've saved me from embarrassment."

"What do you mean?" Anya asked.

"I don't think my business associates would take me seriously if I went around with a disposable pen in my suit pocket. This beautiful accessory makes a statement."

"What's it saying?" Anya teased.

"It's saying, I'm gonna replace this nigga's gun."

"What?" Anya looked puzzled.

"One stroke of a pen can solidify a deal faster than discharging a full round of bullets from a gun," Sergio said wisely.

"I'm so glad you like it. Happy Birthday, Sergio."

"Thank you."

"Now, it's time for your second gift. Would you like a drink before I present it?"

"Sure, why not?" Sergio moistened his lips and furrowed his brows as he wondered what Anya had in store for him.

Anya popped the champagne bottle and poured the sparkling liquid into both flutes. She handed Sergio a glass and then took a quick swig from her glass. Next, she clicked a switch on the entertainment system and "Rocket" poured through the speakers. Swiveling her hips, Anya began her practiced routine.

Grinning, Sergio gulped the contents of his glass and leaned back, ready to enjoy the show.

Anya dramatically extended her left arm, caressing her flesh with the fingers of her right hand. The burlesque moves included hip rolls and sexy slaps on her thighs. By the time she began daintily tugging on the zipper, pulling it downward, a half-inch at a time, Sergio was sitting on the edge of the bed, urging her to take it all off.

But Anya continued to taunt and tease, taking forever to remove her dress, and when she did, Sergio was so worked up, he announced that the show was over and lifted Anya up and tossed her on the bed. He tore off her bra in split seconds and when his large hands worked on the elastic band of her rose-bud decorated thong, Anya surprised him by pulling off the rose, exposing the easy access to her private parts.

"Damn, that's sexy." He hurriedly rid himself of his clothes, and in seconds, he was naked and straddling her. He covered her mouth with his. His tongue was sweet, like champagne, and Anya closed her eyes, savoring the taste, and feeling a sense of peace. She felt safe and protected in his arms. It was time to allow herself personal happiness. It was time to finally let go of her feelings for Brick.

Sharp raps on the bedroom door startled Anya and Sergio.

"What is it?" Sergio barked.

"May I speak to you, Mr. Sergio? It's important," Paloma said on the other side of the door.

"One moment," he said impatiently. Sergio got out of bed and retrieved a robe. Anya covered her nudity by pulling the sheets and duvet up to her chin.

Sergio only cracked the door open. "What is it, Paloma?"

"Mr. Majid is here. He says there's been some kind of emergency involving one of your workers, and he needs to speak to you. I told him you'd gone to bed for the night, but he said you'd be upset if he didn't alert you to the situation."

"He's right. Thanks, Paloma. Tell Majid I'll be downstairs in a few." Sergio closed the door.

"What's going on?" Anya asked.

"Something has come up and Majid is here. It has to be bad news for him to drive here to tell me in person. I'm sorry about this interruption, baby, but it's an important business matter." Sergio put on a pair of briefs beneath his robe. "Hopefully, the matter can be resolved quickly."

Sergio exited the bedroom and closed the door behind him.

Anya resented Majid's intrusion. She disliked the man intensely and sensed that the feelings were mutual. She could tell Majid resented the time Sergio spent with her. If she wasn't in his life, Sergio would have been at the club tonight, spending his birthday partying with Majid and the boys. She wondered if Majid had made up an excuse merely to interrupt her and Sergio's private celebration.

With time to kill, Anya got out of bed and tidied up the room by picking her dress and heels off the floor. She hung the dress in Sergio's closet, mixing it in with his vast collection of suits and casual clothes. She stuck her heels and purse in a spare shoe drawer and stood back with her arms folded, observing Sergio's overflowing wardrobe. She wondered where she'd store her clothes when she and Sergio set up housekeeping together. More than likely, Anya would use one of the spare rooms for her personal closet space.

Sergio had brought up the M-word today, and she returned to bed, imagining what it would be like to be his wife. Sitting up in bed, naked, she took long sips of champagne while waiting for Sergio to return. When forty minutes passed without Sergio even checking on her, she felt somewhat offended. She was also bored and the boredom brought on a sudden appetite. Deciding to try out portions of the feast that she hadn't tasted yet, Anya put on one of Sergio's oversized T-shirts and crept along the hallway to the back stairs that led to the kitchen area. Sergio always received guests in the main room, which was quite a distance from the kitchen. No one except Paloma would know that she was scrounging in the fridge like a starving beggar.

Surprisingly, Paloma wasn't in the kitchen, and Anya assumed she was still tidying up the dining room. The woman was a meticulous worker and kept Sergio's home spotless.

In the microwave, Anya heated up her own creation of Dominican chicken stew and also an exotic-looking dish of rice, lamb, and vegetables that Paloma had prepared. She sat at the island scarfing down the meal that was scrumptiously spicy and sweet.

Being nosey, she wanted to question Paloma about Majid's visit—find out if she knew any details. Surprisingly, Paloma still hadn't returned to the kitchen. Anya washed out the dishes and utensils she'd used before searching for Paloma. Barefoot, she padded toward the dining room. When she neared that area, she heard voices. Angry voices. She tiptoed toward the sound of the voices, and covered her mouth in shock when she saw Sergio and Paloma, on their knees, side-by-side, with their mouths taped and their hands tied behind their backs.

Holding a gun, Majid paced in front of them. A man named Hassan, who was one of Sergio's bodyguards, stood next to Majid. He also held a gun.

Dear God, what's going on? Anya's heart rate accelerated.

"This muthafucka is going legit and trying to leave us hanging," Majid said bitterly.

With the tape across his mouth preventing him from speaking, Sergio could only shake his head in denial.

"Yes, you were," Majid yelled hoarsely. "Man, I got eyes and ears everywhere. I know about the sneaky move you're tryna make." Majid was so angry, he was practically frothing at the mouth.

Natalie! That no-good, treacherous bitch set us up! Anya surmised that Natalie had gone back to Majid, reporting that Anya had mentioned that Sergio was considering going legit. What Natalie didn't know was that Sergio was going to give Majid a top position in his business venture. And that's why Sergio was shaking his head while Majid accused him of betraying their partnership. If only Majid would remove the tape from his mouth, Sergio could explain.

The duct tape could not contain the mournful moans that escaped Paloma's lips. She had nothing whatsoever to do with the beef between the two men. She was merely at the wrong place at the wrong time, and Anya couldn't bear witnessing Paloma trembling in fear.

"Go upstairs and bring that stuck-up bitch down here," Majid ordered Hassan. "She's gonna get it right along with her man and this maid-bitch."

Hassan left the room and went in search of Anya. *Ohmigod, they're gonna kill all of us.* Her stomach seized and dread inched up her throat. As she hid in the shadows, she made eye contact with Sergio. He was trying to use his eyes to communicate with her. His frantic eyes kept darting to the left, trying to give her some kind of signal. Suddenly, she realized he was telling her to save herself—to flee in the direction of his gaze. And she remembered the hidden safe room that he'd shown her several weeks ago. A room he said no one knew existed.

CHAPTER 27

With no landline on the premises and with her cell phone zipped inside her purse, which was stowed in a cubby inside Sergio's closet, Anya had no way of calling for help. But she had to do something. What were her options? Thinking fast, she decided she could either explain to Majid that Natalie had given him incorrect information or she could abandon Sergio and hide like a coward in the safe room. She couldn't leave Sergio helplessly tied and gagged without at least trying to save him. Maybe she could reason with Majid and explain that there'd been a huge misunderstanding. Sergio was a good man and she could vouch for his loyalty to his crew.

Even though Majid's very presence radiated danger, she couldn't stand by and allow him to hurt Sergio over some inaccurate information that he'd gotten from that dumb-ass Natalie, who was trying to win points with Majid by throwing Sergio under the bus.

And poor Paloma! The housekeeper was completely innocent. She'd only been in the country for a little over a month. She was trying to make a better life for herself and had worked late tonight to earn extra money. If Anya hadn't asked her to work overtime, she wouldn't have even been in the house when Majid and Hassan arrived. Feeling an overwhelming sense of guilt, Anya decided she had to say something on Sergio's behalf.

Terrified but willing to risk her life, Anya took one brave step forward but instantly froze when she heard the unmistakable sound of a gunshot followed by the ominous thump of a body hitting the hardwood floor. *Oh, dear God! No!* A quick, stolen glance and she saw Paloma's lifeless form, facedown with blood pouring from a wound in the back of her head.

Majid turned cold, malevolent eyes on Sergio. "Do you see what you made me do to your housekeeper? All of this because you allowed that bitch, Anya, to make you weak. You let her get into your head and turn you against me. When Hassan brings her downstairs, I'm gonna pistol-whip her and rearrange that pretty face—beat it beyond recognition," he said vehemently, holding his deadly gun up and waving it around. "I'm gonna bury this gun deep inside her whoring cunt before I pull the trigger," Majid threatened, his lips curled in hatred.

Anya shuddered. Majid looked positively evil. She didn't understand why he despised her so much, but she believed his hatred for her had been an instant reaction on the first night she'd met Sergio at the club.

Majid suddenly ripped the tape from Sergio's mouth. "I'm running shit, now, yo. So, start talking. What's the combination to the safe?"

Sergio flinched at the sight of Paloma's dead body. "Why would you do that, man? You're taking shit too far. I was planning on bringing you and a few others on board with the new company after everything was established."

"Tell that shit to some other sucker," Majid said sneeringly. "Now, what's the fucking code?"

"I'll tell you; I'll tell you. But you have to promise you won't hurt Anya."

"Man, I'm not sweating that ho. All I want is the money that I helped you make. You been paying me peanuts and I want my share of the dynasty you wouldn't have been able to build without me. Give me the numbers," he growled. "I'm not going to ask you again." Majid pointed the gun at Sergio.

"Eleven-two-sixteen," Sergio blurted, and then exhaled in relief. Without warning, Majid raised his gun and pulled the trigger, blowing a hole between Sergio's eyes.

Eyes bulging, Anya covered her mouth to smother a gasp. Shock and fear flooded her body and she tried to creep backward, but her legs felt weightless, threatening to give out. Unable to move, she leaned against a wall, trembling from the shock of what she'd seen. *No, no, no. Not my sweet Sergio. This can't be happening!*

Anya heard Majid running up the stairs, anxious to grab the money from Sergio's safe. She realized he believed she was in Sergio's bedroom and was also eager to torture her before taking her life. When his footsteps no longer echoed on the marble stairs, she fled to the kitchen pantry and pulled on the shelving unit that doubled as a secret, reinforced door.

The safe room was soundproof, an impenetrable fortress. No one could get in unless she opened the door, which could only be unlocked from the inside by using the combination of numbers that Sergio had given her with his last breath. Majid would be in for a rude awakening when he was unable to open the safe and also unable to locate Anya.

Panicked, Anya looked around the room that was equipped with a portable toilet, nonperishable snacks, bottles of water, soft drinks, and Sergio had even stocked the room with top-shelf liquor.

Her darting eyes landed on surveillance equipment and she let out a sigh of relief when she spotted a disposable cell phone that was connected to a charger inside the safe room. She picked up the phone and called 9-1-1. In a surprisingly calm voice, she reported the murders, gave the dispatcher Sergio's address, and clearly spelled out the names of the victims as well as the murderer and his accomplice. She hung up and turned off the phone, killing its signal after the dispatcher began questioning her about her connection to the murders.

The surveillance equipment inside the safe room didn't have audio, but she didn't need sound to interpret what was going on. Majid was inside Sergio's bedroom, his face contorted as he yelled at Hassan. Most likely, he was blaming his sidekick for Anya's escape. She saw Hassan leave the bedroom in search of her, and she watched as Majid went inside the walk-in closet and worked on the combination lock that failed to pop open. Angry, he kicked a wall and exited the closet.

His eyes darted around Sergio's bedroom as if the mystery of the combination was something he could snatch out of thin air. He took the bottle of champagne out of the bucket of ice and helped himself, guzzling the bubbly straight from the bottle. After he emptied it, he lowered his head, scratching his chin, deep in thought. His lips moved menacingly as he most likely cursed Sergio for giving him the wrong numbers to the safe and for having the last laugh.

Majid returned to the closet and fiddled with the combination again. Hassan reappeared, holding out his arms in defeat with a look of exasperation on his face. Majid stared at Hassan in disbelief, his eyes glittering with rage. He smacked Hassan on both sides of his face and then sent him out of the room again, probably ordering him to check the grounds.

Eight minutes had elapsed since Anya had called 9-1-1 and she wondered how much longer it would take the police to arrive. A few minutes later, while Majid tinkered with the safe, Hassan ran into the bedroom, his mouth stretched wide, yelling something. Majid quickly pushed the pine wardrobe against the wall, concealing the safe. To Anya's amazement, Majid eased deep in the recesses of the closet, hiding behind Sergio's numerous suits that hung in the closet. Hassan looked around trying to find a hiding place and opted for slithering under the bed.

Moments later, police officers stormed into the bedroom with guns drawn.

Anya watched with bittersweet satisfaction as both men were yanked from their hiding places, roughed up, handcuffed, and then led out of the bedroom. Unfortunately, the surveillance in the safe room didn't focus on other areas of the house, only on Sergio's bedroom where the safe was kept.

Holed up in a room that no one knew existed, Anya had to wait it out while homicide detectives and other criminal investigators gathered evidence and evaluated the crime scene. She remained hidden for the next twenty-four hours and after disconnecting the surveillance equipment, she emerged from the safe room. Instead of rushing upstairs to get her clothes and her purse, she spent a few moments in quiet meditation in the room where Sergio's and Paloma's blood was splattered on furniture, artwork, and the walls. Bitter tears ran down her face.

On my mother's soul, I swear to you, Sergio, if by chance Majid beats this case, he's going to have to answer to me. The same goes for Hassan. And that bitch Natalie pretended to be my friend, but was using me to win points with Majid. She's gonna pay dearly for the senseless destruction she caused. Her last moments are gonna be a slow and torturous agony; she's going to beg for death.

Anya raced upstairs, grateful that the police hadn't located her clothing or her purse that contained her phone and her identification. They had no idea she'd been on the premises. If it weren't for the fact that she needed to move with anonymity in order to get to Natalie and unleash her vengeance, Anya would have revealed herself to the police as an eyewitness to murder.

She dressed hastily, and then struggled to move the heavy wardrobe that concealed Sergio's safe. Sergio wouldn't want his money locked up in the police evidence room or divided up between crooked cops; he'd want Anya to keep the money for herself. It went without saying that she'd look out for Paloma's family as well as keeping money on the books for Sergio's uncle.

Tugging and pulling, she finally moved the wardrobe. For security reasons, Sergio changed the code once a month. He'd mentioned that most recent series of numbers was her date of birth. She swiftly punched in the code and the safe swung open.

The stacks and stacks of bills inside the safe were supposed to be Sergio's admission to a legitimate life in the corporate world. With tears flowing once again, she stuffed the money in a drawstring laundry bag and stealthily exited the house.

CHAPTER 28

B rick unlocked the double locks on the front door and walked inside his apartment, tossing his keys on the kitchen counter. The clatter of metal against granite echoed in the empty apartment. He had mixed feelings about Misty leaving. A part of him was relieved she was gone and the other part wished she was still here, if only so he could keep an eye on her and make sure she was all right.

It had been difficult at first for him to accept that she possessed uncanny abilities, but after she healed herself, he became a believer. Still, he had a nagging feeling that somehow she was going to wind up in a world of trouble. Her abilities were gifts from above, but knowing Misty, she'd find a way to abuse and misuse her God-given powers, and sooner or later, she was going to piss off the wrong person.

Thinking about Thomasina's reaction when he had told her that Misty was able to prophesize, Brick laughed to himself as he walked to the fridge and took out a cold beer.

"I saw that article about her in the paper about her touching folks and seeing their future. That ain't none of the Lord's doing; that's Satan's work," Thomasina had said, shaking her head. "That daughter of mine has been touched by the devil's wicked hand."

He had yet to tell her that Misty had also acquired healing powers and was no longer paralyzed. He didn't want to be responsible for giving Thomasina a heart attack from the shock of discovering that Misty had performed a miracle and had healed her spinal cord injury. He decided that Misty would have to be the one to drop that bomb on her mother if they ever started speaking again. Knowing Misty, she was probably anxious to make up with her mother, if only to show off the new wardrobe she'd bought with the donation money.

He and Thomasina were trying to get along and be cordial for their son's sake, but Thomasina's face hardened with fury whenever he spoke about Misty. In order to have the visitations with his son go as smoothly as possible, Brick decided it would be best if he didn't bring up Misty's name in the future. The mother and daughter's animosity toward each other centered on his relationship with both of them. Misty had been his girl for years, but after she'd cheated on him, he ended up marrying her mother.

Although he'd attempted to patch things up between them, neither mother nor daughter was having it. There was no doubt in Brick's mind that Thomasina loved Misty and vice versa, but he thought it best to butt out and allow them to patch up their relationship in their own good time.

Kicked back on the couch with his feet propped up on an ottoman, Brick drank beer and watched TV and inevitably, his thoughts drifted to Anya. Prolonged thoughts of Anya would either have him in the shower beating his meat or send him to the strip club in search of the dancer named Island Girl, who reminded him of Anya.

The way he yearned for Anya, it was a good thing he didn't go to the strip club with the fellas after work tonight. A mere lap dance from Island Girl would not be enough to satisfy his urges. Not tonight.

It was odd how thoughts of Anya had prevented him from giving himself fully to Misty. His dick wouldn't act right; it didn't want Misty at all, and Misty was furious over that. The way she glared at him after his piss-poor performance in bed made him feel like crap. Brick shook his head, thinking, *Man, if looks could kill, I'd be a dead muthafucka!*

"But knowing Misty, she'll get over her anger the minute she finds herself a sucker who's willing to bow down and cater to her desires," Brick said aloud.

His phone buzzed and he glanced at the screen. To his surprise, Misty was calling.

"Speak of the devil," he said into the phone.

"I hope you weren't talking about me to my mother," Misty said with an attitude.

"No, I was talking about you to myself," he said with laughter. "So, what's going on? Are you all right? You need anything?"

"I'm fine. Look, I'm gonna get straight to the point."

"Go ahead."

"I'm pissed off at the way you did me the other night, but I'm willing to move on."

"That's good news. You know you'll always have my heart, but we're not—"

"Yeah, yeah…whatever. I'm not trying to hear that shit. You know me, Brick, and you know I don't appreciate being rejected. But I'm trying to be more mature, so don't be trying my patience by bringing up unpleasant bullshit."

"All right. So, what do you want to talk about?"

"I called to make you an offer."

"Aw, man. Here we go, again," Brick groaned. "What kind of scheme are you tryna involve me in?"

"It's not a scheme. It's business. Big business. Beyond anything we've ever done before. And it's perfectly legal."

"I'm listening."

"I know you could use some extra money with your child support payments being high as fuck, so before I call anyone else, I want to offer you an opportunity to make some under-the-table, tax-free moolah. Money in your pocket that my greedy mother can't get to."

"Doing what?" Brick asked suspiciously.

"Being my bodyguard. I was going to call a personal protection agency, but I don't think there's anyone who will protect me better than you."

"Thanks for the vote of confidence."

"I'm willing to pay top dollar, and I need you to be strapped, so get yourself a gun so you can start taking lessons at the shooting range."

"I don't need any lessons; I know how to shoot a gun."

"I'm not talking about a ghetto shootout with bullets flying everywhere. I need a straight shooter."

"Why? Has anybody been threatening you?"

"No. But I'm going to be dealing with extremely large sums of money. I'll have more money on me than you'll find inside a Brinks truck."

"Fuck outta here."

"If I'm lying, I'm flying," Misty said, laughing as she recited a line she and Brick used to say when they were kids.

Brick laughed with her. And for the first time in a long while, Misty felt like an old friend, again. Like the girl he used to know back in the day. The delicately pretty, but surprisingly tough, little girl whom he could kick it with as if she were one of the boys.

"You're getting paid a bunch of stacks to tell someone's future?"

"Stacks? You're thinking too small, my dude. I'm getting paid a cool million to heal a rich muthafucka."

"A million? Did I hear you right?"

"You sure did," Misty said with a proud grin. "But the next billionaire who wants me to lay my healing hands on him is gonna have to double that price. The miracles I can perform are worth it," she bragged.

"How'd you hook up with this wealthy dude?"

"Through Gavin; his family has connections, you know. The man's name is Jeffrey Backus. He has several homes, and in two weeks we'll be taking a private jet to his vacation spot in Hawaii."

"I want to be there for you; you know I always have your back, but I think you should call a legitimate protection agency. Get someone who's trained in that profession because I don't think I'm qualified. "

"I have faith in you; don't downplay your skills, Brick."

Brick rubbed his head worriedly. "I don't know, Misty. That's some high-level shit you're talking. You need agents with James Bond, high-tech equipment—a whole team with Secret Service qualifications."

"I don't need all that. You can handle this job. You got inside one of Smash Hitz's houses, took out two of his people, and got away with it. This isn't even a dangerous mission, but I want to be sure I have protection if somebody tries to come between me and my money. By the way, I'll pay you twenty thousand for a job that shouldn't take more than twenty-four hours at the most. It's a long flight—ten hours, so most of our time will be spent in the air. But once we get there, we'll be in and out. It shouldn't take long to collect the money and to heal dude. Tack on another ten hours for the flight back home, and that's it. It's easy money, Brick."

Astonished over the amount of money Misty was willing to pay him, Brick was speechless.

"Think of all the nice things you can do for Little Baron with that kind of money," she continued.

"You don't have to convince me, Misty. I'm in!" Brick said enthusiastically.

"By the way, Brick, I realize that what we had ran its course. I was hurt and angry at first, but I made some adjustments and I don't have any hard feelings. We're better off as friends, anyway."

"Misty, I...I'm really sorry things didn't—"

"It's cool," she interrupted. "I'm over it, so drop the subject. Let's concentrate on getting this money," she said brightly.

"I'm all in," Brick agreed.

After Brick and Misty hung up, he thought about her offer. Misty had a tendency to inflate the truth, and he figured she was exaggerating about the private jet, the amount she was getting paid, and also his cut. Twenty thousand dollars for a day's work was as outrageous as Misty claiming someone was going to pay her a million dollars. Still, even if she paid him only a fraction of what she had promised, the extra money would help with his cash flow situation that had taken a big hit after child support had been deducted from his paycheck.

CHAPTER 29

The private jet wasn't exactly the flying palace Misty had expected from Jeffrey Backus, but it was better than a commercial flight. She'd done her research and was aware that Backus owned a custom-designed jet that seated forty people. The décor was cream and white with an elegant staircase that led to a lounge with a 57-inch multiplex screen and white leather seats, a conference room, a master and guest bedrooms, gold-plated fixtures in the bathrooms and kitchen, and other luxurious amenities. She supposed he didn't think she was worthy of traveling in his personal aircraft, and the idea of being snubbed didn't sit well with her.

Though the ten-seater jet Backus had chartered for Misty was comfortable, it couldn't be described as luxurious. After four hours in the air, Misty retired to the bedroom, which wasn't anything special, only a small room with a bed. It would have been nice if Brick joined her and tightened her up like he used to back in the day, but he was more engrossed in the latest *Fast and Furious* movie than in Misty. One hand dug into a bag of microwave popcorn while the other held a container of iced tea. The snacks and movie had his undivided attention.

When they'd first boarded, he tried to snap open a can of beer, but Misty firmly let him know that he could not touch any alcohol during the flight. She needed him focused and of sound mind when they reached their destination. When they were younger, Brick used to drink too much and was known to get the rams whenever liquor was in abundance. The last thing she needed was a drunk-ass bodyguard while trying to handle business in Hawaii. To his credit, Brick didn't protest laying off the alcohol and he seemed content sipping on soft drinks.

Gavin, on the other hand, was acting sullen and bitching about the size of the plane. His grandfather's plane, he said in a brag-gadocio manner, was equipped with a fitness room, showers, and several bedrooms. He also kept pestering Misty about using her abilities to help locate his missing lover. She wanted to laugh and could barely keep a straight face. His missing boyfriend was the last thing on her mind. Besides, she had no way of finding him, even if she wanted to. She had the gift of prophecy and healing power in her hands, and had no idea why Gavin thought she was like one of those kooky psychics who claimed to be able to locate the bodies of murder victims and find missing people.

An hour from their destination, Misty woke, freshened up, and changed into a navy Dior dress and Jimmy Choo heels. After admiring herself for several minutes, she called Brick's phone and told him to come to the bedroom and change from his jeans into the European-cut suit she'd brought along for him.

"Can I get some privacy?" Brick asked before stepping out of his jeans.

"Boy, please. I was sleeping next to your naked-ass only a few weeks ago, so don't be acting like I've never seen you out of your clothes before."

With a resigned shrug, Brick unbuckled his belt and pulled off his pants. Misty's mouth watered as her eyes glossed over his arms, legs, and thighs. Brick was pure muscle. Taking a risk, she stole a glance at the bulge in his briefs. All of that coiled-up dick was going to waste stuffed inside his underwear. A sigh of regret escaped her lips, and Brick looked at her curiously.

"Something wrong?" he asked.

"No, I was thinking that it's a shame we have to turn around and get back on this plane for another ten hours after we handle our business. It would be nice to relax in Hawaii for a day or two," Misty said, coming up with a quick excuse.

"You want to sightsee while you're hauling around a million bucks?"

"It would be nice to see a little bit of Hawaii before we go back home."

"You can see Hawaii some other time. We need to get back to Philly so you can put the money away in a safe place," Brick said with authority as he buttoned the crisp white shirt Misty had bought him. Dressed in a well-cut, black suit, Brick tied his neck tie and then stood back and checked out his reflection in the mirror. "Do I look like an experienced bodyguard?" he inquired, fixing his face in a serious expression.

"Yeah, you'll pass for one," Misty said in a disinterested tone. In reality, she was practically drooling. Brick looked so delicious in the expensive suit that was accessorized with a shiny, nine-millimeter handgun stuck in the back of his pants, she was so worked up, she would have dropped down to her knees and deep-throated him at the snap of his fingers.

The combination of suit, tie, and gun was entirely too much sexy. It was a damn shame that Brick didn't realize how much he still loved and needed her, and it was Misty's responsibility to show him the error of his ways—in due time.

They were meant to be together, but there was no point in rushing the inevitable. She had no doubt that Brick still loved her; he was simply having a hard time adjusting to the drastic changes in her appearance, and her new abilities made him nervous. Including him in her money-making venture was a perfect way to keep him close as well as to keep him dependent. Once he became accustomed to having long paper, he wouldn't want to return to living from paycheck to paycheck. It was only a matter of time before she got her man back. In the meantime, she'd train David to treat her in the worshipful manner that Brick used to.

The house, a ten-acre estate overlooking the Pacific Ocean, was unlike anything Misty had ever seen. With palm trees swaying serenely and colorful exotic gardens that added to the tropical paradise atmosphere, the landscape surrounding the home was as breathtaking as the ocean view. Inside, the home had a Middle Eastern vibe, from the architectural designs to the collection of Islamic art.

A pretty young woman, obviously a native of the island, who was dressed in a maid's uniform, escorted Misty, Brick, and Gavin from the foyer, through the courtyard, and then into the living room with its sweeping views of the lush grounds and the ocean.

The opulence of Jeffrey's Hawaiian retreat infuriated Misty. No single person needed a vacation home as lavish as this one. The place was large enough to house at least five families, and yet (according to an online article) Jeffrey Backus lived here alone, leaving the place empty for long stretches of time.

If Misty owned a house like this, every room would be thoroughly lived in, and she wouldn't abandon it to roam around the world. Some people had no business having tons of money.

Misty checked the time and began to sulk when she realized that she, Brick, and Gavin had been waiting for over an hour for Jeffrey Backus to grace them with his presence. When he finally entered the room, Misty's eyes shot from his tanned face, thick silver hair and eyebrows, down to the dark gloves he wore to hide his affliction. He was a hefty man with a commanding presence.

Gavin jumped to his feet. "How are you, Mr. Backus? I'm Gavin Stallings. We've spoken on the phone several times, and I must say, it's very nice to meet you in person. I believe you've played golf with my uncle, Clark Stallings," Gavin said, clearly kissing up to the billionaire.

Backus brushed past Gavin, giving him only a curt head nod. Being a self-made man, he probably disapproved of trust fund kids who never had to work for anything.

"You must be Misty," Backus said, approaching her and reaching for her hand. She gave him a weak handshake, grateful that the fabric didn't allow their palms to touch. She wasn't there to give him a reading, and since he didn't think highly enough of her to send his personal luxury jet, she didn't want to give him any bonuses. Admittedly, she was envious of his gorgeous home and angry that he'd kept her waiting. Backus would have to be put in his place for treating her like an underling.

"You're a tiny little thing. Not at all the way I pictured you," Backus quipped, giving her a wide grin that probably charmed most people. Misty wasn't charmed and didn't crack a smile. He needed her more than she needed him, and she declined being sociable as punishment for having to travel for ten hours in a cramped, economy airplane.

"Yes, I'm Misty," she replied without a trace of a friendly smile. She nodded toward Brick. "That's my bodyguard, Brick, and you've already met Gavin."

"What happened to the nurse who was listed as part of your entourage?"

Misty shrugged. "When I saw how small the plane was, I decided to leave her behind," she lied. In reality, she didn't feel like being bothered with Ms. Peabody.

Backus didn't react to the insult. "Why do you need a bodyguard? Surely you don't expect to get mugged while visiting my home." Shaking his head in amusement, he took a seat in a plush and roomy, dark blue chair. "Well, let's get down to the business of healing," he said with a smirk, clearly doubting that Misty had the ability to cure his infirmity.

"That's not what we agreed to. I have to get paid in cash before I lay hands on you."

"That's not a problem, but suppose you're unable to cure my condition?"

"Don't worry; I can heal you," she said with confidence.

Backus rose from his seat and plodded across the room toward a library that took up an entire wall. He removed six or seven large, leather-bound books from the middle shelf, revealing a wall safe that was hidden behind the books.

Misty wondered if the two duffle bags and the briefcase they'd brought along would be enough to store the stacks upon stacks of bound bills that Backus removed from the safe. The money covered the surface of a table and numerous piles were arranged on the floor.

Carrying a duffle bag, Brick took steps toward the money. Gavin stood still, looking uncomfortable and unhappy.

"Let's leave the cash in plain sight until Misty works her magic on my hands," Backus said, halting Brick's movement.

"That's fair enough," Misty said, shooting Brick a look that signaled him to back up. She nodded toward the dark blue chair.

"Have a seat, Mr. Backus, and let me have a look at your hands."

"Aren't you going to burn incense and launch into an ancient chant to set the mood?" He gave a loud belly laugh.

"I didn't know you were a comedian, Mr. Backus. Let me assure you, there's no hocus pocus stuff; I'm simply gonna lay hands on you and you'll be healed."

Backus tugged on the fingers of the glove on his right hand. "Okay, let's have a go at it." From his tone, it was obvious he was skeptical about her abilities, but in his eyes Misty saw a glimmer of hope.

Several feet away, Gavin gasped when Backus exposed a hand that was unbelievably misshapen, lumpy, and crooked. Brick averted his eyes, looking down at his glossy shoes.

Misty placed her palm on top of Backus's afflicted hand and closed her eyes. The moment her hand began to tingle, she knew the healing had begun. She kept her hand in place until the sensation subsided.

"My hand feels different," Backus said in an awed whisper.

"Let's see how it looks," Misty said as she removed her hand from his.

"My God! This is unbelievable." Backus balled and unballed his fist, and spread his fingers that were no longer bent and deformed from the effects of arthritis.

"Amazing," Gavin blurted from the other side of the room.

Excited, Backus yanked the glove from his left hand and extended his arm. "Here you, go. Fix this one, too."

"Hold up, mister. Don't get greedy, now," Misty said with a hand on her hip. "I didn't agree to heal both your hands. You're gonna have to cough up some more money for your left hand." She narrowed an eye at Gavin, who had made the arrangements.

"That's exactly what I told Mr. Backus," Gavin said in his own defense.

"Money's not an object. I'll have another million in cash, first thing tomorrow."

"Sorry, I have to get back to Philly. You can make an appointment with Gavin."

"Can't you wait one more day?" he pleaded. "I'll pay you an extra two million if you delay your trip until tomorrow."

Brick let out a whistle when he heard Backus's substantial offer.

"I have another client tomorrow; I can't stay," Misty said with finality.

"You do?" Gavin blurted.

She didn't actually have another client booked, but Backus didn't need to know that. "Yes, I do." She frowned at Gavin for asking her a stupid question. She motioned for Brick to start loading up the money.

"I can fly to Philadelphia in a day or so if that will speed up the process." Backus had a pleading look in his eyes as he continually caressed his newly healed hand with the deformed one.

"Gavin and I have to look at my schedule; he'll be in touch with you."

"I suppose I'll have to be patient," Backus said with a mixture of irritation and disappointment. He turned his attention to Gavin. "Do you have my personal number?"

"No, I only have your assistant's number."

"Take down my number, Mr. Stallings," Backus said, suddenly treating Gavin with respect.

Misty unzipped the second duffle bag after Brick filled the first. "By the way, Mr. Backus…"

"Yes?" he asked, wearing a hopeful expression.

"The next time I travel all the way to Hawaii, I hope you'll make sure I travel in style. That little-ass plane was insulting."

"I apologize. Insulting you wasn't my intention. I'll be sure to send my own private jet. It's a flying palace; you'll love it." He flashed another charming smile. "Can't you trust that I'm a man of my word and I'll make sure you get paid? What's the point in flying all the way back home when you can conduct the procedure right now?"

"I can't do it."

"Why not?" Backus's eyebrows were pulled together as if tremendously perplexed by Misty's stubbornness. He shot an awkward glance toward Gavin, as if he expected him to intervene and talk sense into Misty. Gavin cleared his throat nervously and avoided eye contact with Backus.

"No offense, but I don't trust you or anyone else when it comes to money," Misty said with a shrug.

"I'll give you five million in cash. First thing tomorrow," he offered in a controlled voice, but with a desperate look in his eyes.

"Make an appointment with Gavin, and next time we meet, don't make me wait a whole damn hour," she said with a sneer. She grasped the handle of the duffle bag and handed it to Gavin. "Let's go, guys."

Misty exited with her head held high, ecstatic to have put the smug billionaire in his place. He'd think twice before coming at her with a snobbish attitude.

On the way to the waiting limo, Misty stopped walking, looked at her right hand and grimaced as she wiped her hand against the fabric of her dress. "Do you have any hand sanitizer, Gavin?"

"No, I don't." Gavin shook his head with a puzzled look on his face.

"What about you, Brick?"

Brick scowled. "I don't carry hand sanitizer around with me."

"Did y'all see that man's nasty, fucked-up, disgusting hands? If y'all gonna be making money off of me touching and laying hands on muthafuckas, the least you can do is to keep some goddamn disinfectant nearby."

CHAPTER 30

I t took a lot of persuading for Thomasina to allow Brick to take Little Baron out for the day, and she only relented after he slid her five hundred dollars.

"How you can afford to give me extra money?" she questioned with an arched eyebrow.

"I hit the number. Uh, not the Pennsylvania Lottery, I play the street numbers," he quickly clarified, not wanting Thomasina to get the bright idea to go after any money she considered to be a hidden asset.

"How much did you win?"

Brick gave her a look that told her to mind her business. "So, can I spend the day with my boy outside your home or what?"

"All right," she said with a sigh. Regulating Brick's visits with his son was the only control she had over him. Brick didn't intend to put up with Thomasina's unwillingness to co-parent much longer. They were in the middle of a divorce, and she and her attorney were calling all the shots, but now that Brick had some extra cash, he could finally pay an attorney to speak up for his rights and get him joint custody so he could have regular visits with his son that didn't involve Thomasina watching him like a hawk.

He hoisted his son up in his arms. "You ready to head out, man?"

"Yeah, Daddy," Little Baron said enthusiastically.

"We'll be back in a couple hours," Brick told Thomasina. Thomasina looked like she wanted to be invited along, but that was out of the question. Brick wanted to enjoy his time with his son, not be questioned and accused like a captured terrorist. He could picture Thomasina grilling him about what Misty was up to and whether or not they planned to get married. She didn't know he and Misty had split up, and she didn't need to know.

When Brick drove into the parking lot of Toys "R" Us, his son began pounding on the window. "I want to go in there, Daddy."

"That's where we're going. Calm down, man," Brick replied with a chuckle.

With Little Baron sitting in the seat of the shopping cart, Brick strolled up and down the aisles of the toy store, slinging anything his son pointed to inside the cart. He and his son were attracting a lot of attention, with other kids gazing at Little Baron with envy and single mothers looking Brick up and down like he was a thick, juicy steak.

One very forward young woman with a cute face and rocking a fatty in her tight jeans, pretended to need Brick's advice on what to buy her seven-year-old nephew for his birthday.

"My boy is only a toddler; I don't know what older kids are playing with these days. Maybe you should ask one of the salespeople," Brick replied.

She smiled and thanked him and when she walked away, he noticed she'd placed her name and number on top of a box of Duplo Legos that was inside his cart.

Having been considered ugly and despicable throughout his impoverished childhood and most of his adult life, he doubted he'd ever get used to female attention. Flattered, he put the piece of paper in his pocket. He wasn't sure if he'd ever get around to using it, but simply knowing he was desired was an ego boost.

When he dropped Little Baron off at home with a shit load of toys, Thomasina bitched about Brick wasting money on crap that the child would lose interest in within a matter of days. Brick didn't respond, but wondered to himself how Thomasina would respond to him spending money on a hotshot attorney. Would she consider that a wise investment? He chuckled to himself as he imagined her shock when he fought back on the matter of visitation rights.

After he left Thomasina's, he bought two packs of condoms and headed to the strip club. He was in the mood to make it rain on them hoes. Tonight was the night for him and Island Girl, and with a pocket full of money, whatever she charged for a private party, he was sure he could handle.

Brick spent a little over four hundred dollars on Island Girl at the club, paying for lap dances, buying her drinks, and making it rain every time she worked the pole during her set. "How much is it gonna cost me to get you in my bed tonight?" he'd asked a few minutes before the club closed. She'd quoted a price that was more than fair and now they were in his apartment, sweaty bodies entangled in the sheets on his bed.

Island Girl lay with her head resting on his chest as they both panted, trying to catch their breath after the intense workout. She was more flexible than he'd realized; in fact, she was double-jointed like a contortionist, bending her body in unbelievable positions as she offered Brick the pussy.

At one point, she sat up, wrapped her legs behind the back of her neck, and locked her ankles. Her pussy was on full display—a wide-open, pink hole, begging to be stuffed with some man meat.

Although the pussy was right in Brick's face and appeared easily accessible, trying to get inside it required him to do a great deal of bending and squatting that he hadn't been prepared for. But unwilling to turn down any challenge that Island Girl put before him, he followed her lead, fucking her in every position she presented. That is, until he caught a painful Charlie Horse in the back of his thighs. After the pain subsided, Brick told her they had to fuck like regular folks who couldn't bend themselves up like pretzels.

On his knees and fucking her while she lay on her back, he linked his arms beneath her knees and pulled her closer, and then held her thighs apart. Reminding him that she didn't require assistance, she stretched her legs open until they were like the hands of a clock in the nine-fifteen position. With Island Girl serving up the pussy so generously, Brick was able to concentrate on beating it up.

By the time he exploded into the condom, his body, as well as the sheets, was drenched with sweat. Lying in recovery mode, Brick was surprised when Island Girl quickly got a second wind and began swiveling under the covers, moving downward.

She took the condom off and tied it in a knot at the top and flung it in a waste can. Semen dribbled out of the tip and Island Girl swished her tongue like a windshield wiper across the dome of his dick. She was licking up cum-drops and polishing his thick length like she was giving a luxury vehicle a deluxe wash. Her head game was so serious, Brick gripped the sheets and lifted his butt off the bed like a bitch when she expertly slurped in a mouthful of partially limp dick and a set of balls, working her jaws like a natural-born dick sucker.

"Damn, girl!" Brick groaned as he felt his nuts tightening and his dick jerking as it came back to life. Once he was fully erect, his balls spilled out of her mouth, and Island Girl quickly cupped his scrotum, caressing it delicately as if his nut sac contained a pair of precious jewels.

Feeling his dick gliding down her throat, all of Brick's nerve endings were on high alert and he had an adrenaline rush that was out of this world. With all his senses focused on the sweet sensations inside Island Girl's mouth, he didn't hear the clicking footsteps in the hallway until they reached the threshold of the bedroom.

"What the fuck, Brick!" Misty cried.

Startled, Brick accidentally jammed his dick deeper into Island Girl's throat, causing her to choke and cough.

"Who is this bitch you got in my bed?" Misty shouted, moving swiftly toward Brick and the stripper, and then stopping to take off a stiletto, which she sent sailing toward the stripper's head.

Island Girl shielded her head with her arms. "Who is this crazy woman? What's going on, Brick?"

"You the one who's crazy," Misty retorted. "How you gonna come into another woman's home and put your stank ass in her bed?"

"Whoa. Hold up, Misty," Brick interrupted, jumping out of the bed and holding out his hand defensively as Misty bent to remove her other heel. "I'm about to smack your little ass clean across this room if you throw another shoe in my direction."

Brick's gruff tone put Misty on pause as she recalled the rare occasions when he'd completely spazzed out on her. When Brick went off, he sort of zoned out, and no amount of reasoning could bring him back to reality.

"You moved out and there's nothing else between us now. We agreed to be friends," he reminded her.

"I know, but why you gotta have a bitch in the bed where I slept?" Misty asked in a weak voice. "Damn, it hasn't even been a month and you already moved on."

"That's right, and you need to do the same thing. What are you doing here, anyway?"

"I came to get some of my stuff."

"And it didn't occur to you to call and see if it was okay to pop up on me in the middle of the night?"

"No, I thought you'd be sleep. I didn't expect to catch you fucking a sleazy ho," Misty said, her eyes wandering to Island Girl's hooker boots and skimpy clothes that were strewn about the bedroom.

"Who you calling a ho, you skinny little bitch?" Island Girl barked, her eyes filled with rage.

Misty waved the stripper off like she was swatting a fly. "You need to put some clothes on and take your slutty ass out of here."

"You're out of order, Misty. You don't call the shots in my crib. Grab whatever you came here to pick up and then get the fuck out."

"Fuck it, you can throw my shit in the trash for all I care. I can afford to replace all my clothes, and I can replace you. Good luck on finding another job that pays as well as I do," Misty said spitefully and then flipped her hair as if she'd scored a point.

"Threats don't work with me anymore. If you don't want me to work for you, then so be it. I got a job; I don't need your money to survive. Now, give me my key back and have a good fuckin' life." Brick held out his hand, waiting for Misty to return the key to the apartment.

She dug into her bag, extracted the key and flung it across the room. She retrieved the shoe that had landed next to the bed, put in on, and then stormed out of the bedroom.

The sound of the front door slamming reverberated around the apartment.

"She's hot with you," Island Girl said with a nervous giggle.

"She'll get over it." Brick went into the bathroom and washed up. When he returned to the bedroom, he located his pants and shirt in a tangled heap on the floor between the nightstand and the bed.

"Why're you putting your clothes on? Don't you want to finish where we left off before your girl tried to kill the mood?"

"Nah, I'm good. Get dressed and I'll drive you home."

"I'm comfortable right here," she said, patting the empty spot next to her, attempting to entice Brick back into bed.

"Yo, it's time to go. There ain't no reason for you to hang around like I owe you money."

"It's not even about the money. I like you, Brick. I'm trying to get to know you better. Get back in bed, baby," she urged him gently. "You told that chick that you moved on. Weren't you talking about you and me?"

"I was telling her that *I've* moved on; I didn't mean I was starting a relationship with you." A frown darkened Brick's face. The last thing he needed in his life was a clingy bitch. He thought spending money for pussy guaranteed him sex without emotional complications, but this ho wanted money and a relationship. "You got paid, now grab your stuff and let's go!"

The bass in Brick's voice and the evil look on his face prompted Island Girl to fling the sheets off, hop out of bed, and begin dressing hastily.

CHAPTER 31

Misty's ploy to slip into bed with Brick in the middle of the night while he was sleeping had failed miserably. It was shocking and infuriating to catch him smashing some cheap-looking, gutter bitch.

Sitting in the back of the cab on her way back to her hotel, she replayed the horrible scene in her mind and couldn't believe the turn of events. *Brick not only kicked me out of the apartment we shared together, but he also threatened to whip my ass. The nerve of that man!*

Her phone hummed inside her purse. Determining it was either Audrey or David on the phone, she let the call go to voicemail. Both of her side pieces were like lovesick puppies and had been blowing up her phone during her trip to Hawaii and every day since she'd returned. Up until now, she'd been too busy to return their calls, but the way her coochie reacted—throbbing and pulsating—after Brick had threatened her with violence, she could use a late-night booty call to put out the fire that raged between her legs.

It was weird how she always got horny as hell whenever she pushed Brick to his limit and provoked him to get aggressive with her. Back in the good old days, he always showed remorse after losing his temper with her. To make up for his bad behavior, he would immediately lick the moisture from her hot pussy and then fuck her slow and sensually while begging for her forgiveness.

Whew! Merely thinking about the way they used to be was such a powerful turn-on, Misty had to pat her coochie to calm it down. Damn, she missed the old days with Brick. She used to have that nigga's head spinning with all the games she ran on him. Used to make him apologize and eat her pussy whenever she fucked around and did him wrong.

But the new Brick would curse her out, threaten her with bodily harm, and felt no remorse whatsoever for mistreating her. Despite his unbecoming conduct, she wanted him back so badly, she was racking her brain trying to figure out a way to make it happen. She was going to lose her mind if she didn't figure out how to worm her way back inside that muthafucka's mind, body, and soul.

Misty checked her phone to see whose call she had missed. Hopefully, Brick had gotten rid of the skank and had called to make up. She peered at the screen and groaned in disappointment when she saw Audrey's name. Audrey's ditsy-ass self was only good for a mild orgasm, often leaving Misty sexually frustrated and in need of a big, juicy dick.

David, on the other hand, could deliver big pussy eruptions that had her on the verge of blacking out. Her only complaint about David was that he wasn't freaky enough. Sure, he enjoyed it when she exposed her kinky side and left teeth marks all over his body, but she wasn't always in the mood to act like a damn canine.

She wished he was a more imaginative lover, but since he wasn't, it was her responsibility to teach him how to thoroughly please her.

She waited until she was back in her hotel room to call him. "David," she whispered into the phone, using an urgent tone of voice.

"Whassup, Misty. Are you all right?"

"Not really."

"What's wrong?"

"Something happened with my ex."

"I'll kill him if he put his hands on you," David hissed.

"No, it's not like that. I went to the apartment to get the rest of my things and somehow he seduced me into having sex with him. I feel so bad for being weak and cheating on you; can you forgive me? I promise it won't happen again."

David went quiet for a beat, and then said, "Yeah, I forgive you."

"I need you to come over—not for sex, though. Brick fucked me until I was raw, and now my pussy is really sore. I need you to come over and hold me until I fall asleep. Can you do that for me?"

"Sure. You know, it's not only about sex for me. I care about you. Hell, I might as well admit it, I'm falling in love with you. I'm so into you, I told my wife that I knew about her affair with her co-worker and then I kicked her out of our bedroom. The only person I want lying next to me is you."

"Where does wifey sleep—on the living room couch?" Misty couldn't stifle a giggle.

"No, she put a futon in our daughter's room and she sleeps in there. Since you and I have been together, I lost my desire for her. My marriage is officially over. I've been blowing up your phone, trying to tell you the good news. I'm a free man, baby."

"Slow your roll, David. For the sake of your child, you need to stick with wifey a little longer. I grew up without a father and I know from firsthand experience how devastating that can be."

"I'm not going to abandon my daughter, but I need to get away from my wife."

"Not yet. I want you to be an honorable man and stick by your child." Misty covered her mouth and laughed behind her hand. If having David around her on a daily basis was beneficial, she would have taken him from his stupid little daughter without hesitation. But she didn't need him hanging around her, twenty-four hours a day, and so she convinced him to be a good father.

"You're so understanding, Misty. That's one of the things I love about you."

"Aw, thanks, babe. I have strong feelings for you, too."

"I hope one day you'll grow to love me."

"Let's not rush things; you'll have to earn my love."

"I plan on earning it."

"That's good to know," she said with a smirk.

"As soon as you say the word, I'll file for divorce. I'm serious about you, girl."

"We'll talk about our future plans when you get here," Misty said sweetly.

"I'm putting my clothes on now, sweetheart. I'm gonna be break-ing speed limits trying to get to you."

"Aw, you got me blushing," Misty said, feigning modesty while a sneaky smile crept across her face.

David hugged Misty so tight, she had difficulty breathing. He mistook her gasping for sobs. "Shh. Shh. Don't cry, Misty," he soothed lovingly. "I'm here now; everything's gonna be all right. You had a slip-up with your ex, I trust you and I know it won't happen again."

Seizing the opportunity to play the victim, Misty bent over and began rubbing her crotch. "I'm not upset about that anymore, but my coochie hurts so bad." She was wearing a short, stretchy, body-hugging onesie. She pulled the crotch area to the side, revealing her bare pussy. "Kiss it for me, David. Make it feel better."

Instead of obliging her immediately as she expected, he hesitated, fidgeting uncomfortably. "Um, I know you don't expect me to go down on you after you been fucking ol' boy." David gawked at her with an expression that said he found her request shockingly absurd.

"It shouldn't matter who I fucked; all you should be concerned about is making me feel better," Misty said with an edge to her voice.

"Did you at least wash it?" he asked, his voice climbing an octave.

Misty stared at him unflinchingly. "No, I didn't wash it. Why should I?"

"Because…" David lowered his eyes and made a sound of frustration. "You know, for sanitary reasons."

She sighed. "I thought you loved me."

"I do."

"Then why're you asking me all these questions. If you want my coochie to be clean, then wash it with your tongue." Having nothing else to say, she pressed her lips together challengingly.

Caught between a rock and a hard place, David caved in and said, "Okay, I'll clean your pussy."

Misty smiled as she clamped her hands on his shoulders, urging him to bow down.

David slowly lowered himself until he was on his knees, his face flush with her vagina.

"Did he use a condom?" he asked, looking up at her nervously.

Misty shook her head. "No, he didn't. Baby, stop talking, all right? I'm in pain and I want you to prove how much you love me." She gripped the back of his neck, nudging his head forward until his mouth mashed against her outer lips. The tip of his tongue jutted between his lips and began to timidly flick against Misty's clit.

"Don't be shy. Clean that coochie out for me, baby. Show me how much you love taking care of me," she said in a whispery, seductive voice that persuaded David to delve inside, stabbing in and out of her wetness with wild abandon. Growing accustomed to and starting to like what he believed to be Misty's flavor, mixed with semen from another man, David began moaning.

"Do you like how Brick tastes inside me?" Misty felt that familiar rush that came whenever she took someone out of their comfort zone and lured them into her sexually deviant world.

"Mm-hmm," he murmured, so focused on lapping up her juices, he was unable to give a coherent verbal response.

The fact that David admitted to enjoying sucking out Brick's imaginary cum had Misty's pussy leaking like crazy. Her over-flowing juices poured out of her and David had to widen his mouth in order to capture every drop.

Feeling herself on the verge of cumming, she led David to the bed and tugged on his belt. "Take your shit off and fuck me," she ordered in a bossy tone that she didn't try to disguise with sweetness.

David quickly stripped and mounted her. "I never did anything like that before," he whispered in her ear.

"Would you be willing to do it again?" Misty inquired.

"I'll do anything for you," he vowed with a groan as he plunged inside her.

Simply imagining all the freakish fun she was going to have with David caused Misty to explode on the third dick-stroke.

"Did you cum already?" David asked, surprised.

"Yeah, a big-ass nutt," she replied breathlessly as her heart raced a mile a minute. "Now it's your turn." She smoothed his hair, and then delicately ran her hands down the sleek athletic lines of his arms and back. Without warning, she suddenly dug her pointy fingernails into his skin.

"Ow!" David yelped from the sharp pain and then immediately

began putting in work with forceful thrusts and powerful gyrations.

"That's right; fuck me like you mean it." She bit his chest lightly and then applied a little more pressure. She continued biting him on his chest and shoulders until his convulsing body and loud groan announced that he'd reached the finish line.

Misty nudged him. "Move! You're smothering me, David."

David rolled onto his back, his chest heaving. "You got me doing crazy shit, but I like it. I've never been with anyone as freaky as you."

"Stick around; it gets much freakier than what we got into tonight. But I want you to know that it takes a real man to be with me."

"I'm a real man."

"We'll see. Don't punk out when I make other kinky requests that might sound outlandish to you."

"I'm open-minded. Whatever you want to get into is all right with me."

"You sure?"

"Positive."

"Well, I've been thinking about getting into a threesome."

David propped himself up with an elbow. "A threesome with who? You, me, and your ex?" he asked, clearly appalled.

"Would that be so bad? You already tasted his cum, didn't you?" Misty said with teasing laughter.

"Damn, you don't have to make fun of me. I did that to make you feel better; now you're throwing it in my face," David said with a hurt expression.

"Aw, I'm only messing with you. The threesome I'm referring to would be with you, me, and another chick."

David brightened up. "Oh, yeah? Who's the chick—one of your friends?"

"No, I want to get into a threesome with you, me, and your wife."

CHAPTER 32

It was Friday evening, and Anya knew exactly where to find Natalie. She'd be gorging on free food and cheap drinks during happy hour at Skippy's.

Anya had been waiting in her car for over an hour when Natalie finally emerged from the club dressed in clothes from Anya's closet. Heading toward the bus stop, Natalie weaved drunkenly, the heels of her fake Louboutins clicking on the pavement.

Umph, bitch still can't afford to buy a decent pair of shoes.

"Hey, Natalie," Anya yelled out the window of her Audi.

Natalie was either pretending or was actually too intoxicated to recognize Anya's car. "Who's that?" she inquired in a slurred voice, leaning to the side and squinting as if trying to make out Anya's face.

"Girl, come on and get in the car. I'll give you a ride home."

Natalie hobbled a little closer. "That's okay, I'm good," Natalie said in a nervous voice.

"Natalie, stop acting crazy. You don't think I hold you responsible for what Majid did to Sergio, do you?"

Natalie looked down guiltily. "I don't know what to think," she mumbled.

"Girl, I consider you a friend, and you can't help what your man did."

"That's true."

"I'm so devastated over what happened to Sergio; I need to talk to someone. You want to have a drink with me?" Anya held up a silver flask. "Drinking alone is depressing."

"You got any weed?" Natalie asked.

"No, but I can buy some. Who do you buy your weed from?"

"My weed man's name is Tone. All I have to do is give him a call and he'll meet us outside the Seven-Eleven near my house."

"Okay, give him a call."

"How much you spending? About forty dollars?"

"No, I need more than that to forget my troubles."

"You want to get a quarter pound?" Natalie asked, her eyes gleaming with hope.

"I can do that. A quarter pound ain't about nothing. I could buy a couple pounds of weed if I wanted to, but I don't really smoke that much." Anya didn't typically boast about her finances, but under the circumstances, it was to her benefit to flaunt her bank account.

"You're definitely not a weed head like me, so would it be okay if you let me have whatever we don't smoke up tonight?" Natalie asked, wearing a greedy smile and seeming to instantly sober up.

"Yeah, you can have whatever's left. I want to get nice, so I can forget my troubles."

Lured by the prospect of free weed and liquor, Natalie zipped around to the passenger's side of the car and got in.

Anya pulled into traffic, speeding in the direction of the highway that would take her to Natalie's neighborhood. Instead of taking the on ramp, Anya swerved suddenly and brought the car to a stop on the desolate underpass of the highway, an area off the side of the road where her car was obscured by trees.

"Why're we parking here?" Natalie asked.

"I want to count my cash-on-hand before we place the order. I don't want to be pulling out big bills in front of a drug dealer. I'm not trying to get robbed, you know what I mean?" From her wallet that was bulging with cash, Anya extracted six-hundred dollars and then stuck the money in her bosom.

Natalie licked her lips visibly when she saw the large amount of cash Anya was carrying in her wallet. Her eyes darted around thoughtfully, as if trying to come up with a plan for her and the weed man to stick-up Anya and split the dough.

"Are you straight? You got enough paper to pay for the weed?" Natalie injected concern in her voice as her eyes roved back and forth from Anya's money-stuffed bosom and down to her bulging wallet.

"Yeah, I have more than enough to pay for the weed."

"Okay, I'm about to call Tone and put in our order," Natalie said. She rifled around in her handbag and retrieved her phone. Before she could enter a number, Anya leaned over and pressed a Taser gun into her forearm and held it there, enjoying the zapping sound intermingled with Natalie's shrieks.

Anya removed the Taser and watched with interest as Natalie slowly recovered. Groaning and frantically rubbing her arm, Natalie was wide-eyed as she stared at the welt that quickly appeared on her arm. "Son of a bitch," Natalie exploded. "Look at my damn arm! What the fuck did you do that for? My shit is burning; feels like it's on fire!"

"Bitch, I'm just getting started." Anya tased her again, this time aiming the weapon at her chest. Natalie's legs kicked out, and her arms went limp as her body convulsed. "I'm gonna have a lot of fun torturing your snitch ass."

Natalie gasped and wailed. "What are you talking about? I ain't snitch on nobody."

"Stop lying, ho. You used the information you got from me to set up Sergio. Trying to win points with Majid, you backstabbed my man and got him killed. I barely escaped with my life, but you don't give a damn. You wanted me dead, too."

"That's a lie! I would never do anything to hurt you, Anya. And I didn't set up Sergio; it wasn't me. I swear to God. I didn't say a word to Majid about Sergio deciding to go legit."

Anya looked at Natalie with undisguised hatred. "You told on yourself, you dumb bitch." She zapped Natalie again and again, causing her to flail about and gurgle as if choking to death.

"Stop, Anya. Please! I can't take any more of this torture," Natalie wailed when Anya stopped tasing her.

"You thought I was a soft bitch, didn't you? You mistook my kindness for weakness, but you had no idea who you were fucking with. You shouldn't have crossed me, Natalie," Anya said with contempt. "Anyone who fucks with me or my people ends up getting hurt real bad. So, don't waste your breath begging for me to stop because I'm not gonna stop until I send you back to your maker."

"Are you planning to electrocute me to death with that thing?" Natalie yelled in horror.

"I sure am." Anya grinned maliciously.

Natalie recoiled as Anya aimed the Taser once again. This time, she pointed it at Natalie's abdominal area. Natalie screamed, but with the rush of traffic overhead, her screams went unheard.

"Damn, do you have super powers or something?" Anya asked with cruel laughter. "I thought you would have passed out by now. Maybe I should jolt you with a higher voltage." Anya pulled a larger Taser from beneath her seat. One look at the black Taser gun and tears began to stream from Natalie's eyes.

"Please. Please. Please, I don't want to die," she cried. "I'm sorry.

I didn't know Majid would take Sergio out; I only told him about the situation so he could get a piece of the action, too. I didn't know he'd kill his own friend, I swear."

"Nice speech, Natalie. But your words went in one ear and out the other. You're shady as hell, so be woman enough to own up to what you did."

"Okay, all right." Natalie raised a hand in surrender. "What I did was grimy, I admit it, but my hand to God, I wasn't trying to get Sergio killed."

"What did you think that evil-ass Majid would do if he thought Sergio was trying to move on to greener pastures without him? Huh? And what's really fucked up is the fact that Sergio was going to bring Majid on board after all the paperwork was signed. You didn't have all the facts when you ran back to Majid. Your worthless, whoring ass caused a good man to get killed over some bogus bullshit that you're too stupid to begin to understand."

"You're right. I got in over my head, and all I can say is I'm sorry." Natalie managed to squeeze out some tears. "I'm really sorry, Anya." Hoping for sympathy, Natalie went overboard and began to weep into her hands.

Anya didn't respond; she only stared at Natalie with loathing. Sensing that her crying act wasn't working, Natalie removed her hands from her face, and said, "Please let me get out of the car; I'll walk home and I won't say a word about this to anyone." She touched the door handle and quickly discovered that Anya had used the panel on the driver's side to keep her locked inside.

"You're not getting out of this car until I'm finished with you," Anya said scornfully.

"I can't take any more," Natalie whined.

"You have to pay for your crime against Sergio and Paloma."

"I didn't do shit to anybody named Paloma. I don't even know anybody by that name."

"Paloma was Sergio's housekeeper. Your man popped her for no reason, also. And now, I'm gonna snap, crackle, and pop you until your insides start frying."

Anya raised the Taser and Natalie began moaning, "Stop! No! Please! Oh, God help me from this psycho bitch."

Like a crazed person, she began screaming at the top of her lungs. She jiggled the door handle frantically and repeatedly kicked the door, as if she were trying to kick her way out of the car.

With amusement, Anya watched Natalie have a meltdown. When Natalie finally wore herself out and began panting for breath while her chest heaved up and down, Anya retrieved the silver flask from the cup holder. "Have a drink and calm yourself down. But I need you to be honest and tell me exactly what you told Majid. Think about it and maybe a taste of liquor will help refresh your memory."

Anya reclined her chair as she offered Natalie the flask.

"Thank you. Oh, God, thank you so much," Natalie said, uncapping the flask and turning the lip of the bottle up to her mouth. Suddenly, the flask dropped from her hand and she let out a piercing scream that died down rapidly as the flesh on her lips and tongue ballooned to a grotesque size, and then popped, the deep red flesh appearing to melt.

Anya leapt to the passenger's side, scooped the flask from the floor, and then straddled Natalie. "Drink this shit," she spat as she struggled to force-feed Natalie the remainder of the Liquid Fire drain cleaner that was inside the flask.

Natalie's melted lips secured the flask in place and Anya didn't remove it until it was empty. Anya didn't feel a bit of sympathy for

Natalie; all she felt was a cold rage as she watched her writhing and moaning, her terrified eyes bulging as her insides burned from the drain cleaner she'd been forced to ingest.

"Don't let me die. Take me to a hospital," Natalie said, her pleading words barely coherent.

"Bitch, you're gonna die and I'm gonna sit here and enjoy watching it happen."

"Pleeeeeease," Natalie said in a long, terrible groan.

Anya shook her head. "Fuck you, you dirty ho! Now, you know how betrayed Sergio felt when a gun was held to his head by a man he considered a friend. You know how betrayed I felt when I watched his brains splatter against the walls because a dirty slut I treated with compassion and generosity repaid my kindness by setting up both me and my man. You knew I'd be at Sergio's on the night of his birthday, but you didn't care. You wanted me to die along with him, but I survived and now I'm your worst nightmare," Anya hissed.

Natalie moaned louder, and Anya turned on the radio to drown out the horrible, screechy, animal-like whimpers that rose from Natalie's chemically burned throat. Fighting for her life, Natalie continued to jiggle the door handle, trying to no avail to escape from the car and save herself from the slow and agonizing death that was absolutely inescapable.

After forty-two minutes of moaning and twitching, Natalie became silent and then slumped into death, leaning heavily against the passenger's door. At that point, Anya unlocked the door, opened it, and shoved Natalie's lifeless body out the car, discarding it with repugnance as if getting rid of putrid, week-old trash.

The only attendees at Sergio's private funeral service were the staff of the funeral home, the pastor who was paid to say a few words for Sergio's soul, Anya, Uncle Fabian, and the prison guards who had accompanied him to his nephew's funeral.

At the burial site, Anya cried quietly, but Uncle Fabian wept openly and unashamedly. Trying to give him a modicum of comfort, Anya told him that she'd taken care of the woman who set up Sergio. "I made sure she suffered. Her death was slow and painful," she said venomously.

He let out a long, weary sigh and wiped his tearful eyes. "I knew that behind that pretty face and innocent demeanor, you had a heart of ice when it came to seeking justice for your loved ones." Uncle Fabian narrowed his eyes and said, "I could put hands on that nigga, Majid, while he's locked up in county, but I'd rather wait until after the trial when that scumbag and the coward that helped him snuff out my nephew's life get sent upstate to my house." He smiled maliciously and rubbed his cuffed hands together. "I have special plans for those two traitors. By the time I finish with them, they're gonna beg for a bullet between their eyes."

CHAPTER 33

Jeffrey Backus had changed visibly since Misty had last seen him. The former smug look on his face had been replaced with a humble expression. In his eyes was the glint of new-found respect for Misty, and rightly so. She'd had the gall to invite the billionaire to Philadelphia, booked in the same hotel where she resided, but she'd kept him in his suite for the past five days, making it clear that his vast wealth didn't faze her in the least. She didn't pay him a visit until it was convenient for her.

A powerful man like Backus didn't wait for anyone, yet he waited for Misty, desperate for the service that only she could provide.

This time, Misty visited Backus alone; she felt comfortable and self-assured enough to conduct their business without the benefit of a bodyguard and without Gavin's brooding presence. She'd repaid Gavin all the money he'd spent on her surgeries, yet he still sulked and complained as if he expected Misty to feel indebted to him for the rest of her life. She was sick and tired of hearing about his missing gay lover, and if he pestered her one more time about finding the man, she was liable to slit his throat. She was so over Gavin. Being around Gavin was a chore, and she was relieved that she didn't need him to tag along with her tonight.

In fact, now that she'd gotten her foot in the door, she was pretty sure she could handle her operation from now on without needing Gavin to introduce her to elite clients.

Brick was still upset with her, but she was sure he'd get over it by the time she called him for the next job. Brick wasn't foolish enough to turn down the kind of money Misty was paying.

After Backus eagerly paid her the two-million-dollar fee she'd requested to heal his left hand, and after Misty carefully stacked the cash in two, extra-large duffle bags, she motioned for him to hold out his hand.

Filled with the anticipation of soon becoming whole and healed, Backus stuck out a gnarled hand that trembled with excitement. Misty placed her own had upon it and felt bones straightening and skin smoothing out beneath her palm.

When the sensations subsided, she removed her hand and smiled in satisfaction at her achievement. "It looks good as new," she quipped.

Backus gazed steadily at his repaired hand. Overcome with emotion, he embraced her. Shedding tears, he thanked her profusely, informing her that he considered her a treasured friend for life. "If ever you need a favor, please don't hesitate to ask," he said.

"I'll remember that," Misty said as she squirmed out of his bear hug and grabbed the handles of the heavy money bags. "I do have a small request, if you don't mind."

"Anything."

"Call the front desk and ask them to send someone up to carry these heavy bags for me," Misty requested.

Backus eagerly picked up the phone and in a commanding voice, he demanded that a bellhop be sent to his suite.

Squeezing anti-bacterial sanitizer into her palm, Misty grimaced as she rubbed her hands together. *Ew! I can't believe I had to touch that nasty muthafucka, again.* Her grimace turned into a smile when she saw the hot dude who came to collect her bags.

Outside the hotel, her driver promptly jumped out the vehicle and relieved the bellhop of the bags that he put inside the trunk. Misty penned her phone number on a fifty-dollar bill and tipped the boyishly handsome bellhop.

"Thanks a lot," the young man said with a big smile.

Misty looked him over; he was medium height and strongly built. Seemed like the type who was eager to please in bed. "There's more where that came from," Misty told the bellhop, imagining their naked bodies entwined.

Being chauffeured around was a great inconvenience, but with all her outward bravado, Misty couldn't bring herself to get behind the wheel of a car. The night she was nearly killed was still fresh in her mind, and though she knew it was irrational, she, nevertheless, had an overwhelming fear of being attacked again while driving.

With her cash flow piling up like crazy, she needed to get the money out of her hotel room and into a safe place. She came up with the idea to rent a storage unit to stockpile her cash. Trouble was, she couldn't drive herself and didn't trust a hired driver to help her unload her fortune. The only person in the world whom she truly trusted was Brick. And he wasn't speaking to her, but it was time for him to put aside their differences and stop being so damn petty.

The easiest way to get to Brick was through his son, and with that in mind, Misty called him and began the conversation by saying, "I realize you've been putting away money for Little Baron's college fund, but did you know that a good private school is often more expensive than college?"

"What do you want, Misty?" Brick said in a weary tone.

"Hear me out, okay?"

Brick grunted a response.

"With the pitiful state of the public school system, I know you don't want your son attending a neighborhood school and receiving an inferior education."

"Stop with the sales pitch; what's on your mind?" Brick said impatiently.

"Well, I was thinking about how my little brother is only being stimulated by my boring mother. She probably has him sitting next to her, eating a bunch of snacks while watching hours of idiotic daytime TV shows. If you leave it up to my mother to plan his future, he's going to end up being dumb as a box of rocks."

"Whoa. You're talking about my son, Misty."

"He's my brother; don't you think I care about his well-being? What you need to do is start his education process as early as possible. My mother was too old to be having a child in the first place, and with you only seeing him every now and then, she's the parent who's having the strongest influence on him. Umph, and that's a shame being that she's out of touch with modern times. He needs more youthful and more sophisticated influences in his life. I'm telling you, the only thing my mother has to offer him is food. She's gonna turn him into a chubby, little mama's boy—mark my words, Brick."

Brick became uncomfortably quiet, and Misty assumed she'd given him food for thought. She continued, "I read that what happens between birth and the age of seven defines a child's future. Little Baron should not be sitting up under my mother all day long without interacting with other kids. It's not healthy—some would consider it as a form of child abuse."

"All right, you're exaggerating and taking shit too far now."

"You won't think I'm exaggerating in years to come when your son identifies as a middle-aged female instead of a young boy. If you don't stop him from spending so much time with my mother, he's gonna end up like the son of that famous sports figure…you know that boy who's always on *TMZ*, prancing around, thicker than a snicker, carrying an oversized pocketbook, and wearing boa feathers draped around his neck."

"I'm not homophobic," Brick said.

"Me either, but why allow a kid to go in that direction if he doesn't have to?"

Brick went silent again and Misty knew she was getting to him. "You would be getting Little Baron off to a good start if you sent him to an exclusive preschool where he can interact with smart kids, play sports, and be educated by savvy teachers. I hope you know that many of the Philly public schools no longer have any extra-curricular activities. So, let's get my brother enrolled in a good preschool; I'll be happy to pay for it."

"What's the catch?"

"Well, I have this problem with driving. Since my tragedy, I have this phobia about driving."

"You already have a driver."

"I need you to drive me on special drops."

"What's that supposed to mean?"

"It means I don't trust anyone but you to escort me to the storage unit where I'm going to stash my money."

"You're gonna put all that money in a storage unit? That doesn't seem wise at all."

"As long as I pay the storage bill, my money will be safer than it is in a bank."

"Whatever. It's your dough; you can do what you want with it. When do you want to make that move?"

"Tonight."

"Nah, that's not gonna work. I'm about to go to bed. I have to be at the job early in the morning. We're gonna have to handle that storage business a few days from now."

"Okay, well, I'm in the limo, about ten minutes from your crib. Is it okay if I drop the dough off...leave it with you for safekeeping?"

"Yeah, that's cool. Call me when you get here and I'll come out and get it."

"One more thing, Brick."

"What's that?" he asked cautiously.

"I'm sorry about busting in on you and that gutter slut, and for going off on the trifling bitch."

Brick chuckled. "Damn, you called her a gutter slut; why she gotta be all that?"

"That's what she looked like to me," Misty said sullenly.

"Listen, Misty, I'm not holding a grudge, but you need to accept that there's nothing between us anymore. You have to stop being all up in your feelings. You hear what I'm saying?"

"Yeah, I hear you, Brick. From now on, I'm gonna focus on making money. Can I count on you to be my bodyguard, again? Say yes, please. Nobody's gonna protect me the way you will, Brick. I trust you with my money and my life, and you know that's the truth." She knew she could persuade him by talking about needing his protection.

"Sure, I'll work for you again, as long as it doesn't interfere with my day job."

"Why do you want to keep busting your ass doing hard labor when I can pay you so much more than you'll ever make on a job?"

"I don't mind hard work. Besides, I don't want to be sneaking around piling up money in a storage unit in order to keep Uncle Sam off my ass."

"Touché," Misty said with a chuckle. "I'll see you soon."

Thrilled that she and Brick were back on speaking terms, Misty hung up. Brick had always been weak, and he wouldn't be able to resist her much longer. It was only a matter of time before she had Brick between her legs and working up a sweat as he strived to please her. But their steamy reunion would have to take place at her hotel. There was no way she would get in their old bed that had been tainted when he had sex with that gutter slut.

Brick wasn't going to like being in rotation with David and possibly other lovers, but until he proved his love and devotion, she would hold on to her side pieces. And Brick had a lot of proving to do. At this point, he hadn't even bothered to ask Misty which hotel she was staying in. If she didn't know better, it would be easy to believe Brick had another bitch on his mind.

But that couldn't possibly be true. There wasn't a woman on the planet that could compare to Misty. One way or another, she'd get Brick to her hotel. If things went the way she wanted, Brick would become so addicted to the coochie, he'd pack his bags and move in with her at the Omni.

CHAPTER 34

To Misty's amazement, she received a call from a man named Jacob Mendelsohn. He claimed to be a close friend of Jeffrey Backus and said he was interested in a healing session for his wife. He said he was currently in Mexico, where his wife was receiving alternative treatment for ovarian cancer.

"No amount of money is too much. I'll pay anything for you to cure my wife."

Misty didn't speak for a moment. Cancer was something she couldn't see, and she wasn't sure if she could heal the man's wife. "I don't know. I'm not sure," she said haltingly.

"I have plenty of money. Name your price," he said desperately.

"I don't conduct business in this manner. There's a procedure you're supposed to follow."

"Jeffrey didn't mention anything about a procedure. When he told me about his cure, I begged him for your number. What's the procedure—do you require money in advance?"

"Jeffrey Backus should have called me on your behalf. I don't know you and I don't like the idea of strangers having my number and calling me any hour of the night."

"I apologize for the late hour. I'm calling on behalf of my wife, Catherine. She's very ill and isn't responding to treatment. I'm desperately trying to help her, and I meant no disrespect when I took the liberty of calling you."

"Mr. Mendelsohn, I'm—"

"Call me Jacob, please."

Rich folks sure knew how to be humble when they wanted something from you, Misty concluded. Jacob Mendelsohn was playing nice, but he was probably a real bastard in the business world.

"Jacob," she said wearily. "I'm not sure if I can cure cancer. I don't want to get your hopes up."

"Would you at least try?" he asked, sounding choked up.

"I don't want to waste your time or mine."

"I'll pay you two million in cash if you'd fly to Mexico and lay hands on my wife. No strings attached. If it doesn't work..." His voice cracked. "At least we tried, right, Misty?"

"I'll need four million, plus a private jet. Not a chartered, economy plane, please. I like to be well rested and comfortable when I travel."

"Not a problem. When can you get here?"

"Hmm." She considered Brick's work schedule and said, "How about Saturday?"

"That's four days from now. Can't you make it sooner?"

"No, that's the best I can do. Now, take down this number and call my assistant to work out all the details. His name is Gavin Stallings. Nice talking to you, Jacob," Misty said and hung up.

She was a bad-ass chick. Billionaire muthafuckas were begging to fly her to exotic locations, yet Brick treated her like she wasn't shit. That man had a hell of a lot of nerve, but she had no doubt that the day would come when he would come to his senses and recognize her worth.

Thankfully, there were quite a few people who recognized her worth, and her friend, David, was one of them. Before the Mendelsohn dude had interrupted her, she'd been primping in the mirror and getting ready for a threesome with David and his wife.

She'd applied lip gloss and spritzed herself with perfume when the front desk called, announcing her guests.

The first thing that struck her about David's wife was her homeliness. What the hell was an unattractive chick like her doing cheating on her husband and stressing him out? Bitch should have been glad she had a man who went to work and paid the bills. And what was David's problem? Why had he been so distraught over this fugly, cheating heifer?

She and David had agreed to dupe his wife into thinking they were participating in a couple's therapy session. He'd told her that Misty was a sex therapist who could fix their relationship.

"Misty, uh, I mean, Ms. Delagardo, this is my wife, Tamia," David said.

"Hi, Tamia. I've heard David's version of what went wrong in your relationship, but as we all know, there're two sides to every story… so what do you have to say about the breakdown in your marriage?" *Damn, I'm good. I sound like an authentic therapist!*

"You don't look like a therapist," Tamia said, giving Misty the side eye.

Misty was dressed in a black tank top, skintight black jeans with rips on the thighs, and black, stiletto-heeled, ankle boots. Black was Misty's color, and she looked shockingly beautiful, especially compared to dog-faced Tamia.

"Do you want me to help repair your relationship or do you want to throw slurs at me?" Misty frowned at Tamia. The woman had a bad attitude, and didn't seem to be the least bit contrite. If David didn't know how to put this ho in her place, Misty sure knew how, and she was eager to get the therapy session started.

"Answer her question, Tamia," David prompted gruffly. "She's trying to help us and you're giving her attitude."

Tamia folded her arms across her chest defiantly. "This is stupid. I don't even want to be here. I never heard of a therapy session late at night in a hotel."

"The work I do is unconventional, and it won't be successful if only one partner is willing to participate, so feel free to leave," Misty said, waving a hand dismissively.

"That's fine with me." Tamia picked up her purse and stood. "Let's go, David. We can find a certified marriage counselor with an office; someone who has daytime hours."

"Excuse me, Miss Thang, you can leave all you want, but David isn't going anywhere—are you, baby?" Misty turned her attention to David, who seemed to melt when Misty smiled at him.

David drew closer to Misty and put his arm around her. "I'm not going anywhere with her." He gazed at his wife scornfully.

Tamia looked dumbfounded. "You have to give me a ride home, David. I don't know what's going on here, but you need to take your arm from around that bitch, and let's go," Tamia said in a voice that quavered.

"I'm sorry, Tamia, but I'm going to have to ask you to leave. Clearly, your husband wants my sex therapy, and since you don't want to take part in trying to heal your relationship, you need to understand that you're interfering with the process, and it's time for you to go."

"I love the way you handle shit, baby," David whispered in Misty's ear, now wrapping both arms around her possessively.

"David, get your hands off that bitch," Tamia bellowed, tromping toward them.

"Back up, bitch," Misty warned. "If you even think about putting a hand on me, David will beat the shit out of you, and after that, you'll find yourself under the jail after my team of lawyers get through with you."

Taking heed, Tamia stopped in her tracks.

But Misty wasn't finished threatening her. "I don't know much about raising kids, but I'll have to learn after David and I get custody of your little girl."

"You're not a therapist," Tamia accused through lips that were twisted in rage. "David, what's going on? Why'd you bring me here?"

"He brought you here because I've taken a few online sex therapy classes and I was kind-hearted enough to volunteer to use my knowledge on your failing marriage, but since you don't appreciate my efforts, you can get the fuck out. In fact, I want David to pick up my new little daughter and bring her here, first thing in the morning." Misty turned to David. "What's your little girl's name?"

"Caitlynn."

"I don't know if I like that name, David. I might have to change it," Misty said, casting Tamia a sly smile.

"You're crazy. You're not taking my daughter and you're not changing her damn name," Tamia shouted.

"I have a lot of pull with Philadelphia judges, and after I show one of my judge friends the tapes that I have of you sucking dick when you should have been taking care of your daughter, he's not going to hesitate to give custody to David. And I'm not going to hesitate to legally change my new daughter's name from Caitlyn to something more appealing."

Misty smiled up at David. "You don't mind if I legally change *our* daughter's name to something prettier, do you?"

"She's gonna be your child, so you can do whatever you want with her," he responded, looking love struck as he ran his fingers through the long, silken waves of Misty's hair.

"Good. We're gonna get married immediately after you divorce this adulteress wife of yours," Misty cooed.

"Sounds good to me," he said, kissing all over her, revealing to his wife how much he idolized and adored Misty. "My daughter will be in good hands with you as her mother."

"After I get papers on you, I want to do something totally unconventional, but only if you want it," Misty said in a soft, sweet voice.

"What's that, baby?" David asked, lovingly stroking the side of Misty's face.

Tamia watched the bizarre interaction between her husband and Misty with her mouth gaped open, too shocked and appalled to speak.

"After we get married, I want to give both you and your daughter my last name. What do you think? Do you like the sound of David Delagardo?"

"I love it."

"We can pick out a new name for our daughter, together."

"No, you pick the name. You have good taste. I'm gonna love whatever you decide to name her."

Tamia clutched her stomach. "Ohmigod; I'm gonna be sick. You two are both crazy."

"Crazy in love," Misty taunted, and then turned her mouth up to David. He obliged by planting a kiss on her lips, slipping in his tongue.

Tamia burst into tears. "Okay, okay. You win. I can't take any more of this. What do I have to do to keep my family together?" she asked Misty.

CHAPTER 35

"Now, you're talking like you have some sense," Misty said. "The first thing you need to do is to get honest and tell David why you cheated on him in the first place."

"I cheated because I wasn't happy at home," Tamia said tearfully.

"Now, you're lying," Misty cut in.

"It's the truth."

"No, you cheated on this good, hardworking man because you're an ungrateful, dirty, grimy ho. Now, tell him the truth about why you cheated."

"What kind of therapy is this?" Tamia blurted.

"It's online therapy and it fucking works. Now do what I said."

Tears of humiliation spilled from Tamia's eyes. "I cheated because I'm ungrateful. You're a hardworking man and I didn't respect that."

"Hold up. Ain't nobody tell you to start freestyling; follow the damn script," Misty said in an outburst of anger.

David patted Misty's back soothingly. "Calm down, sweetheart; don't let her upset you. She's always been hardheaded, and that's why our marriage fell apart."

"Your marriage fell apart because she has loose morals," Misty countered. Then she eyed Tamia who was sniffling and crying as she came to realize that she'd already lost her husband and there was a strong possibility that she might also lose her child to the wicked woman whose outrageously pretty face didn't match her ugly, cruel heart.

"Now, I'm gonna ask you one more time, Tamia; why did you cheat on your husband?"

"I cheated because I'm an ungrateful, dirty, grimy ho," Tamia recited with her head hung down.

"That's better. Now, let me ask you something?"

Tamia looked at Misty reluctantly.

"When is the last time you sucked your husband's dick?"

"She hasn't done that in over a year," David complained.

"Shh. Be quiet, David. Let Tamia answer for herself."

David pantomimed zipping up his lips.

"I don't remember," Tamia said curtly.

"Okay, well, when's the last time you sucked your man's dick?" Misty inquired.

Tamia sighed. "A few weeks ago."

"Then you need to give your husband head two to three times a day to make up for the way you neglected your wifely duties for so long. Now, if you can't handle it, I'll be more than willing to take him and your daughter off your hands," Misty reminded, her words an unveiled threat.

"That's not a problem. I'll start giving him head, again," Tamia agreed.

"I want you to start, now," Misty said coldly.

"In front of you?" Tamia was mortified.

Misty responded by unbuckling David's belt and shoving his pants down. She stuck her hand inside his briefs and fondled his dick until it was throbbing and rigid. As Misty stroked him, he caressed her small breasts, squeezing and groping at the clasp of her bra. The way he was breathing heavily, Misty knew he was yearning for a mouthful of her titties, but it wasn't the right time for that.

Misty pulled away from David's groping hands and hungry, searching lips. "Come handle this," she said to Tamia while holding David by the base of his dick. Tamia stepped forward and attempted to caress her husband's dick.

"No, I got this. Drop down on your knees and open your mouth," Misty directed in a bossy tone.

Doing as she was told, Tamia assumed a position on her knees. With her eyes squeezed shut in deep humiliation, she opened her mouth. Misty guided David's dick inside his wife's mouth. David groaned in delight as the head entered the moist warmth.

Still holding his dick and controlling the tempo of the blowjob, Misty could feel him swelling and thickening inside her grasp. David began to thrust, trying to jam more dick length into his wife's mouth.

Misty smacked his ass cheeks. "Be still. I'm running this show."

David's body went still as he allowed Misty to control his dick thrust, using her hand to drive his length in and out of Tamia's open mouth at a pace that she determined.

Growing hot and bothered by the kinkiness of the sexual activity, Misty couldn't help from getting more involved in the action. She grabbed a handful of Tamia's hair, forcing her head to bob up and down at a rapid rhythm while she used her other hand to jam David's dick down his wife's throat.

"That's enough, bitch," Misty said as she withdrew David's dick from Tamia's mouth. "Now, you can fuck me, baby," she told him as she pulled him toward the bed.

With tears in her eyes, Tamia stood and watched helplessly as her husband swept Misty into his arms and carried her to the bed. After pulling off her boots, he kissed her feet. He helped her wriggle out of her tight pants and thong and like a magnet pulled to metal, his lips fastened against Misty's pussy. David made loud, wet sucking sounds as he slurped the moisture from between her legs.

Misty beckoned Tamia. "Come sit on the bed and get a close look at how much your husband loves eating out my coochie. Now, I need you to help him out."

"In what way?" Tamia asked warily.

"I want you to lie down on the bed and let my baby straddle your face."

"Why does he have to straddle my face?" she asked in a scared voice.

"He cums quick the first time; so let him bust that first nutt on your face, you know, to get off some of the aggression he feels toward you for dogging him out the way you did. That's part of the therapy, understand?"

Resigned to do whatever warped ideas Misty had in store for her, Tamia nodded her head.

"After he busts that first nutt, then he can fuck me the way I like it, with those long, hard strokes."

David straddled his wife, but he wasn't allowed to touch his dick. Misty masturbated him, and then aimed his erupting member at Tamia's face. Seeing sticky ejaculation sliding down her nose and her cheeks was a powerful aphrodisiac for Misty.

She grabbed David by the arm, pulling him off his wife and onto her. With their bodies pressed together, Misty humped and writhed with lust as she frantically filled her pussy with David's thickness.

Sobbing, Tamia staggered to the bathroom to clean her face. For Misty, hearing Tamia's pitiful weeping was like listening to romantic music. The sound set the mood, heightening her lust, and prompting her to wrap both legs around David's waist as she threw the pussy at him.

CHAPTER 36

Anya had been certain to park her car on the side of Skippy's where there were no cameras, and she felt certain no one had seen Natalie getting inside her Audi.

Bags crammed with shoes, clothes, and Sergio's money were piled in the trunk of her car. She had one stop to make before hitting the road, headed for Philly.

On a residential street that hadn't been ravished by the poverty of the inner city, Anya pulled to a stop and parked. Outside, older people tended to their yards or sat on their porches shooting the breeze. All eyes were on Anya as she got out of her car and walked to the house with the water sprinkler spraying the grass.

The woman dressed in bright colors and with smooth, dark skin was obviously Paloma's Aunt Harriet; the resemblance to her niece was startling. She was expecting Anya, and welcomed her inside. Neighbors craned their necks, wondering about the identity of the well-dressed young woman visiting Harriet.

Harriet discreetly closed the door and offered Anya a seat. "So, you're Mr. Sergio's girlfriend?"

"Yes, I am…I was," she corrected, dropping her eyes. The idea that she'd never see Sergio again…that she had to speak of him in past tense still hadn't fully sunk in. "I'm not going to beat around the bush. I came to give you something." She pulled an envelope from her bag. The envelope was stuffed with thousands of dollars. "There's more than enough money here to cover sending Paloma's body back to Santo Domingo, to pay for her funeral, and for round trip tickets for you to fly back with her body. And I'd appreciate if you'd give the remaining money to her family back on the island."

"That's very kind of you," Harriet said.

"It's what Sergio would have wanted."

"I knew his mother. Mr. Sergio was generous like she was. They're together, now…in heaven. His father, eh, I'm not so sure where he ended up. He wasn't a nice man. But Mr. Sergio had his mother's kind heart."

"I hope he's in heaven," Anya said in a voice barely above a whisper.

"Of course, he is. The good Lord has already forgiven his sins."

Anya left Harriet's house feeling comforted. The average woman would be nervous about driving across country in a car that had millions stashed in the trunk, but Anya felt safe and protected. No harm would come to her. Her two guardian angels—her mom and Sergio—were looking out for her.

After driving 644 miles without stopping to sleep, Anya arrived in Philly, and checked into a hotel. She could feel her eyes trying to close as she made her way to the elevator with the bellhop trailing behind her, pushing her assorted pieces of luggage on a gold baggage carrier.

A very pretty young woman, who appeared around Anya's age—no more than five years older—got on the elevator. "I must have missed your phone call," the woman said to the handsome bell-hop flirtatiously.

"Oh, I didn't think you were serious," he responded, blushing.

"I never kid around. When I see something I want, I make it very clear."

"Cool. I'll give you a call." He looked embarrassed for Anya to overhear him making a hookup with a guest of the hotel.

Minding her business, Anya searched her phone as if expecting a text from Sergio. Glimpsing old text messages was so heartbreaking, Anya closed her phone and stuffed it in her bag. She glanced up and found herself looking into the face of the woman who was flirting with the bellhop.

Not only was she stunningly beautiful, but she looked eerily familiar. Anya felt a chill so strong, her body shuddered. The old folks said someone was walking on your grave when you felt a sudden and powerful cold chill. The woman had a hostile vibe and she defiantly stared Anya down, forcing Anya to break her gaze and look away.

She was relieved when the elevator reached the twelfth floor, and the strange lady sashayed through the sliding doors, head held high. Though she was petite in stature, she walked with the air of a much taller person. In fact, she gave the impression that she was quite fond of herself. Putting it bluntly, the bitch had an ego problem.

In her room, Anya kicked off her shoes and collapsed on the bed. Too tired to take off her clothes, she got under the covers, fully dressed. Before drifting off to sleep, she pictured the woman from the elevator again, and wondered why she seemed so familiar. She racked her brain trying to figure out why she felt so connected to her, but fell asleep before she could figure out the answer.

Refreshed after sleeping twelve hours straight, Anya contacted Jonathan Whitman, the private detective she'd hired to find her father. "I'm in Philly and since I'm in such close proximity, I was wondering if there's anything I can do to help you with the search for my father. Do you have any leads? Are there any homeless shelters that I could visit?"

"Actually, I was going to give you a call today," Whitman said.

"Really? Do you have news?" she asked hopefully.

"Yes, but I'm afraid it's not what you want to hear."

She pressed a hand against her heart. "Oh, no, don't tell me he's dead," she blurted with apprehension creeping into her voice.

"I'm sorry. He passed away several years ago," Whitman said.

"No. No. No," she cried. "What happened; how'd he die?" It was devastating to imagine her father slumping over dead on a park bench or dying alone on the streets while living inside a cardboard box. The imagery of him being an anonymous derelict that was seemingly unwanted and unloved, with no family members even claiming his body, caused her unbearable grief.

"He had lung cancer that had gone untreated. He collapsed in the streets and spent his remaining months in a very nice hospice facility in Pottstown, Pennsylvania."

"Pottstown? How'd he end up there?"

"Who knows? The homeless tend to move around a great deal. On a brighter note, the facility kept his personal effects and I was going to have them mailed to you, but since you're in the area, perhaps you'd like to pick up his things."

"Sure, I'd love to," Anya said, wiping away tears with the back of her hand.

"Hold on for a sec while I look for the director's name and the phone number of the facility."

Placed on hold, grief took over, and Anya broke down sobbing again. Her poor father had died with no one who loved him by his side. He must have felt so terribly afraid and unloved. *I would have been there to hold your hand, Daddy, if only I'd known where you were.*

Whitman returned to the phone and gave Anya the contact information for the hospice facility. Before hanging up, he extended his condolences. Tearfully, Anya thanked him. She set the phone down, and stared into space.

My father's gone, and I have absolutely no one. All the money I've acquired means nothing now that I can't share it with him.

For the next two days, Anya stayed in her room, having meals delivered as she shut herself off and mourned alone.

CHAPTER 37

Brick had the foresight to stop at Home Depot and pick up sheets of plastic to store and preserve the bundles of money that Misty wanted to hoard in a storage unit. He'd never seen so much cash in his life.

"Isn't it beautiful, Brick?" Misty gestured to the covered money stacks. "That money represents the power I've always wanted. There's close to three million right there, and there's more to come. I have an appointment with some guy in Mexico. He wants me to heal his wife of cancer. I told him I wasn't sure if I could cure cancer, but he's willing to pay me a fortune merely for trying. Isn't that something?"

Misty gazed at Brick with a proud expression. Brick grunted a sound that was supposed to express agreement, but worrisome thoughts plagued his mind.

He imagined that most billionaires made their money from being ruthless, and Misty could possibly be in over her head without even realizing it.

"You should be careful in your dealings with those people. Rich folks love money even more than you do. They're feeling vulnerable while they or their loved ones are unhealthy, but who's to say how they'll react if someone dies after one of your healings?"

Misty waved her hand through the air. "This money is proof that I'm the bomb-dot-com, but you love being negative."

"That's not true. I only want you to be careful."

"I am being careful; that's why I hired you as my bodyguard."

The preschool that Brick selected for his son was located in the Society Hill section of the city and was near his work site. The annual tuition of twenty-eight thousand dollars was a drop in the bucket for Misty. Of the many perks, the elite school offered early exposure to foreign languages, such as Latin, German, and French. The previous year, the children had successfully built a robot, and that was something Brick felt his son would love getting involved in. There were three libraries, four art studios, and five music studios. The kids were urged to learn an instrument. In addition to academic and fine arts, there were a variety of special programs for children including gourmet cooking and leadership classes.

Despite her ulterior motives, Misty had come up with a fantastic idea. Getting Thomasina on board with the idea of enrolling their son in nursery school was a lot easier than Brick had expected. He led her to believe that part of the tuition was being covered by his vague lottery winnings and the other portion was a scholarship the school offered for minorities.

The first day he dropped his son off at school, Brick felt a tremendous sense of pride. His son was getting an opportunity that he could never have dreamed of. Who knows where life would have taken Brick if he'd had caring parents and had been provided with a quality education?

Although the other parents were wearing business attire and carrying briefcases when they dropped their children off in the morning, Brick, dressed in work coveralls and carrying a lunch tote, didn't feel out of place in the least. He figured his money was as good as theirs, and his son deserved the same privileges as any other kid.

At the end of the week, when Misty reminded Brick that she needed him to accompany her on the trip to Mexico, Brick readily agreed. He had no intention of relying on Misty to pay Little Baron's tuition year after year, and he was eager to earn more money to put aside for next year's school fee.

The trip to Tijuana, Mexico via a luxury jet could have been pleasant and relaxing had it not been for disgruntled and inebriated Gavin Stallings. Brick had no idea what dude's problem was, but he seemed to be muttering profanities under his breath as he guzzled down shots of tequila. Hearing Misty's name mumbled and also seeing Gavin casting angry looks toward the jet's master bedroom, where Misty was getting in her beauty rest, it appeared to Brick that she was the target of the man's drunken ramblings.

What had Misty done to piss off Gavin? Brick wondered. He'd have to speak to Misty about his suspicions after she woke up. In the meantime, he'd keep a watchful eye on Gavin, and he wouldn't hesitate to jack him up, if he displayed any sign of violent behavior toward Misty.

Upon arrival at their destination, Gavin was ordered to stay behind at the hotel while Brick and Misty were chauffeured to the alternative medical center where the Mendelsohns were waiting for them.

Compared to the abject poverty of the neighborhoods and the people he'd glimpsed through the darkened window of the limo he'd ridden in, the facility was a complete contrast. Surprisingly, the facility looked more like a rich resort than a medical center.

Misty and Brick were escorted to Mrs. Mendelsohn's private suite of rooms by smiling professionals who seemed eager to please.

They were met by a grim-faced Jacob Mendelsohn in the living room area. "She's not doing well today," he said, rubbing his forehead anxiously. "She can't keep any food down…" His voice trailed off as he shook his head grimly. "These alternative treatments worked for a while, but my wife's going down fast." He gazed at Misty with watery eyes. "I need you to do whatever you can to save my wife. She's only forty-three years old; that's too young to die."

"Okay, well, I have a policy," Misty said, causing Brick to cringe.

Please don't let her bring up money right now while this man is in despair.

"I don't lay-on hands until I've been paid in full and in cash," she said in a tone that didn't contain an ounce of compassion.

Damn, his wife is dying, Misty. Have a heart! Mortified by Misty's callousness, Brick's gaze shot downward.

"Sure. I…I…have the money right here," Mendelsohn stammered as he pointed to a large, zippered piece of luggage.

Misty motioned for Brick to check the bag. Brick wanted to offer the grief-stricken man a thousand apologies for Misty's coldblooded attitude, but having to act out his role of hardened bodyguard, he maintained an impassive expression as he strode across the room and examined the cash that was stacked inside the suitcase.

Since getting involved in Misty's healing venture, he'd learned to calculate amounts of money by eyeballing stacks of large denominations. "It's all here," he concluded in a serious tone.

"I'm going to take you to see my wife, Elaine." He led them through a kitchenette and a small dining area to get to the bedroom. In the dining area, two teenagers sat at the table looking forlorn.

"These are my kids," Jacob said, without slowing his stride. Brick was relieved that Jacob hadn't bothered to make proper introductions. He doubted he could look those kids in the eyes.

Inside the wife's official hospital room, Brick was overcome by the showing of love that was demonstrated by an extensive array of flower bouquets, and what appeared to be over a hundred get well cards were atop tables and thumbtacked to every available wall space.

Elaine Mendelsohn was nothing more than skin and bones, Brick noted. She looked much older than her actual age. Her room had an odd smell that Brick assumed was the overwhelming scent of the flowers combined with the scent of impending death. Had it not been for the slight rise and fall of her narrow chest, Brick would have assumed Elaine was already dead. He didn't believe there was anything Misty could do for the cancer-ridden woman and he intended to strongly suggest she get over her greed and return Jacob Mendelsohn's money. It was the right thing to do.

Scowling, Misty approached the bed where the sick woman lay with her eyes closed, and Brick could tell from Misty's expression that she was creeped out by the woman who looked like a breathing corpse. With her aversion to anyone who wasn't glamorous, let alone people who were deathly ill, Misty was definitely in the wrong field, Brick surmised.

"She's been sleeping a lot for the past few days," Jacob explained.

Misty pulled back the covers and then to Brick's and Jacob's utter shock, she lifted up the woman's nightgown, exposing an adult diaper.

"What're you doing?" Jacob demanded.

"The cancer's in her vagina, right? So, I'm going straight to the source."

"She has ovarian cancer," he corrected with annoyance.

"Same thing," Misty said with a shoulder shrug. She undid the tape that held the diaper in place and Brick immediately averted his gaze.

"Is this necessary?" Jacob asked in a raised voice.

"It can't hurt," Misty responded as she covered Elaine Mendelsohn's pubis with her palm. She kept her palm in place for what seemed like an unbearably long time to Brick. Never had he felt as uptight and uncomfortable as he felt in that moment. He'd have to figure out another way to pay his son's tuition. Being an accomplice to Misty conning this desperate family was not what he'd signed up for.

After removing her healing hand, Misty retaped the diaper. A few moments later, Elaine's eyelids began to flutter, and finally opened, revealing vibrant brown eyes.

"Jacob," she said in a surprisingly strong voice. "Who are these people?"

"Uh, they're friends of mine. How're you feeling, honey?"

"Hungry. In fact, I'm starving," she said, struggling to sit up.

"Do you think you could hold some soup down?" Jacob asked, looking surprised.

"I have the strongest urge for a big plate of spaghetti or maybe Chinese food," she said with happy laughter.

"We're in Mexico, remember, hon? I don't think we'll find those dishes on the lunch menu here." Jacob clasped his wife's hands and kissed her on the cheek.

"What kind of treatment are they using on me? I honestly feel like I could get out of this bed and run a marathon." Elaine laughed heartily.

Jacob glanced at Misty and mouthed the words, *Thank you!*

CHAPTER 38

Anya's father's worldly goods included a battered wallet that contained his Pennsylvania identification and appointment cards for the city health clinic. But he'd left behind a gift that she'd cherish for the rest of her life—a small photo album with pictures of her parents and her, depicting happy times together. Some pictures brought back wonderful memories and others were taken too far back for her to recall. But seeing her parents together, smiling and happy, gave her a warm feeling inside. They were together now in the afterlife, and one day she'd join them. Until then, at least she had some proof that she'd once been the cherished child of loving parents.

Brick wanted to come clean with Thomasina and tell her about Misty's miraculous healing capabilities and her ability to walk, but Thomasina had so much animosity toward her daughter, he doubted if she'd be happy about the turn of events. If she found out that Misty was earning millions of tax-free dollars, she was liable to alert the IRS, and so Brick refrained from bringing up Misty's name.

After returning from Mexico, he was suffering from jet lag and was running a little late to pick up Little Baron for nursery school.

When he arrived, he was dismayed to find his son dressed preppy-style in a button-down shirt, a vest, Dockers, and even a bow tie. "Why you got him looking like he's on his way to Oxford University or somewhere?" he asked Thomasina.

"He's going to that fancy school, and I figured he should look the part," she responded.

"The other kids don't wear designer clothes. They dress in regular play clothes."

"My son is not any regular kid. He's taking leadership classes with a bunch of white kids and I want him to stand out. He's gonna have to learn to work twice as hard and to dress to impress."

"You got my little man looking crazy. He's gonna stand out like a sore thumb, looking like he's ready to play polo or a game of croquet," Brick said sarcastically, and then removed the bow tie and tossed it on the coffee table. "We're running late and there's no time for him to change, but in the future, dress him in clothes that he can rough-house in. Dressing him like a little scholar will make him a target for bullies. Is that what you want?"

"No, but I think he looks suave and handsome," Thomasina said stubbornly.

Brick groaned and said, "Come on, Baron. Let's go to school, man." He told himself that from now on, he'd have to keep an emergency change of clothing in the car for his son.

After getting Little Baron strapped in the back seat, he noticed a late-model, light-blue car pull up across the street. The car moved shortly after he pulled off and proceeded to tail him to the expressway. Though the driver stayed three or four car lengths behind, Brick was certain he was being followed.

He wondered if he was being followed by someone working for Jacob Mendelsohn. Had the man's wife taken a turn for the worse, causing him to want to seek revenge on Misty? Fucking around with Misty always brought chaos into Brick's life. He bitterly recalled how his face had gotten carved up by a ruthless drug dealer back when he and Misty were teens. Misty had screwed the drug dealer over, going on shopping sprees with his money, but Brick had been the one to pay the cost. Having his face disfigured had turned him into a monster that people pointed at, and his reckless behavior had been a reflection of shame and self-loathing.

Thomasina had given him back his confidence; for that, he'd always have love for her.

Glancing in his rearview mirror, he could no longer see the blue car. Maybe he'd overreacted. With all the supernatural occurrences he'd witnessed with his own eyes, there wasn't any wonder that he was edgy and somewhat paranoid.

The only drawback to his son attending school in Society Hill was the horrendous parking situation in that area. Forced to park several blocks away from the school, he cursed when he realized he didn't have any change for the parking meter. Running super late, he had no choice but to lift Little Baron in his arms and speed walk to their destination. When they neared the school, he lowered his son to the ground and held his hand as they entered the building. The moment they arrived in his classroom, Little Baron let go of his father's hand and scampered off with his classmates.

It was a joy to see his boy fitting in and enjoying the new environment. With all her faults and flaws, Misty made a good call when she suggested enrolling Little Baron in an exclusive nursery school.

With less than fifteen minutes to drive to work in the crawling, downtown traffic, Brick hustled back to his car. He was braced to see a ticket plastered across his windshield, but was totally unprepared for a sight that was so glorious and so surprising, he let out a shocked gasp.

The mysterious blue car was parked behind his, and standing outside the car was Anya, and her whole face lit up when she saw Brick. Fearing that his eyes were deceiving him, Brick rushed forward, arms extended, his groping hands anxious to touch and hold her. It was a dream come true when seconds later, Anya was in his arms.

"Baby, baby, baby! It's so good to see you. I thought you were in Trinidad," Brick said in a rush of words as he squeezed her tight.

"There wasn't anything for me in Trinidad, and so I went back to Indiana, but that's a long story. I know you told me to stay away, but I was in Philly, and I needed to see you before I left town."

"Did you find your pops?"

Anya shook her head. "He's dead. All my searching was in vain; he passed away from cancer a few years ago." Tears sprang to her eyes, and Brick held her closer, rubbing her back as he comforted her. She wiped her eyes, and attempting to lighten the mood, she said, "I saw you with your son. He's getting big; he's handsome, and looks exactly like you."

"That's my little man," Brick said proudly. He glanced down at his watch and realized he'd never make it to work on time. *Fuck it, I'm calling in sick today.*

"I didn't know if you were locked up or not and I asked the private investigator who looked into my father's situation to get me an address for you. I'm sorry if I seem like a stalker lurking outside your house and following you to your son's school, but I was desperate to see you once more."

"It's okay. My wife and I aren't together anymore."

"You're not?"

"No, we're in the middle of a divorce. I have my own place. I stop by her crib in the morning to take my son to school."

"What happened with Misty? Did she pull through?"

"Misty's doing fine. Came out of the coma. Her story is so incredible, you're not even gonna believe it." Brick looked around as if suddenly noticing the passersby that were briskly walking up and down the sidewalk, and having to navigate around him and Anya. "I'm skipping work today, so let's get out of here. I'll tell you everything over coffee and breakfast. There's a place I like that's not too far from here."

"Why don't we go back to your place? I'd love to cook you breakfast. For old time's sake," she added with a bright smile.

Sitting on a kitchen stool, Brick couldn't take his eyes off Anya as she bustled around the kitchen. "This can't be real. I know my ass is dreaming, and I'm gonna be mad as fuck when the alarm clock wakes me up," Brick said, grinning at her.

Anya returned the smile and then her expression went serious. "What's going on with Misty? Is she able to communicate? Is she in a rehab facility?"

Brick inhaled deeply. "Man, I don't even know where to start. Well, first of all, yes, she can communicate and, no, she's not in a facility."

"Where is she?"

"She was living here for a hot minute."

"You're kidding."

"She had nurses taking care of her. But anyway, let me back up and tell you how it all went down. When she came out of the coma, I was so relieved that she was all right, my feelings got confused and the two of us sort of hooked up again."

"Hooked up? In her condition?"

"It wasn't about a sexual relationship. I was prepared to commit to her unconditionally, you know. Then weird shit started happening."

"Like what?"

"First of all, she developed the ability to read people soon after coming out of the coma."

"I've heard of people emerging from comas with new abilities."

"It freaked me out."

"I can imagine."

"The way it worked with Misty…well, if she touched someone's hand, she could see scenes from that person's past and future."

"Wow," Anya said incredulously.

"There was a big write-up about her in the newspaper and people started sending her donations. Long story short, a dude from a rich family paid for cosmetic surgery to fix her face. After her surgery, we moved in this place together. Shortly after that, she had dental surgery, and when she came out of anesthesia, she had another ability."

Anya raised her brows in curiosity.

"She was able to lay hands on her paralyzed arms and legs and suddenly she could walk."

"Brick, that sounds impossible. Do you think she was faking her paralysis the whole time?"

"No. She had a severe spinal cord injury. As strange as it sounds, it's true. Misty is making a killing healing rich folks. I work with her as her part-time bodyguard, and I've seen the miracles she can perform with my own eyes."

"Okay," Anya said doubtfully. "So, did you two end your relationship on good terms?"

"Kinda, sorta. We had some bumps in the road, but we see eye to eye now."

With her back to Brick, Anya flipped pancakes and scrambled eggs in a frying pan. "I was in a relationship also. With a drug dealer. He got killed," she said softly, leaving it at that. The pain was too raw for her to provide details, and Brick didn't push.

Brick walked up behind her and embraced her from behind. "I'm sorry to hear that, babe, but on the bright side, I'm happy to have you here with me."

Anya turned around and faced him. "His name was Sergio Travares, and although I had strong feelings for him and despite the fact that I miss him so much, I have to admit, that I never stopped loving you, Brick."

"I feel the same way, and I realize I was foolish to let you go. But I thought I was gonna get locked up, and I honestly believed that I was doing what was best for you."

"Things worked out the way they were supposed to. If we were together when Misty woke up, what would have happened between us?"

"It's hard to say."

"I think you know the answer, Brick, and that's why we had to go our separate ways."

"But things are different now. Misty and I are over. Nothing more than business associates."

"I believe you. I know you wouldn't lie about something like that."

"You mentioned that you were only passing through Philly. Where are you going?"

Anya shrugged. "No idea. I'm gonna travel for a while, and maybe one day I'll find a place to settle down in—a place to call home."

"Home is right here with me, baby. If you give me another chance, I swear, I'll never let you down again."

Anya didn't respond, at least not with words. She lifted her chin, offering him her lips, and Brick delicately pressed his lips against hers. The sexual chemistry between Anya and him had always been powerful, and he should have been prepared for the jolt of passion that shot through him, and the immediate hardening in his groin, but he wasn't.

Not wanting to appear that he was trying to rush her into something she wasn't ready for, he pulled away. "Is the grub ready, yet?"

"The food can wait, but I can't," Anya said, turning off the burners and covering the pots and pans.

CHAPTER 39

After a barrage of voicemails and text messages from her former nurse, Audrey, Misty finally allowed the desperate woman to visit her at the hotel. With David and the hunky bellhop taking care of her sexual needs, she didn't have any use for Audrey, and she made it clear to the nurse that there'd be no lesbo action between them in the future. If she wanted to massage Misty's feet or rub down her back, that was fine, but no more cat-licking. Misty had lost her desire for girl-on-girl activities. She'd only used Audrey when she was in a sex-bind, but she had plenty of good dick at her disposal, now.

"Hey, Four-Eyes, long time, no see," Misty taunted when Audrey entered her suite. Audrey ducked her head down, self-consciously, and when she recovered from the slur, she began showering Misty with compliments.

"You look more beautiful than ever," Audrey said worshipfully.

"I know, right. I was looking in the mirror this morning and thought to myself that I get prettier and prettier every day," Misty bragged, flipping her wavy hair.

"I missed you, Misty. Why'd you make me stay away? I did everything you ever asked me to do. I don't understand what I did wrong."

Misty sucked her teeth. "If you get all mushy on me, you're gonna have to leave. I was nice enough to let you come visit me, so don't start whining and acting ungrateful," Misty scolded.

"I'm sorry; I didn't mean to sound ungrateful," Audrey said, her face composed in humble contrition. Then her expression brightened, and her eyes scanned Misty from head to toe. "That blue nail polish looks good on your pretty feet."

"Well, that shows that you don't have any taste whatsoever," Misty said contemptuously. "I hate this polish and plan on getting a different color later on today."

"You're right; that's not your color at all. Do you want me to paint your nails for you?"

"No, I don't have time for that right now. One of my fans—a dude who works here at the hotel, is gonna stop by for a quickie. You can help me get out of these clothes and get ready for him. I want to be naked when he gets here, and I want my body glistening with this handmade, scented lotion I picked up when I was in Mexico."

"You've been to Mexico?" Audrey asked, looking dejected.

"Mexico and Hawaii. Girl, I'm so famous and in such demand, I've been traveling all over. I'll be flying out to Japan soon to spend some time with a new fan," Misty boasted.

"I wish I could go with you."

"If you play your cards right and do the things I need you to do, you might get to take a trip with me one of these days. A working trip, of course. You won't get to sit back and chill; I'll expect you to take care of me."

"I love taking care of you."

"You'll have to prove your worth."

"I can start by helping to get you ready for your fan," Audrey said, swallowing down a knot of jealousy as she followed Misty into the bedroom. Misty sat on the bed as Audrey kneeled down to remove her sandals. Misty stood while the nurse tugged off her tight jeans and top. Misty giggled derisively when the nurse pulled off her panties with trembling hands, her tongue darting out and inadvertently licking her lips.

"What's wrong, Ms. Peabody? Why're you shaking and licking your lips? Does seeing my coochie make you nervous and hungry?"

Audrey looked at Misty with a pitiful expression. "I miss what we used to have," she uttered in a squeaky voice.

"Damn, you're a needy bitch." Misty flopped down on the edge of the bed and spread her legs wide open. "Come on, and eat some of this pussy, with your dyke-ass self. But remember, I got shit to do, so don't get too comfortable slurping between my legs."

Audrey removed her eyeglasses and squatted between Misty's legs. She worked hard to please Misty, stretching her tongue as far as she could.

Simply for the sake of being spiteful, Misty repeatedly yanked on Audrey's bang, pulling her head forward and causing the nurse to groan in pain. With each groan, she released a rush of hot breath that warmed Misty's sensitive pussy in a freaky, new way.

In the midst of receiving oral sex, Misty made a sound of annoyance when a knock came at the door.

Audrey yanked her head up. "Is he here already?"

"Probably so. My fans are always so anxious to get with me."

Audrey nodded in understanding.

"Go get the door and tell him I'll be with him in a second."

"Do I have to leave now that he's here?" Audrey asked, looking gloomy as she put her glasses back on and tried to smooth down the front of her hair that was sticking out in different directions from all the tugging Misty had done to it.

"You can wait around if you want to."

"I want to very much," Audrey said eagerly.

"All right, you can watch TV in the other room while we're in here smashing."

"Are you gonna let me finish what I started after your fan leaves?"

Loving the idea of Audrey getting sloppy seconds, Misty gave her a big smile and said, "Absolutely."

The bellhop had beat the box up to such a degree, Misty could barely move. All she wanted to do was sleep. And when Audrey came in the bedroom, trying to lick on her tender pussy, Misty berated the nurse, calling her all kinds of perverted names.

"Do you want me to leave?" Audrey asked unhappily.

"Actually, I want you to run an errand for me. I'm sick of this hotel food and I'm weary of the nearby places that deliver. I'm in the mood for an authentic cheesesteak from Jim's on South Street."

"What do you want on it?" Audrey asked enthusiastically.

"Extra cheese, fried onions, hot peppers, salt and pepper, and ketchup."

"Anything to drink?"

"No, I have plenty of juice in the fridge. Now, get a move on. That bellhop wore my ass out and I'm starving."

"I'll be as quick as I can. Oh, can you call the steak shop and see if you can place an order for pickup?" Audrey asked.

Misty looked at Audrey as if she'd lost her mind. "I know you don't expect *me* to call the steak shop."

Audrey smiled sheepishly. "No, I don't know what I was thinking." She laughed nervously and said, "I'll call them right now." After finding the number online, she made the call and inquired about pickup. She hung up and wearing an apologetic smile, she turned to Misty and said, "They don't take orders over the phone."

"Well, now you know," Misty said with a shrug. "Oh, I thought of something else I want. While you're on South Street, stop by that cupcake place called Scandalicious, and get me two Passionate Kisses."

"Two what?"

"Passionate Kisses; it's the name of a cupcake. All of the bakery items have sexy names; I love the ambience in Scandalicious."

"A cheesesteak and two sexy cupcakes coming right up for the beautiful lady," Audrey said in a cheerful voice, seeming to somehow think that Misty's desire for a cupcake with a provocative name was a reflection of the kind of evening they'd spend together.

Misty rolled her eyes at Audrey. "Would you please stop running your mouth and get your ass moving!"

Audrey pushed her sliding glasses up the bridge of her nose and grabbed her purse before swiftly departing.

A few minutes after she'd gone, Misty's phone rang. Seeing Gavin's name on the screen, Misty scowled. Gavin was drinking a lot lately and she had begun to consider him unnecessary to her fast-growing business. She'd gotten a call from Jacob Mendelsohn, telling her that the doctor had given his wife a clean bill of health, and that she was now cancer-free. Thanks to Misty's magic hands, of course. Mendelsohn wanted her permission to refer her to one of his associates, a wealthy Japanese businessman. With word-of-mouth business from her satisfied clients, she definitely didn't need Gavin anymore. And it was time to let him know that his services were no longer necessary.

"Hello, Gavin," she said in a curt tone.

"You lying bitch!" he exploded.

"I beg your fucking pardon!"

"You told me you foresaw a future where Randolph and I ended up together and happy."

"I did," she lied.

"Then explain to me why Randolph is back in town. He's out of the closet, openly gay, and has asked his wife for a divorce."

"That's what you wanted, isn't it?"

"He's planning a commitment ceremony with a twenty-one-year-old. A vegetarian, Rollerblading, beach bum he met at Venice Beach in Los Angeles, while he was there trying to find himself." Gavin spat the words with cold contempt.

With Gavin being in such a foul mood, Misty determined that it wasn't a good time to fire him. Attempting to calm him down, she soothed him with more lies.

"He's only trying to make you jealous, Gavin. He's given up so much for you, and he wants to find out if you feel he's worth fighting for."

"How do I do that when he's hosting a dinner party tonight to introduce his boy-lover to *our* friends at *our* favorite restaurant. The restaurant where we shared our first meal together. It's so demeaning. Such a horrible slap in the face."

"You should crash the dinner party and declare your undying love for Randolph in front of everyone. That should do the trick," Misty said, laughing to herself as she imagined Gavin making a fool of himself. "Call me tonight and let me know how it went," she said sweetly, though she planned to ignore his calls and possibly move to another hotel under a fictitious name. Though she could afford to buy an elaborate home, and pay cash for it, she hadn't taken the time to look at any places, yet. At the moment, hotel living more than suited her needs.

Still, Gavin was behaving like a loose cannon and she didn't want him stalking her and seeking revenge after he publicly disgraced himself. Misty had no choice but to find an alternative living situation.

CHAPTER 40

In bed all day and into the night, Brick and Anya shared the most intimate details of their lives during the time they'd been apart. Anya sobbed as she recounted the horrifying specifics of Sergio's execution-style murder, but she became deadly calm as she described her brutal method of revenge against Natalie.

"Do you think I'm a monster?" she asked Brick.

"No, I think we're very much alike. We love hard and we're trusting to a fault. When that trust is betrayed or if someone we love is harmed, we become ruthless killers."

Brick proceeded to tell her how Misty had deceived him into believing she'd changed; how she'd pretended to be a wiser and more loving version of her former self. But it had all been a guise. She was the same self-involved Misty that she'd always been. Maybe worse. He admitted that he still had a soft spot for Misty, but no longer had romantic feelings for her.

"Our relationship is sort of like sister and brother. She's like a stubborn little sister who thinks she knows everything, but always manages to get herself in trouble," Brick said, shaking his head. "I agreed to be her bodyguard because I genuinely want to protect her. And the money she pays doesn't hurt. My son's school isn't cheap."

Anya frowned. "What are you protecting her from? Seems to me that she's a danger to others."

"She's not dangerous. She's egotistical and she uses people, but she's not a killer," Brick said, defending Misty.

"Does that make her better than us?" Anya asked.

"No," he admitted. "We're passionate people. Maybe too passionate, whereas Misty is pretty much heartless."

"I want you to stop working for her, Brick. There's no future for us if Misty is in your life in any capacity. You don't have to worry about money. I have plenty of it."

"You did enough for me already. You spent a lot of dough helping me track down the dude who hurt Misty. I have to tell you, it blew me away when I discovered you had slipped a chunk of money inside my bag before we went our separate ways. It touched my heart that you were still thinking about my well-being even though I broke your heart."

"My love is unconditional, Brick. I don't give love in order to get something back."

"That's a new concept for me."

"Well, get used to it. I can pay for your son's school and I can take care of anything else you need."

Brick shook his head adamantly. "I can't let you spend any more of the money your mother left for you."

"My mom's money is in the bank, accruing interest. I have Sergio's money. Millions in cash. I have more money than I could ever spend. Aside from taking care of Sergio's incarcerated uncle and his housekeeper's family, I plan to give a lot of the money away to various charities." Anya looked Brick in the eye. "It's time to part ways with Misty. I don't know her, but I can feel her negative energy, Brick."

"It's a wrap, babe. You don't have to worry about me working for Misty anymore. I'll give her a call first thing tomorrow."

"There's one more thing," Anya said. "I don't want to stay in this apartment you shared with her. We need our own place."

"I'm not gonna argue that point. I have the day off Saturday. Do you want to start looking then?"

"No, I can't wait that long. Being in Misty's space gives me the creeps. I'll find us a place tomorrow. Is there any particular area that you prefer? Any amenities in the apartment that you simply must have?" Anya said, going from a serious expression to a big smile.

Brick thought about it and said, "Instead of an apartment, I'd prefer a house in the suburbs. Nothing elaborate. A cozy place with a big back yard for my boy. My divorce is up in the air right now because I haven't signed yet. Thomasina only allows me to see my son on her terms, but I plan on getting a lawyer to fight for my parental rights and get me joint custody in the divorce settlement."

"That sounds fair to me. Don't put it off much longer, Brick. Hurry up and get a lawyer so we can move forward without any attachments to your ex-wife or her daughter."

With so much on his mind, Brick couldn't get into the groove of working. It was finally ten o'clock, time for his morning break, and it hadn't come soon enough. He needed to make a call to Misty, to let her know she needed to find a new bodyguard, but it was too early in the morning to listen to her bitch about him quitting. The time could also be spent talking to a divorce lawyer, but he needed a strong cup of coffee before he'd be in the mood to deal with a shady, money-hungry attorney. Deciding to wait until lunchtime to make the calls, Brick left the work site and walked over to a food truck that served the best coffee and egg and sausage sandwiches in the area.

After placing his order, he absently pulled the *Philadelphia Daily News* from the rack in front of the food truck and stared at the headlines in disbelief: *Heir to Stallings Fortune Killed In Lover's Spat.* Beneath the headline was a photo of Gavin that appeared to be about ten years old. The subheading mentioned a gay love triangle. Brick quickly read the article, determining that Gavin had interrupted a celebratory dinner at a posh restaurant, yelling that Randolph Bingham was his lover and soul mate and that he was willing to fight for the man he loved. A twenty-one-year-old California man, a psych patient who had walked away from a mental health facility three months ago, became incensed and beat Stallings over the head with a silver candelabra, bludgeoning him to death before stunned diners.

Forgetting about the coffee and food he'd ordered, Brick walked away from the truck as if in a daze. He leaned against a telephone pole, pulled out his phone, and called Misty.

"Have you heard the news?" he asked her.

"What news?" she responded in a sleepy voice. "I haven't gotten out of bed yet. I had an orgy in my room last night with some of my fans, and we partied until daybreak," she said in a boastful tone designed to make Brick jealous.

"I don't care about your orgy. I called to tell you about your friend, Gavin."

"What about him?" she said irritably.

"He got killed last night. Some psychotic white boy from Cali beat him over the head and splattered his brains in a public restaurant."

"Whaaat? I saw that shit when I first met Gavin, but I didn't know who was gonna do the deed," Misty said with excitement in her voice.

"Misty, your boy got murked and you act like you want to be congratulated for foreseeing his death. Why didn't you warn him?"

"I'm only one person, and I can't save the world. I can't change folks' destiny either," she said somberly. Then her mood suddenly became upbeat. "Oh, by the way, I've been meaning to tell you, we have a trip coming up. We're going to Japan! Isn't that exciting? This time we're going to stay over and enjoy the nightlife and do some shopping. Can you get a few days off from your job? You must have some personal time you can use."

Brick was stunned by Misty's lack of concern over Gavin. "No, I can't get any time off. In fact, I don't want to work for you anymore. You're gonna have to find yourself another bodyguard."

"Brick! You can't leave me hanging. Who else is gonna look out for me the way you do?"

"I don't know, Misty, and to be honest, I don't give a fuck," Brick growled and hung up on her.

CHAPTER 41

The only thing Misty would miss about Gavin was the efficient manner in which he dealt with her clients. She'd been on the phone with Mr. Oshiro, the rich, Japanese bigshot, for ten minutes and she was ready to tear her hair out from having to listen to his bad English. Gavin had picked a hell of an inconvenient time to get himself murdered.

While Misty struggled through the conversation with Mr. Oshiro, Audrey, sensing that Misty was getting stressed, took it upon herself to massage Misty's scalp to relieve her tension.

Aggravated that Audrey's fingers were in her hair while she was conducting important business, Misty swatted the nurse's hands and shoved her away with her foot.

Instead of taking a hint and making herself useful in a less annoying way, Audrey approached Misty again, this time massaging and kissing the foot that Misty had kicked her with.

"Excuse me, Mr. Oshiro," Misty said politely into the phone. She glared at Audrey, snatched her foot from the woman's grasp, and said through clenched teeth, "Can you keep your goddamn hands off me for a few minutes? Damn! Get out of here and go sit in the other room and watch TV until I call you."

Audrey nodded contritely and left Misty's bedroom. "Get back here and close my door!" Misty yelled before returning to her important phone call.

When Misty inquired about flying in style, Mr. Oshiro assured her that she'd be traveling in his new Gulfstream V, a high-performance aircraft. The staff that would be at her beck and call included a chef, a masseuse, and a manicurist.

"Okay, I'm sold," Misty said with titters of happy laughter. "Oh, one last thing, make sure you pay me in American money. I prefer bundles of one-hundred-dollar bills."

After sealing the deal with Mr. Oshiro, Misty felt like celebrating. But with David at work at the hospital, the bellhop holding up his post in the lobby, and with Brick being obnoxious and stingy with the dick, Audrey was the only person available for Misty to share her moment with.

"Pour two glasses of wine, Audrey! We're gonna celebrate!" Misty yelled from the bedroom.

Audrey didn't ask what they were celebrating. Accustomed to doing whatever Misty ordered her to do, Audrey hustled to the kitchenette. The sound of clinking glassware announced that she was doing as she was told.

Her phone rang and Misty hoped Brick was calling to make up with her, to tell her that he wanted to go to Japan with her. It was a damn shame the way she couldn't let go of him. It wasn't exactly love that she felt; it was more like ownership. And his desire to want to cut ties with her felt like the worst kind of betrayal.

She glanced at the phone, and felt let down when she saw David's name on the screen.

"Hey," she said dully.

"Misty, I'm in trouble," David blurted in a frantic tone of voice.

"What kind of trouble?" she asked, though she didn't care. She had troubles of her own and couldn't be bothered with other people's problems. She sighed as she thought about Gavin no longer being available to handle the business end of her operation. And with Brick acting like a temperamental asshole, she no longer had a bodyguard.

"What do you want me to do about your troubles?" she said in a gruff tone.

"Misty, your vision came true. I shot Neil."

"Who's Neil?"

"My wife's coworker; the man she was having an affair with."

"Why'd you shoot him? You got your wife back. You should have been satisfied with that."

"Tamia was afraid you were going to take Caitlynn from her, and so she kidnapped my daughter and ran to Neil. They were on their way to the airport, trying to leave the state and I couldn't have that. I shot out two of his tires and then ran up on him and popped him in his temple. I would have shot Tamia, too, but my daughter was crying and clinging to her."

"I told you not to buy a gun."

"I didn't; I borrowed one."

Misty groaned. "This is ridiculous. I wasn't actually going to take the child. I was only fucking with her, so she'd start treating you with more respect."

"I thought you wanted to marry me and adopt my daughter?"

"Hell, no. I don't want any bratty kids." Misty was thoroughly disgusted with David.

"What am I gonna do?" David asked miserably.

"Turn yourself in. What else can you do?"

"Can you help me get out of the country?" he asked desperately.

"That would make me an accessory. You're on your own, David. All I can say is good luck." *And good riddance with your nutty, unstable self.*

"Don't hang up!" he bellowed. "This is your fault! You ruined my life!"

"Fuck you!" Misty shouted and ended the call.

Audrey burst into the bedroom, carrying two glasses of red wine. "What are we celebrating?" she asked cheerfully.

"We're not celebrating anything. Get that fucking wine out of my face, you goofy, four-eyed bitch."

Audrey scurried away and Misty slammed her bedroom door. The day couldn't get any worse. All her prophecies were coming true at the most inopportune time. It was a good thing she'd never touched the bellhop's palm. Not wanting to know his future, she'd avoided palm-to-palm contact with him. *At least I have one good dick left*, she thought, attempting to console herself.

Still, none of the men she'd been fucking with could take the place of Brick. Somehow she had to convince Brick to come back to her. Once she got him in her clutches again, she would literally drug him and lock him down with shackles until he got it through his thick skull that he belonged to her.

CHAPTER 42

It was dusk by the time Anya and Brick arrived at the house on Orchard Lane in Rose Valley, Pennsylvania. Brick was still dressed in his work uniform. They stepped outside the car and observed the exterior of the home. "Isn't it beautiful?" Anya said. The secluded stone colonial home sat on two acres of land. "Your son will have lots of leg room to run around and play if we buy this house."

"Wow!" Brick exclaimed, taken in by the stately elegance of the house. "I'm straight from the hood, and never imagined living anywhere as quiet and peaceful as this."

"I'm sorry you can't see the inside until Saturday, but take my word, it's a gorgeous house. I was sold when the realtor showed me the kitchen! That kitchen is so amazing, it'll inspire me to step up my game in the cooking department." Anya looked at Brick. "Do you like what you see?"

"Love it. My boy will thrive, having all this outdoor space to romp around in. With all these trees surrounding the place, I can build him a tree house. That's something I always wanted as a kid. Seemed like a cool getaway when the adult world was too much for me."

"Maybe you can retreat to the tree house when you and I get into it," Anya said jokingly.

"We never get into it, babe. There's never been drama between us. It's all love."

"I know, Brick. And I feel so lucky to have you back in my life."

"I feel the same," he admitted.

"You should have seen the realtor's face when I told her we were willing to pay the three-hundred eighty-five-thousand-dollar asking price in cold cash. Dollar signs seemed to light up in her eyes and twirl around." Anya laughed when she said this. "It's up to you, Brick. The house is vacant, and if you like what you see, we can move in real soon."

"I don't have to see the inside. I trust your judgment, and if you love it, then so do I. Cancel the appointment Saturday. Tell the realtor we'll take it."

Anya and Brick held hands on the drive back to the city. They rode in silence except for the soft music that played from the radio. Each was in a state of bliss and conversation wasn't necessary. At the wheel, Brick smoothly veered off I-495 at exit 5, and glided onto Township Line Road, which would take them directly into Philadelphia.

"As you know, I'm not comfortable being in your apartment, so why don't you stay in the hotel with me tonight?"

"That's not a problem, Anya. Whatever makes you happy. Where are you staying?"

"The Omni, Fourth and Chestnut."

"That's perfect. It's near my work site. I'll call Thomasina and let her know she has to take our son to school tomorrow."

"Do you think she'll mind?"

"Not at all. But without me overseeing things, she might dress him like a mini college professor," Brick said with laughter.

"I'm glad you two are getting along and co-parenting."

"We're getting better," Brick said pensively. "It's gonna take some time before all the wounds are healed."

Anya nodded. "Do you have to stop at your apartment to pick up a change of clothes or toiletries?"

"Nope, I'm always prepared with extra work clothes and a bag of essentials in my trunk."

"Okay, then let's head to the hotel."

Brick and Anya pulled into the hotel's secured indoor garage and surprisingly found a spot immediately. Brick cut the engine and turned to look at her. "It seems too good to be true, the way everything is working out for us now that we're back together."

"We've been through a lot; don't you think it's time for things to finally flow smoothly? I don't know about you, but I'm ready for a blissfully happy life," Anya replied as they both got out of the car. She moved close to him and slipped her hand in his.

"Yeah, it's time for me to let go of the past and all the hurt that I experienced as a child. That was the hand I was dealt, and—"

"And now you've replaced those cards with a different hand," Anya interjected wisely. "In this moment and from now on, no more regret. We're living in the moment."

"You're right, and I'm gonna make it my business to enjoy every moment I spend with you," Brick said cheerfully, although he had a vague feeling that the harmony they were experiencing was only the quiet before the storm.

A car rolled into the garage and Brick protectively pulled Anya close as the car whizzed past. Suddenly, tires squealed as the car came to an abrupt halt, and then began speedily backing up, causing Brick and Anya to have to jump out of the way.

"What the fuck!" Brick exploded. The window to the passenger's side rolled down and Brick was stunned to see Misty. Her nurse, Audrey, was driving.

"Well, well, well. Fancy meeting you here, Brick," Misty said sarcastically as she got out of the car.

Anya recognized her immediately as the woman she'd seen in the hotel elevator. And then with a sinking heart, she realized why she'd seemed so familiar. This gorgeous woman was Misty. She was Brick's childhood sweetheart and the love of his life. Anya had sat in Misty's hospital room, checking on her on Brick's behalf while she was still in a coma. She'd also seen pictures of what Misty had looked like before she was beaten and disfigured. A surgeon's diligent work had restored her looks, but her carefully crafted features were now distorted by rage.

"Who's this bitch?" Misty scowled at Anya.

"You're the fuckin' bitch," Anya barked, stepping toward Misty.

"No, baby. Don't get into it with her." Brick grabbed Anya by the arm, holding her back.

"I must be hearing things? You've been treating me like a pariah, but you call this average-looking slut *baby!*"

"You got a lot of mouth, bitch!" Infuriated, Anya tried to yank away from Brick, but he held her firmly. "Let's walk away. Come on, think about the future we're planning together, and you'll realize it's not worth it," Brick said sensibly.

With his arm around Anya, Brick turned her around and guided her away from Misty who was fuming mad and cursing up a storm. Enraged, Misty ran behind the couple and sucker-punched Anya in the back of her head. The blow from Misty's small fist was more annoying than painful, but it was degrading.

"What the fuck is wrong with you, Misty?" Brick shouted.

Going around Brick, Anya quickly retaliated, drawing her hand back and landing a punch in Misty's face, knocking her on her ass.

"Oh, my God. Are you all right, Misty?" Audrey screamed and leapt out of the car. But instead of running to Misty's aid, she attacked Anya with a sharp object, stabbing her with amazing speed, puncturing her neck, her side, and then plunging what turned out to be a long screwdriver in the center of Anya's chest.

Brick ripped Audrey away from Anya and tossed her in the air. Her body hit the hood of her car with a loud thud. But he hadn't acted swiftly enough. The damage to Anya had already been done. Anya lay gasping and bleeding profusely as her life appeared to be slipping away.

Brick dropped down to the ground, trying to staunch the blood from the deep wound in her neck with a bandana he wore on the job that had been stuffed in his back pocket. The screwdriver, covered in blood, rolled ominously across the concrete and under Audrey's car.

"I'm gonna get you help, baby. Stay with me," he pleaded to Anya as he called 9-1-1. "I need help. My girl got stabbed in her neck, her chest—all over. I don't think she's gonna make it. Send an ambulance. Please. Hurry!"

"Where are you, sir?" asked the dispatcher.

"Inside the garage at the Omni Hotel on Chestnut Street. Hurry up and get here before she stops breathing," Brick yelled and hung up.

Sitting on the ground and cradling Anya, Brick gave a sharp intake of breath when he noticed Anya's eyes roll into the back of her head. "Anya! Come on, baby, stay with me. Please, baby, please."

"Why're you crying over her, when you can have me?" Misty asked. She got up and dusted herself off before slithering over to Brick with a look of triumph in her eyes.

"Why's the fucking ambulance taking so long?" Brick shouted hoarsely, looking wild-eyed. "You have to help her, Misty. Lay hands on her."

"Fuck that shit," Misty said fiercely. "Let her go, Brick. Stop worrying about that random bitch. I can't help her; she's already dead."

"No, she's not. There's life still inside her; I can feel it. Please, Misty," he begged with tears pouring from his eyes. "Heal her. Do it for me—for old time's sake."

"She's dead," Misty insisted.

Brick gazed upon Anya and her eyes were half-closed and vacant. Her mouth was open, as if she'd tried to take a final breath of air.

Sobbing, Brick began bargaining with Misty. "Touch her; you can at least try to heal her."

"And what do I get out of it?"

"I'll come back to you. I'll be the man I used to be. Dedicated to you and only you. I'll place you above all others, Misty—even my son," Brick said, bargaining with everything that was dear to him. He glanced down at Anya again and her complexion was turning a ghastly gray. Fearing she would soon utter her last breath, he was prepared to make a deal with the devil if that's what it took to spare Anya's life.

Misty arched her brow suspiciously. "So…what you're saying is, all I have to do is lay hands on this dead bitch and you'll be humble and devoted the way you were before my mother ruined you and got you to thinking you're God's gift to women?"

"Yes, I swear. I'm all yours, Misty. All you have to do is lay hands on Anya, and I'll become the old Brick—your faithful lover, exactly the way you trained me to be," Brick pleaded urgently.

Misty had a look of excitement in her eyes. "Okay, but I'm curious about when you started seeing this chick. Who the hell is she?"

"Her name is Anya. She's a friend who helped me out when I was down. She financed the trip we made to L.A.; she helped me get inside Smash Hitz's world. I would have never got my hands on Horatio and gotten revenge for what he did to you if it wasn't for her. She even visited you in the hospital when your mother wouldn't allow me anywhere near you."

"Oh!" Misty said, suddenly enlightened. "So that's where I know her from. She was lurking in my hospital room, talking to me while I was in the coma. I remember that now but, at the time, I didn't know who the hell she was, and couldn't understand why she was talking to me." Misty shrugged. "It didn't matter since I couldn't respond anyway."

"You're wasting precious time, Misty! Her pulse is getting weak. You have to heal her before she stops breathing."

Misty sighed. "Okay, I'll try, Brick."

"Stop talking and do it!"

Misty placed a hand on the open wound on Anya's neck, and it miraculously closed.

"Touch her chest and touch the spot where she was stabbed on her right side," Brick prompted, his words coming out in a rush of desperation. Misty complied, and although the wounds closed, Anya continued to lie still and lifeless in Brick's arms.

Misty shrugged. "I tried, but it was too late. I told you she was dead." Misty removed her hand, and was about to stand up when Anya took a deep, strangled breath.

"Anya!" Brick cried out. "Breathe, baby. Take a deep breath."

"Don't be talking that *baby* shit to her. We have a deal, Brick," Misty said, her eyes brimming with fury.

"I know," he said, nodding grimly as he caressed Anya's face.

Misty attempted to stand, but her legs gave out. "Ohmigod, something's wrong with my legs," she said, her eyes wide with alarm. She lifted her arms to reach for Brick, but they fell uselessly at her sides. "I can't move, Brick." Misty looked around in abject fear. Unable to sit up any longer, she toppled to her side. "Oh, no! I can't walk and I can't move. I'm fucking paralyzed again. Fucking with that dying bitch took everything out of me."

She shot a hateful look at Anya whose clothes were bloodstained, yet she miraculously had no wounds.

Misty began struggling to breathe. "I'm scared, Brick. Everything's getting dark. I can feel my soul leaving, but I'm not ready to die. Oh, no. Shane is here and he's beckoning me, telling me it's time. Make him go away, Brick," Misty whimpered.

Her eyelids fluttered vigorously as she struggled to hold on to the life that was quickly slipping away.

"Can you help her, Brick?" Anya asked in a weak voice.

Kneeling over Misty, Brick spoke her name softly, afraid that the sheer volume of his natural voice might hasten her demise. "The ambulance is on the way. You're gonna be all right, Misty."

"I don't think I'm gonna make it—not this time."

"Don't say that, babe."

"You called me, babe," she murmured dreamily.

Brick caressed Misty's face and stroked her hair. "Ain't nothing changed, you'll always be my baby."

"Really, Brick? You still love me?"

"I never stopped."

Through sheer will, and despite her irregular and shallow breathing, Misty forced her eyes open and scrutinized Brick's face, searching for something she could trust. Maintaining a loving and reassuring expression, Brick tried to give her what she needed.

"I love you, too, Brick, and I'm not scared anymore. I'm ready."

"Ready for what, Misty?" There was fear in Brick's voice. Despite her many flaws, Misty was a part of him, and he wasn't ready to lose his former lover, his sister, his friend.

"I'm ready to go back," she said with a faint smile. With one last, croaking gasp, her body went limp.

"Misty!" Frantic, Brick checked but couldn't find a pulse. Misty's eyes were wide open and staring vacantly, and it was obvious that she was dead.

"Where's the ambulance?" Anya asked, looking around. "Maybe she can be revived."

"She's beyond help. She's gone," Brick said, teary-eyed.

He reached beneath the car and using the clean part of his bloodied bandana, he wiped Anya's blood from the weapon. "You're not gonna like this, Anya—I don't like it, either—but it's something I have to do. I'll explain later."

The muscles in his face visibly tightened as he savagely drove the screwdriver in and out of Misty's body.

"Why'd you do that?" Anya asked, horrified.

"To cover our tracks. When I made the nine-one-one call to get you help, I told them you'd been stabbed, but Misty healed you, and I need that call to make sense when the police get here," Brick explained. He moved to the hood of Audrey's car, where she remained knocked out. He placed the handle of the screwdriver in Audrey's hand and folded her fingers around it.

Regaining consciousness, Audrey slid off the hood of the car, and jumped to her feet, ready to resume battle. Audrey shrieked when she glanced at Misty, who was deathly still and covered in blood. "You killed her," she accused, wielding the deadly screwdriver as she stalked toward Brick, looking at him with outright loathing.

At that precise moment, the dual sirens of an ambulance followed by a police car filled the parking garage.

CHAPTER 43

Although she couldn't get along with her daughter while she was alive, Thomasina became a concerned and doting parent after Misty died. "I don't want you to spare any expense in preparing my child's body for the grave. Make sure she looks beautiful," she instructed the mortician.

Dressed in a satin and lace white gown, Misty was laid to rest in an all-white coffin; she looked like a sleeping angel.

The choir sang "Heaven" by Beyoncé and both Thomasina and Brick shed bitter tears.

After the burial, church members and friends gathered at Thomasina's house, offering condolences as they filled their plates high with fried chicken, greens, and potato salad.

"I still can't understand why that crazy nurse would kill the patient she was supposed to be caring for," Thomasina said to Brick, sniffling and wiping her eyes. "The way she stabbed my child repeatedly was unforgiveable."

Brick grunted and nodded.

"I can't thank you enough for being there. If you hadn't called nine-one-one, the police wouldn't have caught her red-handed, holding the weapon. That nurse needs to be underneath the jail; I pray to God she never gets out. It's shameful the way that hussy is trying to play crazy, claiming that she killed your friend, Anya and not Misty. What a crock. Anya is alive and well while Misty is dead in her grave." Thomasina shook her head disgustedly. "Why didn't Anya come to the service?"

"She wasn't comfortable with that. She's my girl, now, and uh, we're planning a future together."

Thomasina looked surprised. "I thought she was only a friend from your past. How did you move so fast from being with Misty to starting a relationship with Anya?"

"It's a long story, Thomasina, but the short version is: Misty didn't want me anymore—not after she got her looks back and was able to get out of that wheelchair. I turned to Anya during my time of heartbreak and one thing led to another." It wasn't the full truth, but it sounded believable.

"Oh, so you got with her on the rebound. The same way you and I hooked up," Thomasina observed with a sad smile. "You were always weak for Misty. What was it? Her looks? It had to be her beauty because we both know she wasn't a very nice person."

"Her looks attracted me when we were kids, but after a while, it was her feistiness…the way she believed she could do anything. Misty had some good traits, Thomasina, but you had to dig deep to find them. I was an expert at overlooking her flaws."

Thomasina gently patted Brick on the arm and then squinted in bewilderment. "I still don't understand how it was medically possible for Misty to be walking around."

"There isn't any medical explanation. According to Misty, she developed healing powers from the coma and was able to heal herself."

"Why'd you keep important information like that from me? Despite the differences between Misty and me, I was still her mother, and it would have thrilled my heart to know she wasn't confined to a wheelchair any longer."

"When I told you about her gift of prophecy, you said it was the work of the devil, so I decided to keep my mouth shut."

Thomasina became pensive. "Maybe I was wrong about her when I said she was touched by the devil; maybe she had a gift from God, after all."

"Maybe so."

"By the way, you're not the only one in a new relationship. I met someone at my line dancing class. Someone my age. It feels good to be out with someone and not being stared and frowned at for robbing the cradle," Thomasina said with a chuckle. "So, I want you to know that I'm through fighting you over the particulars of the divorce. We took our marriage as far as it could go. I got a fine son out of the deal and hopefully you gained some wisdom."

"I did."

"My only regret is that I didn't make up with Misty and spend some time with her. It was foolish of me to allow pride to prevent me from having a relationship with my daughter. I don't know if I'll ever forgive myself for not making up with her."

"She knew you loved her, Thomasina. She loved you, too."

"You think so?"

"I know so. She told me she was going to surprise you with a visit on your birthday." Brick was lying; Misty only cared about herself, but he wanted to remove some of the guilt from her mother's heart.

"People can say what they want about Misty, but she packed a lot of living in her short life. It's a shame Little Baron will never get to know his big sister," Thomasina said remorsefully.

"We'll keep her memory alive for him," Brick replied.

Brick turned over the millions that Misty had stockpiled in the storage unit to her mother, telling her that Misty had received the money from donations. Being financially secure, Thomasina was able to move out of the city and into a lovely suburban home that was only a few miles from Brick and Anya's house. Little Baron didn't have to travel far when he rotated between his parents' homes.

Five inches of snow blanketed Brick and Anya's property. After helping Little Baron build a snowman, and then participating in a family outing where Anya and Brick ran behind Little Baron as he sledded on a plastic disc down a small hill with a slew of other exuberant kids, Anya's fingers were starting to feel frostbitten, despite her fur-lined gloves.

"I'm going to head back to the house and start wrapping the Christmas gifts for the women at the shelter."

"Do you need some help?" Brick asked.

"No, I'll be fine." Anya gave Brick a quick kiss and began the five-minute trek back home. She and Brick had a wonderful life and it sometimes weighed heavily on her heart that their financial blessings came from two people who had succumbed to violent deaths: Anya's mother and Sergio.

Though she couldn't bring them back, she did her best to show her gratitude by spreading the wealth around and contributing to numerous charities.

In the midst of wrapping gifts, Anya was surprised when Brick and his son returned home sooner than expected.

She stopped what she was doing and undid the scarf around Little Baron's neck and helped him out of his outerwear. "Do you want some hot chocolate, honey?"

Little Baron nodded enthusiastically and ran toward the kitchen. "I can make it, myself," he squealed. When he visited his dad and

Anya, he was allowed to be more independent. Popping a K-cup into the Keurig brewer and fixing his own hot chocolate made him feel like a big boy.

Brick and Anya trailed behind Little Baron to the kitchen, but hung back while keeping an eye on him.

"What's wrong?" Brick asked.

"Nothing."

"Yes, there is; what's on your mind? Talk to me."

Anya sighed. "Our life is perfect, yet I can't seem to find complete happiness. We've both done so many horrible things, and I'm terrified of the bad karma we've created."

Brick clasped both Anya's hands and stared in her eyes. "You have to stop judging us and allow the Man above to measure our sins. We all have to meet our maker eventually, but until then, we have an obligation to live life to the fullest."

"But I've seen and done so many horrible things, I'm terrified that as soon as I start to enjoy life, something horrible is going to happen. What goes around comes around, and I feel like it's only a matter of time before the dirt I've done catches up with me. I don't know how you manage to be so optimistic."

"Would it be better if I beat up on myself on a daily basis and fell into a state of depression? If I punished myself like that, do you think it would help me become a better husband and father?"

"No."

"So, you understand why it's important for me to remain optimistic and look on the bright side?"

Anya nodded. "I get your point, but I'm not like you. I have a conscience and I'm haunted by my actions in the past. I want to move forward, but it's hard."

"We made a promise to each other; remember?"

"When we said our wedding vows?"

"Our vows were heartfelt, but that's not what I'm referring to. Do you remember the promises we made to each other right before Misty's nurse tried to kill you?"

Anya was pensive for a moment. "It's all a blur. Misty attacked me and I was defending myself. I don't remember getting stabbed; I sort of blacked out, and the next thing I consciously remember was hearing Misty pleading with you to save her life." Anya gazed up at Brick with worried eyes. "And I remember the brutal way you stabbed her with that screwdriver," she recalled with a grim look on her face.

"I explained to you why I had to do that."

"I know you did, but it's such a confusing story."

"I'm gonna explain it again, and hopefully we can move past it." Anya nodded.

"Misty's nurse attacked you with the screwdriver. She stabbed you in three places, and you were dying. I begged Misty to heal you, but you were so far gone that when she laid hands on you, it drained the life out of her."

Though Brick had recounted the incident on several occasions, each time he mentioned that Misty had lost her life while saving hers, Anya felt a knot in her stomach the size of a fist. "Oh, God, I feel horrible about that."

"It was her time," Brick said bluntly. "She beat death on a couple of occasions, but this time, she was ready. She left this earth with a smile on her face. Since I'd already called nine-one-one and reported a stabbing, I knew we'd have big problems if your blood turned up on that screwdriver. What you have to understand is Misty was already dead when I stabbed her. It wasn't an easy thing to do, Anya. It took all my strength and willpower to drive a fucking screwdriver into her lifeless body. But I did it so that we could have a chance at love and all the good shit that life has to offer."

Anya looked at Brick with sorrow in her eyes, still hesitant about taking a plunge into happiness that more than likely, wouldn't last.

Trying to convince her, Brick said, "You seem to think that self-punishment is going to change the past and wipe the slate clean, but it won't. Being happy is a choice, and it's what I want; I thought you wanted to be happy, too."

"I do, Brick. With all my heart, but I can't help feeling that I don't deserve to be happy. Not after all the harm I've caused others."

"Neither one of us ever harmed an innocent person, and you know that's the truth."

"But we're not God."

Brick fell silent briefly. "When we were in that parking garage, before it all went down, I complained about being dealt a bad hand during my childhood and you wisely suggested that I replace those cards with a different hand."

"Yeah, I remember saying that."

"And we agreed that from that moment forward, we'd be happy and live in the moment. Do you remember that?"

Anya nodded. "I do."

"We only have to choose happiness, Anya. It's that simple. You seem to think it's noble to wallow in guilt and regret." Brick eyed her intently. "So, what's it gonna be—are you willing to move forward or are you going to linger in the past?"

"I'm going to try my best to put the past behind me. Just bear with me, please," she said, snuggling up to Brick. "It's going to take a little time for me to live in the moment, but I promise that my ultimate goal is to hold on tight to you and our family, and to accept all the joy that life has to offer."

"You're my wife, Anya, and I love you more than life," Brick said, lowering his head and kissing her.

Little Baron made a face as he waited for his hot chocolate to finish brewing. "Ew, you two are always kissing."

"That's because we love each other very much," Brick explained.

"And we love you, too," Anya added. "And I'm about to cover your face with a bunch of sloppy kisses," she said, playfully chasing a squealing Little Baron around the kitchen.

Brick smiled warmly at Anya and his son, relieved that he'd convinced his wife to let go of her gloom and the ghosts of the past. Life was a precious gift and it would be a shame to not enjoy it. One day, the two of them would have to answer for their sins, but until then…only God could judge them.

ABOUT THE AUTHOR

Allison Hobbs is a national bestselling author of twenty-three novels and has been featured in such publications as *Romantic Times* and *The Philadelphia Inquirer.* She lives in Philadelphia, Pennsylvania. Visit the author at www.allisonhobbs.com and Facebook.com/Allison Hobbs.

MISSED ANY OF MISTY'S DRAMA?
SEE HOW IT ALL GOT STARTED IN

DOUBLE DIPPIN'

BY ALLISON HOBBS
AVAILABLE FROM STREBOR BOOKS

Along with an exotic dancer named Star, Brick, Misty, Shane, and Tariq had all piled into Brick's borrowed car. After dropping Tariq off, Brick weaved wildly through traffic, swerving like a drunk. He struggled to steer the car toward Star's apartment on Pulaski Avenue.

"Do you mind if my friends crash at your place? My man's too messed up to drive." Shane asked the dancer, with a worried gaze fixed on Brick.

"Sure, if they don't mind sleeping in the living room. I only have one bedroom."

"That's cool," he responded and then scowled at his friend. "Yo, Brick. You want me to drive, man?" Shane shouted.

"Naw, I'm straight, man. I got this." Brick's words came out slurred.

"He ain't got shit," Misty interjected. "Pull over, Brick; let Shane drive."

Jumping the curb when he pulled over, Brick hit the brakes. "Damn, that was fucked up," he said, cussing as if the car was at fault.

Shane took the driver's seat. Misty got in the back with Star while Brick slid drunkenly into the passenger seat.

"You dance real good." Misty sidled next to Star. "I wish I could dance like that."

"It ain't even about dancing; it's working your body like you getting some good dick. Anybody can do it."

"Yeah, but I'd be so scared to take off my clothes like that." Misty made her voice sound small, like the voice of a little girl.

"Girl, as pretty and young as you are…" Star paused and shook her head as if Misty had no idea of the untapped goldmine she possessed. "Girl, you wouldn't even have to work up a sweat. The only thing you'd have to do is come up on stage, swivel your little hips, and rub your crotch. If you showed those perverts just a little bit of tits, they'd break their necks to stuff your thong with cash."

"For real!"

Star nodded with a smile.

"But is it worth it? You know…do you make enough to really get up there and take off your clothes?"

"If you get some lap dances in to supplement what you get on stage, you can make out pretty good. Like tonight. Here it is a Monday night. Most people don't think of Monday as a money night. But I made out pretty good."

Misty's dark, round eyes grew large; her heavy silky lashes fluttered with interest. "So you're saying this is a career I could think about getting into and I could make enough green to survive?"

"Survive! Girl, stop playin'. I made three hundred in lap dances and a buck twenty on stage. On a Monday night! That ought to tell you that you can make some real nice change."

"Do you think you could get me in there?" Misty asked, her voice filled with hope.

"Um. I can put in a good word, but you're still gonna have to audition for the manager. I'll give Shane my number; give me a call tomorrow and I'll try to set something up."

"Oh, that's so nice. Thank you," Misty gushed.

Star was tall and slender. She looked to be in her mid to late twenties. She wore a curly ponytail and had a nice-looking face. Her body wasn't spectacular but she worked it so well, the men forgot that they'd been initially disappointed when she turned around and revealed an ass so flat it looked like someone had beaten it with a board.

"Right there," Star said, pointing. "Pull up behind that white van."

Misty and Star walked together like two best girlfriends while Shane held up Brick, who was so drunk he could hardly stand up.

Star waved to her leather sofa, indicating that Brick could lie down there. "Oh, hell no," Misty said. "I'm sleeping on the couch; let his drunk ass sleep on the floor." Everyone laughed at Brick's expense.

Shane tried to ease the big man down to the floor, but unable to hold the dead weight any longer, Shane dropped his friend. Brick's body hit the floor with a great thump. Brick lay sprawled, but didn't awaken, which caused more titters of laugher.

"I'm sorry I don't have an extra blanket, but I have plenty of clean sheets," Star said, her faced fixed in an apologetic expression.

"That'll work. Girl, I'm so tired I'm gonna pass out in about five minutes," Misty informed Star as she pulled off her sneakers and make herself comfortable on the leather sofa.

She threw a sneaker at Brick when he began to snore. They all erupted into more laughter when, after getting clunked in the head with Misty's sneaker, Brick's snoring grew even louder.

Shane and the willowy exotic dancer went into her bedroom and in a matter of minutes, Shane had Star hitting high notes, chanting, praying, and begging for more. Her cries of passion continued until the sun lit up the bedroom. Satisfied, Star fell asleep in Shane's arms, wearing a contented smile that looked as if it were permanently in place.

Shane woke her up around nine in the morning, "Baby, I gotta go. Can I get your number? You know I want to see you again." He was holding a cell phone.

"Why you gotta leave?" she asked, lifting her head slightly.

"I'll be back tonight if I can borrow my man's car."

"Okay." Star gave Shane her number, reciting each number slowly and deliberately. Shane pressed the numbers, each button making a different musical sound. "All right, baby. I got you on lock."

Shane kissed her and hugged her tight. Contentedly, Star turned over and snuggled into her pillow. "Damn, I hate to leave you," he said, patting her flat buttocks. "You better have that ass ready for me tonight."

She smiled dreamily and went back to sleep.

In the car, Misty counted the money that Shane had lifted from Star's purse.

"That bitch can lie," Misty accused and sucked her teeth. "This is only three hundred and fifty dollars; she said she made four twenty."

"It's cool, though," Brick said, grinning. "I gripped her jewelry box." Brick displayed a blue wooden musical box.

"Now, that's what I'm talkin' about. You go, boy!" Misty squealed with glee. She sat in the backseat, but stretched her arm across the front seat to investigate the pieces inside the jewelry box.

"Yo, stop grabbing everything," Shane said, giving Misty an evil look.

"Y'all dumb asses don't know fake stuff from real, so hand me the muthafuckin' jewelry box," Misty replied, snatching the jewelry box from Brick.

"And your violent ass better not hit me with your stinkin' sneaker no more," Brick said, laughing. "Won't even let a black man get his snore on."

They all let out big guffaws. "Damn, you was convincin' like a muthafucker when you be playin' your drunk role," Misty complimented him.

"That's how niggas get robbed. They be thinkin' I'm twisted, but I be all up in they shit, taking everything," Brick bragged.

More laughter followed and then Misty took out a sparkly tennis bracelet and solemnly handed it to Shane.

"Aw shit. This jawn is worth some money. That bling is about three or four carats, right, Misty?"

"Look at it real good, Shane. You know that dancin' bitch can't afford no real bling. Chips maybe, but not three or four carats. "

Shane held it in his palm as if weighing the bracelet. "It's heavy; it's blinging like crazy. It looks real to me."

"Turn it over."

Shane turned it over and shrugged.

"That shit is set in silver." Misty sucked her teeth in disgust. "Real diamonds are not set in no damn silver. Fucking fake-ass bitch!"

"Well maybe we can sell it to some knucklehead who don't know no better. How much you think we can get?" Brick asked.

"I don't know. Let's see what else is in here." Misty rifled through the seemingly worthless pieces of jewelry. She held up a pair of diamond earrings. "These look real?" she asked, contemptuously.

"Damn, I don't know. Just hand me the fuckin' jewelry box," Shane suggested.

Misty sucked her teeth and shoved the box toward Shane. He looked through it and then, shaking his head in disgust, he gave the jewelry box back to Misty.

"So what did you get, Miss Know It All?" Brick asked.

"Man, I clipped that bitch in the backseat of the car last night." Misty proudly held up a wallet and extracted two credit cards. "Now let's go spend some money before that lap dancin' ho wakes up and starts canceling these credit cards. Yeah, she's gonna be madder than a muthafucker when she finds out how much Shane's dick cost her."

Headed for the Gallery Mall, Brick sped out of Germantown, Misty threw the jewelry box out the window.

"Whatchu do that for?" Brick asked, astonished.

"There wasn't nothing but a bunch of worthless costume jewelry in there. The box was wooden; that should have told you something."

"She ain't have no gold chains or nothing in there?" Brick asked, obviously disappointed.

"She ain't have nothin' but a bunch of bullshit in there. But don't worry, baby. We gon' see how much she got on these cards. I hope she got enough for a shopping spree for all of us."

Twenty minutes later, Shane and Brick hung out in the food court while Misty tested one of the cards at a woman's boutique. She met up with them swinging two bags.

"Look at this greedy bitch, she done bought up the whole store." Brick's gruff voice carried, causing diners to turn their heads toward Misty.

"Okay, genius. Go ahead and bring a lot of attention to us." Misty sat down and took a bite of Brick's sandwich.

"So how much is on the cards?" Shane inquired.

Misty shrugged. "No way to tell unless I have her PIN number. But here's how we can work it. Y'all can't use a female's credit card, so go look around and see what you like. Go in separate stores. Then come tell me and I'll go make the purchases."

Shane nodded.

"Sounds like a plan," Brick agreed, bobbing his head up and down as he gobbled down his food.

The two men got up to do some window shopping. Misty stuck

out her hand. "Split the cash, Shane. I know you don't think you're keeping that hooker's money all to yourself."

"I did the work, didn't I?"

"Oh, that's how we're playin' now? Okay, I didn't know the rules. But I'll remember the next time y'all want me to lure some nut to a hotel or some dark alley somewhere. Uh huh. I'm sure gonna remember this shit." There was no mistaking the threat behind Misty's words.

Slowly, Shane pulled out the knot and gave Misty and Brick one hundred dollars apiece. "Y'all know I was just playin'." He laughed sheepishly.

"I don't know. You can be real shiesty when you wanna be." Misty gave him a smile and hopped up from her seat. With her two bags hanging from the crook of her arm, she went to investigate the myriad of choices in the mall's food court.

During the drive back to West Philly, the trio was exhausted. "Y'all feel like stopping for a minute so we can hollah at Wayne Gee?" Shane asked. Wayne Gee was a friend as well as their weed connection.

"We'll have to hollah at the Gee man later," Misty said, shaking her head. "I'm too tired to stop anywhere."

There wasn't much conversation until they got close to the house where Shane had been staying off and on.

The red pickup truck parked in the middle of the block indicated that Paula, Shane's latest benefactor, wouldn't be able to admit him into the premises. Unfortunately, her husband was home.

Misty sucked her teeth. "What's that muthafucker doin' home?" She sighed deeply. "Oh well, I guess you'll have to come to our place. My mom's at work. You can get some sleep until she gets off and then call that bitch Paula and see what's up with her husband. Ain't he supposed to be on the road driving an eighteen-wheeler?" Misty questioned Shane.

"That's what I thought. Fuck it. I'll call her later."

Shane, Misty, and Brick piled their packages in Misty's bedroom. Her mother didn't like Brick staying there, and she'd made it abundantly clear that putting a roof over the heads of two male slackers was absolutely out of the question.

Misty locked her bedroom door. "Can't have my nosey mother all up in our business."

The three friends, too exhausted to undress, fell asleep in Misty's queen-sized bed.

"Misty!" her mother yelled as she banged on her daughter's bedroom door.

"What?" Misty sat up, cracked open an eye, and looked at the clock. The red digital numbers announced that it was 8:30 and the darkened bedroom was evidence that the day had turned to evening. "Damn," Misty said, shocked that they'd slept so long.

"I know you and that Brick ain't still laying up in that bed 'sleep. Get the hell up, Misty. Brick, you, too. Both of y'all get out that bed right the hell now."

"Okay, Mom. But damn, you ain't gotta be all loud and bangin' on my door."

"Who pays the bills around here?"

Misty sighed and rolled her eyes. "All right, Mom. We're getting up now."

"I'm getting ready to go get a drink around the corner at the bar. When I get back, I want y'all up, dressed, and out!"

Brick slept through the bickering and continued to sleep.

Shane woke up instantly, stretched his sinewy body, and cut his eye at the clock. He sat up and massaged his head. "Who got the weed?" Shane sat on the edge of the bed. "Damn, my whole body hurts; cramped up in this bed with you and Brick ain't no joke."

"Me? How much room did I take up?"

"I know you tiny and all, but you sleep wild and crazy. You be moving all over the place. And that big ox," he said, pointing to Brick. "My arm is numb; feels like him and all his ten tons was laying on my shit all night." Shane grimaced as he rubbed his arm. "I need some weed."

"We didn't stop and get none, 'member?" Misty reminded him. "We'll have to hollah at Wayne Gee later on."

"Damn, I don't like waking up with no weed," Shane grumbled as he worked his hands upward and began to massage the top of his head.

Shane took out his cell phone and called Paula. When she picked up, he said, "Is your old man still at the crib? No? Well next time the plans change, hit me up on my cell; give me some kind of warning. That shit was fucked up. Yeah, aiight. I'll be over soon." He paused. "Oh, now you trying to rush me? I'll get there when I get there. Damn."

"What did she say?" Misty asked when Shane hung up.

"Said her husband's trip got delayed. But it's cool, the muthafucker's on the road now."

"For how long?"

"I don't know. Probably three or four days. I gotta take a shower. Did your mom leave yet?"

"I don't know; let me check." Misty unlocked the bedroom door. "Mom! Mom, are you still here?" She closed the door. "She must have left."

"Aiight; I'm gonna take a quick shower." They both cast a curious gaze at Brick, who had rolled over on his side.

Misty pulled open one of Brick's eyes. It was unfocused as if he were dead.

"Come on; he's out for the count. He took a couple Xanies on the way home. He ain't waking up no time soon."

Misty and Shane got in the shower together. "You know you gotta tighten me up before you go fuck that bitch." She closed the shower curtain and turned on the water.

Brick startled them when he stumbled into the bathroom. With his eyes closed, he lifted the toilet seat and began to urinate. When he finished, he didn't flush the toilet and he didn't wash his hands. Like a zombie, he went back to the bedroom.

Misty and Shane, crouched in a corner as they hid from Brick, doubled over in laughter when he left. Misty's drenched hair was plastered to her face.

"You look so beautiful right now," Shane said in a tender voice. "I really don't want to go over Paula's."

"I know you don't, Shane, but we spent all the money. You gotta go get some more." Misty washed Shane's well-developed shoulders and back. She handed him the washcloth, which he soaped up and gently washed her small breasts, and stomach, He stopped when he got to her groin. He placed the soap and washcloth on the plastic shower rack.

Misty put a foot up on the side of the tub as Shane delicately separated the folds of her vagina, got down on his knees, and licked it clean.